THE PARIS BOOKSHOP FOR THE BROKEN-HEARTED

REBECCA RAISIN

Boldwood

First published in Great Britain in 2025 by Boldwood Books Ltd.

Cover Design by Cherie Chapman

Cover Images: Shutterstock

A CIP catalogue record for this book is available from the British Library.

Paperback ISBN 978-1-83533-520-8

Large Print ISBN 978-1-83533-521-5

Hardback ISBN 978-1-83533-519-2

Ebook ISBN 978-1-83533-522-2

Kindle ISBN 978-1-83533-523-9

Audio CD ISBN 978-1-83533-514-7

MP3 CD ISBN 978-1-83533-515-4

Digital audio download ISBN 978-1-83533-517-8

This book is printed on certified sustainable paper. Boldwood Books is dedicated to putting sustainability at the heart of our business. For more information please visit https://www.boldwoodbooks.com/about-us/sustainability/

Boldwood Books Ltd, 23 Bowerdean Street, London, SW6 3TN

www.boldwoodbooks.com

For the drippiest boy who ever did live, Will, I love your mad rizz and sigma energy. It's lit. (Sorry, I had to!)

1

Never in my wildest dreams did I expect my life would implode in such spectacular fashion. How does it happen to a person like me, who plots every move with military precision? I have systems in place, and I trust those systems will keep me safe. Spoiler alert: they have not.

Not only do I have myself to worry about, there's also my thirteen-year-old daughter Eloise to consider. She's not coping with the sudden move from London back to our hometown of Paris. I don't blame her. Who wants to be wrenched away from their friends and all they know?

Despite my efforts to salvage the situation, my finances are in dire straits. I can't pay next month's rent and the bills are piling up, so I had to take drastic action and get us packed up and on the move quick smart. Deep down, Eloise knows returning to Paris is *truly* the last resort, but that doesn't mean she's happy about it. What teenager would be?

Me, well, I'm grateful we've got somewhere *to* go, in the midst of all this upheaval.

Although fleeing like this, admitting defeat, is incredibly

difficult under the circumstances. To say I feel like a failure would be an understatement. My entire adult life, I've strived to get ahead so my daughter has a stable and secure homelife.

And now here I am, my worst fears realised. Almost penniless, no home to call our own, and no job. I've got whiplash from the latest plot twists in this saga, but this is real life, not a lofty piece of fiction that I can close the cover on.

It's a scary place to be when you're a solo mum, but I do my utmost to shove those worries aside for now and focus on what I can control. My daughter's happiness. Starting over.

It's not all doom and gloom though; my parents are waiting for us in Montparnasse with open arms.

As the Eurostar chugs closer to Gare du Nord, I lean back in my seat as Eloise's head lolls softly on my shoulder. When she sleeps, all the anger she holds falls away from her pretty features. Anger that has been solely directed at me. Understandable. There *is* no one else for her to blame in our little family unit of two.

I've done my best to defuse her temper by explaining our shiny new (uncertain) plan and all the reasons it will serve us well, but she insists leaving London is 'lame' and that I've ruined her life. At these times, I find myself resorting to humour, admittedly not the strongest weapon in my arsenal, but it's what most 'parenting a modern-day teen' books suggest – *Get on their level. Make it fun!*

When that inevitably fails, I highlight the many adventures we can share, like spotting the Parisian gargoyles that scare away evil forces from sacred places. In reality, the gargoyles have a much more practical purpose: they channel rainwater away from walls to prevent erosion and water damage. I prefer to think of them as sentinels sitting high on their lofty perches, keeping the city safe from all manner of dark forces.

At these types of suggestions, I'm met with an eyeroll from Eloise and a screwed-up moue that quite puts me back in my box. Still, I press on with my efforts because I've paid a fortune for those parenting books and I'm not willing to admit defeat. Not again, that is. Everything can't go belly up, or what does that say about me?

We're nearly home now. The closer we get to Paris, the more I can breathe. The knots that have been tying up my shoulders slowly release. I never thought I'd leave London, especially under a cloud of suspicion, but here we are. At least I'll have my parents to lean on.

My *maman* and Eloise are as thick as thieves, so I'm hoping she'll be able to get more than a monosyllable out of my daughter while I dust off the past.

Or possibly have a breakdown.

Why not both? It's best to keep my options open, I've learned that much from these last hellish months where I've pasted on a smile for so long it's resulted in lockjaw, which will probably end with me needing dental work as I grind my teeth to dust. I remind myself not to succumb to panic.

I attempt some box breathing, a technique my former therapist taught me to help with anxiety. I've found myself using these calming methods more frequently lately, probably due to the fact my carefully laid plans HAVE BEEN DOUSED AND SET ON FIRE. That's the rage rearing its ugly head again. All the while I'm stuck on this train pretending to read a novel while my heart beats staccato and my thoughts race too fast. The sudden onset of these wild swings of emotion have been tricky to navigate while I outwardly try to appear serene. In control. Steadfast. Just like always. I am a together person and I will remain that way, dammit.

In the quiet of the moment, I mull over the fact my beloved

systems let me down. Actually, let me rephrase that: how a *man* I loved and trusted manipulated the systems and let me down. The way I'd set up the computer program, there should have been an alarm, a flashing neon sign alerting me: *Doom approaching! Humiliation not far behind.*

Stupid, *stupid* me in love-bubble land got lax and fully trusted in the man I'd given my heart to. My partner in love and business, Alexander, took a wrecking ball to both and then did a midnight flit. I'm (usually) a sane and rational person but there have been moments since when I've been tempted to exact revenge on the guy for his crimes. Luckily for him, Eloise needs me most evenings, if only to tell me all the ways in which I've failed, so I've been a little busy, a little too *frazzled*, to find his hideout and swap his toothpaste with haemorrhoid cream. That's probably the broken heart talking. In the chaos of untangling his deceit, there hasn't been time to process my own private hurt. Now he's out of my life for good, I can pretend he never existed. *Alexander who?*

I've aged about a decade since the fallout and all I really want to do is rant and rave and stomp my feet, but of course I can't because it's not in my nature. I haven't *planned* for that and my daughter would have a conniption if she saw her very calm, very poised mother lose her grip with reality. Sometimes being the adult is grossly unfair.

Right now, a guttural cry, fists raised to an expanse of blue spring sky, eyes bulging as I expel all that pent-up rage would be just the ticket. Instead, I sit ramrod straight on this rollicking train, pretending to read while I sip water that dribbles down my chin because of that previously mentioned lockjaw.

The book I'm struggling with is a romance novel. Every word is like a stab to the heart. I'm only reading this lovey-dovey tome as it was a parting gift from my upstairs neighbour, who said reading romance novels is the only *proven* cure for a broken heart. I'd pressed her on the veracity of such claims, disappointed when she didn't have hard evidence to back that up. Instead, she huffed and puffed, thrust the book into my hands and quickly shut the door.

If I didn't believe burning books was a crime, this adorable enemies-to-lovers tale would already be engulfed in flames as I did an anti-love chant at the top of my lungs to warn others just me like me who *thought* love at first sight was real.

Guess what? It's not.

It's a lie that all those romantic novelists spin for their own financial gain. How *very* dare they! I've got half a mind to send out a press release about the matter, until I remember that I don't have a business any more and I'm also a persona non grata and thus the book trade would probably assume I'd lost my mind. Which could be the case, since I've edited and enjoyed romance novels for the last ten years or so and am *complicit* in this love story farce!

Well, not any more. Eloise and I have left London with only two suitcases and a backpack full of books. I also have a couple of extra bags, but those are under my eyes and here for the duration. Belongings that we couldn't part with have been shipped over ahead of us, mostly things that are important to Eloise, keepsakes and sentimental items.

After all this drama, I feel decidedly ancient at the ripe old age of thirty-three. I had my daughter relatively young at twenty. Her 'papa' Etienne, my high school sweetheart and absolute love of my nineteen-year-old life, took one look at the positive pregnancy test and ran away screaming, never to be seen again. I learned the hard way that no matter what precautions are in place, accidents *can* happen. But somehow it felt more divine than that. I'm not a believer in woo-woo, but when

Eloise popped out earthside I knew it was meant to be, no matter what hardships I faced being a young and solo mum.

Still, Etienne's abandonment only firmed up my resolve that men were the devil and not to be trusted. From then on, I'd need a laser-like focus to achieve my dreams with a baby in tow. Not long after Eloise's birth, it was back to university to continue with my degree. It wasn't easy juggling motherhood and study, and some days I wanted to give it all up and just be with my baby, but I'd picture her future and knuckle down and get to work.

There wasn't the time or inclination for a romantic relationship, and honestly, I didn't miss it. Becoming a mother was a masterclass in learning to accept that you can't plan everything. You have to learn to be a little more flexible. Men were out, routines were in.

After university, I worked my way up in the French publishing industry over the course of the next few years. When I was offered an entry-level publishing position in London, I jumped at the chance. The move was only doable because I had a small inheritance from my aunt, which helped make ends meet what with the exorbitant cost of living and daycare expenses in a big city like London. I learned the true meaning of the word frugal and kept my eye on the prize. Levelling up. Ambition filled my gut when food didn't.

And who enters the second act, but a handsome bibliophile with a bad boy swagger, Alexander. He loved words, but was trained in numbers, dressed preppily but spoke seductively. Had that whole 'take charge' energy that appealed. It helped he was the total opposite of my teddy bear teenage boyfriend who'd done a runner before my belly had had a chance to swell. In my mind that equated to teddy bears bad, bad boys good.

Really, the science behind it was seriously lacking, I see that now.

I, Coco Chevallier, hesitantly allowed myself the gift of returning to love-bubble land. A place where nothing good happens. Why didn't I *remember* that? Alexander promised me the world and delivered nought, setting fire to everything on his way out.

It's also kind of ridiculous that a woman who edits sweeping love stories for a job has only *had* two longish relationships. Is it me? It must be me. Or it's them. I suppose having only two real loves means that the results aren't quantifiable. But I've always felt I couldn't just rush into love. I didn't want to risk introducing my daughter to a deadbeat. Except I accidentally did. Well, never again.

The Eurostar screeches and hisses its way into the station, the pneumatic sound not dissimilar to the shrieking my daughter made when I told her we were leaving London. The racket jolts Eloise from her nap. She yawns and stretches her arms high above her, gracefully, like a swan unfurling.

They say when you have a child you wear your heart outside of your body, and it's true. Your heart is suddenly at risk, vulnerable, because it beats not just for you, but for the emotional connection to your child. Everything is magnified. It's all at once strange, intense and beautiful.

'I hate trains,' she says, rubbing at her reddened eyes, still swollen from an earlier crying jag because her friends surprised her today to say yet another farewell. 'Is Mémère meeting us at the station?' Eloise asks.

'No, darling. I told her we'd get the bus and meet her at the apartment to save her the trouble. We can go to Marché Edgar Quinet and buy a baguette, olives and brie for *apéro*.' My parents live in an apartment in Montparnasse right in the thick of all the action.

The area is steeped in literary history. It was once a hotspot for impoverished artists in the twenties and was much less salubrious than it is now. To this day, it's a literary hub and with my bookworm sensibilities, I love every square centimetre of it. It's also a foodie paradise and has open-air produce markets, high quality but budget friendly. I have accounted for Eloise wanting to splurge on some snacks when we arrive, so the market fits the bill and the finances, or lack thereof.

'I hate Paris.'

Sometimes it feels like teenagers hate everything, but according to the literature, they're figuring out their identity and grappling with being more independent. Makes sense to me, so I follow the script I've been taught: *be sympathetic.*

'That's the spirit. Paris *is* a hellhole.' I hope that by agreeing with her she'll see I'm on her side. We're a team of two. *Go team!*

She wrinkles her nose. 'Are you *trying* to be funny?'

I wrinkle my nose to mimic hers. 'What? No. I'm being *supportive.*'

Conversing with Eloise is like walking on tightrope; it's such a balancing act between getting it right and getting it wrong – I always seem to get it wrong, but I'm hopeful the more I learn about these tumultuous teenage years, the better equipped I'll be.

I remember being a gangly teen where small annoyances were heightened as those hormones roiled inside, so I do my best to be agreeable and slap on a smile that gives me a tension headache. Lockjaw is rearing its ugly head again. 'Let's eat our body weight in *fromage* and see if that helps matters.'

Eloise rolls her eyes and harrumphs. This is such a fragile age. I wish I could say it was just the collapsing of our London life that provoked this sort of behaviour from my daughter, but alas, it was not. As soon as night became day on the dawn of her thirteenth birthday, my happy-go-lucky goofball changed, developed big emotions, big feelings that she still doesn't quite have a handle on. All totally normal, of course, but the swiftness of the transformation took me by surprise. Hence the scramble to educate myself so that we'd both come out the other side relatively intact.

'Cheese? *That's* your answer?'

How can cheese ever be wrong? It's cheese! By the curl of her lip, I surmise she isn't impressed. 'It can't hurt, can it?' Buying food at the local market is more cost effective than dining out in bistros. Until I find another job, things are going to be tight financially. And so far, the job hunting is not going well. In fact, I have the sneaking suspicion I've been blacklisted in the publishing industry in London, another reason to hurry home and hope my job prospects are more successful in Paris. But I don't share any of that with my daughter as she's likely to throw the hissiest of hissy fits and I don't have enough paracetamol for that today.

Surely returning home to Paris is the answer? I only hope news of the thefts hasn't reached the City of Lights. I've been cleared of any wrongdoing, but still that taint remains. It's an actual nightmare that this has happened to me when I'm wholly innocent. I try not to dwell on it or I'll self-combust.

The train comes to a stop. 'Grab your bag, darling. Let's go.'

I step from the train onto the hectic platform and help Eloise down with her suitcase. We make our way through Gare du Nord station; the chaos, the intensity of so many bodies rushing about, even the gendarmes with their ginormous rifles and serious faces, put me strangely at ease. I feel comforted by the familiarity of being on home soil once again.

Outside the station, I walk ahead of Eloise as she fumbles with her phone. A rather good-looking man approaches; we do a two-step shuffle to avoid walking into each other but misstep into the same spot. We pause, and it's almost as if the world tilts, or I'm off balance. But I can't help feeling a sizzle of attraction as we lock eyes. That's until Eloise slams into the back of me, shooting me into the warmth of his arms.

'Watch where you're going!' my daughter shrieks, and the moment is lost. The man slides out of my way and is gone.

What *was* that? I've never felt a spark like that before; a *coupe de foudre*. I turn to search for him on the crowed pavement, but he's gone.

'Will you *move*?' Eloise spits. 'I need Wi-Fi.'

I exhale the intensity. *Coupe de foudre*. Love at first sight is a myth! A lie! My poor bruised heart is clearly malfunctioning. Why then did that brief interaction feel like a romance novel come to life?

2

'There they are, *mes belles filles.*' Maman takes me into her arms, holding me tight, as if she senses my nerve endings are frazzled to the extreme. Perhaps it's the permanent pinched expression on my face that makes me look like I suck lemons for fun in my spare time. That and the good old lockjaw that really is becoming a painful reminder that I'm holding on to my stress by my back molars alone.

After Maman releases me, she pulls Eloise into a hug. 'You've grown so tall and it's only been a few months since I saw you last. *Tu es jolie.*' She's right, my daughter *is* very beautiful, with poise like a ballerina, whereas I stand more rigid like a tin man, a soldier. My dad says I have good bearing; my *maman* says I need to drink more wine to loosen up. She's French. That's her answer to everything.

'*Merci,* Mémère,' Eloise says, smiling wide, the sight warming my soul. It's the first real smile I've seen from her in a while and it gives me a much-needed boost. Isn't it strange the way your child's happiness is inextricably and forevermore linked with your own?

When they part, I hand Maman the bag of goodies from the produce market. Her face lights up as if I've done her a momentous favour and not the other way around. '*Merci*, Coco. What a treat.'

I follow her to the kitchen. She unwraps the various wedges of *fromage* and places them on a wooden board to allow them to come to room temperature, which is proper cheese etiquette.

Cheese is hallowed in France. There are rules one must follow to preserve these long-standing traditions, such as which order to eat cheese – usually you start with the milder cheeses such as Comté and end with the strongest like Roquefort. Each style of cheese is sliced in a particular way depending on the shape. Then you must navigate when it's suitable to eat the rind and when to avoid. I enjoy the fact there is a system for *fromage*. It makes perfect sense and I do take exception if someone cuts a wedge of brie across the middle of the triangle. You can't *uncut* a poorly cut wedge of brie – the damage has been done.

'I took the afternoon off so I would be here to welcome you both, but Dad had a new client meeting so he had to stay on.'

'Oh, Maman, you didn't need to do that. We could have let ourselves in.'

'Any excuse to sneak out of work is fine by me.'

I squeeze her shoulder in thanks as I survey their compact apartment and wonder how we're all going to cohabit in such a small space. There's no way we can avoid disrupting my parents' lives with four of us living in such confined quarters, which isn't exactly fair on them.

My parents are 'couples' goals', as Eloise says, in business and in love. They taught me the value of being passionate about what you do, committing to a goal and striving to achieve it. They're entrepreneurs who work hard, always have, but it's never taken away from family time. As a kid, I wasn't social, I didn't fit in; I suppose I still don't in a way, but when they introduced me to books, life suddenly made sense. I loved those early readers, and that love for literature only grew with each year. The cadence of a sentence, the rules of grammar, the beauty of a well-placed metaphor; I'd found my raison d'etre.

And now, I might have returned, a failed venture behind me, but I'll always be proud of what I did manage to achieve. This *is* an adventure, an extended sleepover with my parents. And right now that sounds like just the tonic.

Their quiet encouragement has allowed me to take calculated risks in business, knowing they'll be there – like now – if it doesn't work out. Recently, they've reminded me that reward comes with risk, and I've got plenty of time to start over. It's also a relief knowing I'll never have to hear an 'I told you so' from them.

Maman is born and bred Parisienne, and my dad is a Brit. I speak both languages fluently but we mostly use French when we're all together.

Growing up, we travelled back and forth across the pond many times as they dabbled various business ventures, before returning to our hometown of Paris for good when I was about Eloise's age after they purchased a commercial laundry. I'm dead proud of what they've achieved, turning a small business on the brink of collapse into a thriving success. They're big on the whole jump outside of your comfort zone thing. I'm a little more risk averse but have still learned from their example.

'When is Dad due home then?' New client meetings usually involve long bistro lunches where deals are made over a glass of *vin rouge* and the *plat de jour*.

'Around five, although he said he'd try and sneak off earlier if he could. He's desperate to see you both.'

Alongside Eloise, my parents are a bright spot in my life,

always have been. I could announce I'd inadvertently killed Alexander by spooning arsenic in his tea instead of sugar and they'd simply pull me in a for a hug and say accidents happen and ask if I need help getting rid of the corpse.

They're good people, inside and out.

'Why don't you put your things in the guest bedroom, and I'll make *apéro*?'

Apéro, from the word *apéritif,* is the lull a few hours before dinner, when friends and family come together and share a drink and finger food. 'Sure, but Dad won't be happy he's missing out.' I get my obsession for *fromage* from him. There's not a cheese too pungent for his tastes. I'm sure my French *maman* found this endearing. If you don't revere cheese in France, there's a very good chance you'll be booted out, such is the passion for it.

'I'll make him a plate for later or he'll never forgive us for eating all the Roquefort.'

'I've never known anyone who eats as much blue cheese as he does.' If I imbibe too much, the sharp tangy flavour makes my eyes water, but my dad can eat an entire wedge of it with no adverse effects.

'You'd swear he had French blood.' Maman's laugh follows me down the hallway as we drag our suitcases to the spare bedroom. It's on the smaller size, but typical of a Parisian apartment, and a double bed takes up most of the space. We hoist our cases on the bed and unzip them.

'I'm not sharing a bed with you, am I?' Eloise says, her tone implying sharing a bed with her mother is the very worst outcome she could imagine. I suppose it's 'cringe', as she says on the daily, a generational slang thing, where they cut words in half. For what purpose? To save time? It doesn't make sense and the editor in me twitches, but I can't fix a whole generation; I know, I've tried on my own daughter and didn't get far. 'You're delulu if you think I am.'

I'm especially confused by the phrase delulu, aka delusional. Is it so much harder to say an extra syllable? I know I'm missing the point and language has been altered since the dawn of time, but still, it's a head scratcher.

She stares me down with so much intensity it gives me pause. It's so grown up, so jarring to see such a look from her. '*Well?*'

Usually, I can internally brush off these Eloise-isms, but right now my patience is taut. I remind myself to take a deep breath and think of the turmoil she's suffered because of my choices. Maybe I *am* delulu! 'Yes, darling, we'll be sharing this room and this bed as there are no other options right now. It's not ideal, but it's not forever. We're lucky to have a fallback like this.'

'I'm not sharing a bed with my *mother*, for crying out loud.'

I recall the advice from the parenting books. Smile, give short practical solutions in a moderated tone of voice. 'OK.' I paste a genial smile on my face that gives me a headache. 'You can sleep on the sofa if you wish.'

'I hate this.' Eloise flicks her long blonde hair and skulks out of the room. With a sigh, I unpack our belongings into a set of drawers so I can stow away our suitcases under the bed.

In time, I'm hoping Eloise will understand the relocation is for the best. Who wouldn't want to live in the 14th arrondissement of Paris? There are *les catacombes des Paris* on one side – just macabre enough for her sensibilities – and *La tour Eiffel* on the other, perfect for Instagram-worthy happy snaps she's fond of. It's close to Jardin du Luxembourg and the Panthéon, and there are hundreds of other little gems tucked away around every turn.

After I'm finished unpacking, I sit on the edge of the bed and slip my phone from my pocket to check my emails, hoping I've reached the interview stage of any of jobs I've applied for in Paris. All I find is a plethora of rejections. I can almost *taste* the worry. But I remind myself, I'm home now, we have a safe space to stay and that is one very big obstacle that I don't need to stress about for the moment.

It might be better to get out there and pound the pavement, putting feelers out. How does one go from the stunning heights of publishing director of their own publishing house to completely unemployable?

It's best not to dwell on the unfairness of it all, as that will achieve zilch. Instead, I picture myself finding a job, settling in, my daughter blooming in Paris and telling me she loves it here. One can only hope.

I leave the phone on the bedside table, vowing not to check my emails again today, and join Eloise and Maman in the kitchen.

'Coco, can Eloise have a small glass of wine?' Maman arches a regal brow as she makes the joke she always does, ready for my usual retort. It's a myth that French children grow up drinking wine; it's not the case at all.

'Absolutely not! She's only thirteen, and I've got a feeling she'd be a *mean* drunk.' I throw a big smile my daughter's way and almost fall over backwards when her own lips quirk upwards.

Maman gives me a wink. Will Eloise settle here under the supportive gaze of my parents? Part of me thinks so. While my daughter breathes fire at me, she's always respectful towards her grandparents.

I pour wine for us, and an apple juice for Eloise.

'Welcome home.' We clink glasses.

'*Merci,* Maman.'

She pats my hand, the way mothers do, a gesture that speaks a thousand words without uttering even one. Tears prick the back of my eyes. I want to tell her I'm going to fix my life. This is just a blip. That I'm so grateful for her and Dad and their unwavering support. But the words won't come. I have a feeling she knows when she hugs me tight.

There really is no place quite like home.

3

A few days later, despite Eloise's many protestations, we walk together for her first day at a new school in the 6th arrondissement, Saint-Germain-des-Prés. It's a little further away than expected but they have a music programme, so it's worth the extra distance as Eloise is musically inclined even though it's mostly self-taught with the help of YouTube.

The school is a twenty-minute walk from the apartment, or there's the option of catching the bus, which Eloise has point-blank refused. 'The bus would be more efficient,' I say, thinking of my parents who have offered to walk Eloise to and from once I'm gainfully employed.

'Urgh. Buses are so mid.'

'Mid? What does that mean?'

'Mediocre, I guess.'

'How do you get mid from mediocre?' I'm genuinely curious about Gen Z slang. It can be clever at times, but mostly it makes no sense, like this 'skibidi' word nonsense that belies translation, at least to me.

'Who cares?'

'I do. If it's from mediocre wouldn't it be med not mid?'

'You're overthinking it.'

'I guess so.' I let it go with the other unanswered questions to the great unknown. This morning, the air is perfumed by spring flowers and it's bright and sunshiny, and it makes it feel like my bones are defrosting after a long, cold London winter. Of course, it's spring in London too, but when we left it hadn't exactly sprung yet.

We walk along the bustling Boulevard du Montparnasse. The neighbourhood has changed, yet somehow stayed the same. Cafés as far as the eye can see that all have the ubiquitous weaved rattan bistro chairs in the Maison Drucker style of yesteryear. I love that about Paris; the good things don't change.

The yeasty scent of fresh baked baguettes permeates the air as we pass a *boulangerie*.

Traffic is heavy, cars toot, people hurry, and tourists meander, snapping photos. Eloise's eyes widen as we stop at the window of a patisserie where petit four cakes sit in colourful rows, like miniature artwork.

Up ahead, I notice one of my favourite haunts is still open and doing a bustling trade. 'Ooh, Eloise, see the shopfront with the blue and white striped awning? Le Crêperie Bretonne? That's where I'd go after high school to regroup and read.'

'By eating your feelings?'

Illogical but true. '*Oui*, I've been known to partake in a bit of comfort eating. School wasn't always easy for me.'

'Because you're a nerd?'

'Am I a nerd?'

She manages to screw up one side of her face, which I've come to learn means *duh, obviously*. 'You got straight As, you read your textbooks before the school year started—'

'Just for fun!'

'—you graduated at the top of all of your classes. Nerd behaviour.'

'I see.'

'You were ahead of your time, Mum. Nerd culture is mainstream now.'

'Trust me to have peaked too soon.' Always the way.

She laughs, a tinkling musical sound, as we walk past the *crêperie*.

'We should've had breakfast there,' Eloise says as the syrupy scent of sugar assails us. There's nothing quite like the humble *crêpe au sucre*, a plain crepe with lashings of melted butter and sprinkled with icing sugar.

'Why don't we go after school?' I'm conserving funds but have allocated a small amount for first day of school celebrations.

She considers my offer. There's such a dichotomy to this age; the push and pull of child to teen. Her first expression is one of anticipation and childlike wonder about simple pleasures such as a sugary crepe, but it's soon replaced by hard mask of a teenager, as if she's railing against getting excited about something so basic as food. This strange age of development is a gut punch at times. There's that sense of an ending; the innocence and glee of childhood vanishes without warning one day.

'No, actually I hate crepes.' A mere minute ago she was of a different opinion. Teenagers *are* contrary. But I've learned the hard way it's best not to point this out, as being contrary in nature they will often disagree.

I've done the research. This behaviour stems from wanting to fit in. Although I do want to assure her it's perfectly acceptable to find happiness in a crepe, to get icing sugar over her face and crow about how delicious every ooey gooey sweet buttery morsel is, but I do not.

It's the way of things. It's probably *me* who needs to accept thirteen is the new thirty and the little girl with pigtails is gone.

The *crêperie* disappears behind us.

'Are we close to school?' she asks. 'I don't want to be late on my first day.' She's a lot like me in that respect: punctual, organised – as much as her age allows.

'*Oui*. It's just up there.' I point to the imposing black gates of the school.

I'm thankful she's bilingual and speaks fluent French so this transition won't be marred by any language barrier. Right now, she's speaking a mix of both languages, as if she's not quite sure which words to use when it's just us two.

We approach a group of teens who have their eyes glued to mobile phones while they push and shove in that joking tactile way teenagers do. It's my worst nightmare, others encroaching on my personal space like that, but it doesn't seem to worry these kids.

Eloise stops and turns to me, dropping her voice to a hiss. 'Why can't I do this on my own? When I holiday here, Mémère doesn't follow me everywhere. I'm allowed my independence.'

I give her my well-practised ever-patient mothering smile. The one that shoots pain into my skull. Now that she's seen the other students, she doesn't want to lose face having her mum here. I get it, but still, she might have holidayed here, but she hasn't lived here since she was a toddler. She doesn't know how to navigate this area yet.

'I want to make sure you get to school safely each day, if that's OK with you?' I'll miss her today, but a break from each other will do us both the world of good. 'Come on.' I nimbly dodge groups of teens to get to the entrance. 'I'll pretend I don't know you, if you prefer?' I don't want her first day marred by the fact her mother is a nerd.

I'm rewarded with a scowl. Eloise often reminds me of a fire-breathing dragon. A totally normal part of development precipitated by an influx of hormones. 'It's too late for that what with you incessantly talking to me and all.'

Teenagers have the unique ability to believe that the entire world is hyper fixated on them. I steal a glance around us and not one person is looking our way, so I feel her assumptions are incorrect, but I keep that to myself. 'OK.'

Cars are double parked on the pavement and traffic whizzes by. There's the screech of brakes, a siren wailing in the distance; the cacophony of Paris life. Just inside the gates, a few parents mill about chatting.

'I'll walk myself home, now that I know the way.'

I have an internal battle with myself. Fight or accept? Eloise knows the Montparnasse area well, but she hasn't ventured around the 6th very often, and definitely not alone. She is creeping closer to fourteen, which in my view is still too young. I assess how I feel about it from a safety perspective and decide that I'm just not comfortable yet with her walking so far from the apartment without an adult. It might be different once she makes friends and they walk in a gaggle together, but not right now, not by herself.

'I'll be waiting at the bench by the park over there for you after school. We can stop at Le Crêperie Bretonne or perhaps an ice cream shop as a treat to celebrate your first day at school.'

She scoffs, contempt marring her pretty features. 'A *treat*. What am I, like... four?'

I paste on a smile when all I really want to do is admonish her for being a brat, but maybe her nerves are the driving force and I need to give her some grace. 'No, you're not four, darling!

When you *were* four, you were a joyous little thing, always smiling and happy. You're not like that now.'

'And whose fault is that?'

I pinch the bridge of my nose. 'I know the answer to this one. Mine?'

'*Oui.*' And just like that, she spins on her heel and enters the gates. No au revoir, no sign of *la bise* – the French custom of brushing cheeks in greetings and goodbyes. I take a shuddery breath and try to exhale all the worry. Nerves, that's all it is. Not for the first time, I wish she had a father figure in her life. Someone to help me with the weight of things. To shore me up when I'm depleted. Be a sounding board for Eloise. But so far that hasn't happened. Even Alexander refrained from any parenting responsibilities with Eloise, claiming he had no experience and that Eloise would only incinerate him with her galactic-force stare and he'd really rather not be involved.

When she'd argue with me, he'd disappear down the local pub for a few beers. I'd felt oddly abandoned at those times. Like he didn't quite love me enough to try and be part of our little family.

As I fight negativity from hijacking the bright spring day, I walk around Saint-Germain-des-Prés, my mind on my daughter hoping she has a great first day. I stop by a patisserie and order a café crème. While I wait, I check my emails, hoping there's a sparkly new job interview waiting patiently for me.

My coffee arrives as I scroll down my inbox.

We're sorry to inform you that you were unsuccessful at this time...

It's a concern. I've made allowances for four weeks of nominal living expenses. What if I'm not employed by week five and my funds are depleted entirely? The last thing I want to do is ask my parents for monetary help. It would be yet another failure and proof that I'm grossly incompetent at forward planning, a skill I once prided myself on. My life is glitching. Is the solution a power down and reboot? If only it were that easy!

I keep scrolling and find an email from a French publishing pal named Fleur from her personal account. We haven't spoken in an age, but I texted recently to give her the heads up that I'd applied for an editorial position at the same publishing house as her, in a different division, and asked if she could vouch for me. Fingers crossed the tide is turning!

> Bonjour Coco,
>
> I'm sorry to email instead of speaking in person but things are hectic, and I wanted you to know ASAP. There's been much chatter in the office after you applied for the editorial role here. Unfortunately, after the London difficulties, the powers that be think it best to keep their distance. I'm so sorry. I did speak up for you, but they wouldn't be swayed. I hate being the bearer of such awful news, but I thought you should know what you're up against. I know you've got Eloise to look out for. Let's catch up when you're settled in?
>
> Bien amicalement,
> Fleur

Mon Dieu! The tides aren't turning, they're gathering into one almighty tsunami. I bite down on a scream while I contemplate what this means for my future.

I am a publishing pariah.

How did I get embroiled in a mess such as this? Alexander, with his seductive eyes and smooth tongue, that's how. He often called me ambitious as if it was a negative trait and not aspirational. He bandied terms like 'workaholic', as if it was a character flaw and not that I had the forethought to schedule my daily timetable in an effective manner so that I completed tasks in an efficient fashion. Shouldn't those skills be lauded?

I shoot a reply to Fleur thanking her for the insider information and the chance to catch up in the future. I finish my café crème and leave some coins on the table, waving au revoir to the waiter as I go.

The news having evidently spread to Paris significantly shrinks my chances of finding editorial employment. Though, as a former publishing director myself, I'd take a wide berth too when hiring someone who'd been embroiled in such matters, so I'm not surprised about their stance. The simplistic part of me had, I suppose, hoped my experience would speak for itself and that someone would let me explain face to face. Alas, that's not to be.

What can I do to support my daughter? It's time to rethink the plan.

4

The last day of the school week arrives as I'm helping Eloise find her backpack, sports uniform and library bag. I walk her to school as she chatters away ten to the dozen, her mood buoyant, which makes me very happy indeed. Maybe this move *has* been for the best? Can she have slid into a new environment so easily? So quickly?

I'm further convinced she has when she gives me a fluttery little wave and joins a trio of smiley faced girls waiting by the school steps. I've only heard her mention one of them so far, a brunette by the name of Léa, who is also a Swiftie and loves friendship bracelets and boy talk. The winning trifecta, it seems.

I'm lost in a daydream as I wander aimlessly along Rue du Maréchal Harispe and come out by the Champ de Mars, the large public greenspace between the Eiffel Tower and the École Militaire. I zigzag hordes of tourists who gather to take pics of *la dame de fer*, the iron lady, as locals call it. I've wandered further than I meant to and gaze around, working out if it's best to take the Metro back to Montparnasse or walk. What else is there to do all day? I've applied for every job in publishing that I can find, even ones I'm overqualified for, but haven't managed to snag a single interview. Having swathes of the day unaccounted for is strange. I'm so used to be being busy, time running away from me. I suppose my confidence has taken a hit and I'm in a state of flux. And after Fleur's email, I'm not quite brave enough to face any more industry pals.

Before things turn dire with my finances, I must take action. It's time to broaden my parameters – finding a job outside the only industry I have ever felt at home in. Whatever it takes, I'll do it, so I can save for our own Paris *pied-a-terre* and get some semblance of normality back.

My heart is full of hope as I gaze at the Eiffel Tower. With the sun on my face, I feel relaxed, lulled by the sights and sounds of my home city with jovial holiday makers all around.

A disturbance pulls me from my reverie, and I'm jostled forward. A stream of curse words ring out as I turn to an angry Frenchman who I can only see in side profile as he holds a proprietorial hand in front of me. Who is this then? He argues with the three obscenely tall men who wear dark hoodies pulled up over their heads despite the sunny weather. 'Give those back, *immédiatement!*'

While the Frenchman berates them, I take a moment to survey him; he's got fire in his eyes as if ready to fight, but he's far too handsome to be putting his good looks at risk like this! So why is he? And then I recognise him. *Mon Dieu*, it's the guy from outside the train station whose arms I literally fell into. Truthfully, I've replayed that first brief encounter a few times since then. Is this some sort of sign? Fate? I don't usually believe in all that mumbo jumbo, and yet...

I blank the mêlée, mesmerised by every small detail about this man, from the sultry curve of his lips to his deep tan, as if he spends his summers in the French Riviera. He's got a Jude Law in his *Talented Mr Ripley* days look about him, and for a very brief moment I fall a little bit in love, before I catch myself. *The sultry curve of his lips?* I clearly miss editing romances, that's all it is! *A little bit in love with him?* I shake my head, hoping to dislodge the fugue. There's a quarrel happening before me and I am making goo-goo eyes at some stunning stranger. My life is already a shambles; I don't need to add any more complications into the mix.

The Frenchman gives the tallest guy a great big shove. I gulp, wondering what I've inadvertently stepped into. Should I help? What if it's a drug deal gone wrong? I could be an unwitting accomplice! Could it be a domestic dispute – perhaps the hot French guy stole one of their girlfriends? And I will not support a cheater, no matter how sultry their lips are. No, it's best I stay well out of the fray, since it doesn't concern me.

The trio dart glances over their shoulders and speak fast and low to one another in the shadiest of ways, while the Frenchman continues rebuking them, seemingly not concerned for his own safety. It's then I notice the zip on my handbag is open. *Je suis un idiot!* Being pick-pocketed is always a risk in the tourist hotspots of Paris if you're not aware of your surroundings. Usually this is easily avoided by using common sense: keeping your bags zipped up and placed to the front of your body, *not* forgotten, blowing about in the breeze behind you, like I've just done – an open invitation for those with the gift of sleight of hand to steal without the victim feeling a thing. All my systems are breaking down, as if someone else is in control of the motherboard. I am *never* this stupid! Usually, that is.

With great reluctance, one of the gang hands my purse and phone back, only because my rescuer is yelling – nay, roaring – for the *gendarmes*. They take off running and I turn to the blustery red-faced Frenchman, who blows out a breath before his features relax into a more amiable expression. In perfectly modulated English he says, 'I'm so sorry that happened to you. You must be very careful around the highly trafficked tourist areas.'

I mean, it's good advice but I already know that. Just a small lapse in concentration. '*Oui. Merci beaucoup!*' My voice peters off as his smile drops away. Why the sudden change in demeanour?

I'm about to tell him this is actually our second chance meeting when he says, '*Etes-vous Francais?*'

Am I French? '*Oui?*' I must look like a tourist. Has my time away changed me so dramatically that I'm no longer recognisable as one of them? '*Je suis Parisienne.*'

His features twist in anger. Does he not gauge the threat is over? 'You're Parisienne?'

He's really belabouring the point, but I let it slide out of politeness. '*Oui.*'

'Then you should know better!' My earlier estimation of him falls. Jude Law, hardly! Unless this is some kind of villain edit, and honestly, that doesn't surprise me – men are always a disappointment in one way or another. Even casual flings I've partaken in have been with the wrong type. Brooding bad guys. Smouldering-eyed alpha males. And for a moment I believed seeing this guy, *the* guy, was fate. How ridiculous! When will I *learn*?

I need a factory reset!

Why on earth am I attracted to such hostile men? Am I secretly a hopeless romantic who always thinks these love affairs will turn out like they do in the books? Have I got some fatal flaw that makes me sensible in every other area, except choosing a man? Not that I act on these feelings very often, but they're still there, lying dormant, waiting to strike.

Just like this specimen, who is very much main character material but suffers from an extreme case of bad manners.

'Usually in conversation one person speaks and then the other replies.'

Sarcasm? He's reading right out of the broody macho man handbook. '*I'm* the victim here and you're mad at me? That's rather problematic.'

His cheeks redden. 'You may as well wear a sign saying target *moi*, if you're not going to pay any attention to your surroundings. Not only would they have your purse and phone but all of your personal details too. They could steal your identity. Drain your bank account.' *Too late, another man has already drained it!* 'And all sorts of nefarious things. And you're just standing there with a smile on your face.' Oh God, that stupid love-struck grin was a byproduct of falling in love with this fool's sultry lips for all of five insanity-filled minutes. Blame the love at first sight books that I read on the daily. Or did.

That sudden enthral has now subsided.

Worse, he's right about me being lax about my surroundings; *however*, he doesn't need to harp on about it. 'It's my first week back in Paris and I was distracted by my life and my...' Why am I justifying myself to this belligerent man?

His eyes blaze as he continues his tirade. 'You should take more care. You're asking for trouble.'

My chest heaves. Who knew that was a real thing? It *actually* heaves. 'I'm asking for trouble because three men decided to steal from me? *That's* victim blaming and well out of order. You're a dinosaur! Stuck in another era!'

He shakes his head as if talking to a recalcitrant child. 'If you *were* a tourist, I would understand, but you're not and... Wait – didn't you bump into me at the train station?'

'What? No?' I lie, otherwise I'm bound to hear about my lack of spatial awareness next. A pressure in my head forms. I try not to catastrophise that it's the beginning of a tumour caused by undue stress, but, well, what if it is? The pain is not helped by this man who just won't let it go, will he? 'You are clearly not listening, like a typical *man*.'

He skipped right over the victim part and straight back into the blame. He's *such* a cliché. If this were a romance novel, I'd be enjoying the conflict, cheering the heroine on, willing her to get the last word in, but this is real life, and I find myself somewhat flummoxed in his presence, as if I'm two steps behind.

From experience, I know I'll conjure sharp witty comebacks around midnight, which will be entirely too late. The curse of *espirit de l'escalier* – to leave your wit on the stairs – I'm proficient in this particular skill. There's no way to prepare for this kind of conflict.

'I suggest you keep your wits about you in future,' he says.

'I suggest *you* refrain from offering unsolicited advice in future.'

He scrubs his face as if frustrated, when really I'm the one who is being mansplained to all over the place as if it's still the nineties and women have progressed nought.

'I guess you can thank me later?' he says, jumping on his high horse. I can almost hear the *neigh*.

I press my lips together and try my best to burn him with a glare. He won't be getting another word from me, and definitely not one of thanks. He expects to be lauded for his rescuing skills, for me to bend and scrape on my knees for my momentary lapse in concentration while he plays the part of knight in shining armour. Well, news flash: I don't need a rescuer! I'd have figured out the crime eventually and I have the lungs of a swimmer when I need to scream for help.

'Not even a single word of gratitude?'

Someone has a saviour complex, that's for sure, and a penchant for holding on to conflict. Alarm bells clang. This is an avoid-at-all-costs situation, because some self-sabotaging part of my psyche lusts after men who are no good. Why? Honestly, it stems from living in fictional worlds where the bad guys are marshmallows underneath, but I'm living in nonfiction land where the bad guys are just plain bad. So why do I get a small thrill at this exchange? It's obviously my subconscious not getting the memo.

He shakes his head and storms off, muttering to himself. All I catch is the word '*Banane*'. Is that obnoxious man calling me a banana? How rude.

I spin on my heel and head the opposite way, hoping I never run into him again. Which *should* be unlikely in this bustling metropolis. I zip up my bag and hold it firmly in front while I walk around the 7th arrondissement, looking for a place to hide, to cool my white-hot rage.

I'm rather ruffled. My confidence is already at an all-time low, and he's just highlighted the fact I almost got pickpocketed by the Eiffel Tower, a hunting ground for thieves.

As I'm idling, getting lost in side streets, I come to a cobblestoned laneway that is as pretty as a postcard come to life. There's an array of pastel shopfronts, as if each business coordinated so the colours that would complement one other. There's a florist on the corner, with a trolley laden with vibrant blooms, and the exotic perfume of roses permeates the air. There's a *paperterie* and *fromagerie*, but my eye is drawn further down to an ornate golden door. A riot of soft pink blooms spill from pots and I see the fluttering of pages atop a display table. A bookshop? I must investigate. I wander down the cobblestones and grin when I find I'm right. Above a pot of pink ranunculus, a sign waves back and forth in the breeze that reads: *The Paris Bookshop for the Broken Hearted.* I'm intrigued by the rather gimmicky name. Is it a clever marketing ploy for tourists? What else *can* it be? Although I've lived in Paris for the majority of my life, I've never seen this laneway. It's not exactly central to the main attractions and I've only found it because of my efforts to hide from that man.

The golden door squeaks as I push it open. As I step inside, I'm met with the unmistakable perfume of old books; an evocative citrus aroma with honeyed vanilla notes. Every bookshop has its own special scent, just like a well-thumbed novel has its own fragrance, from leathery to lavender, or a spicy nuttiness, each note an olfactory clue to its past, its rich history.

As my eyes adjust to the dim lighting, I take in a mahogany bar along the back wall. Bottles of spirits are lined up like the colours of a rainbow as twinkling fairy lights sparkle above. Well-worn leather stools sit empty awaiting patrons. A chalkboard is written up with the daily menu of charcuterie, I smile as I read it:

Romance *plat du jour, because what is life without love and sugar?*
A sweet range of petit fours and macarons.

Crime *plat du jour, because it would be a crime not to snack while you read!*
Saucisson, pâté, terrine and aged fromage served with a sliced baguette.

Fantasy/Sci-Fi *plat du jour, because sometimes we all need to escape to other realms...*
An extravaganza of sweet and sour bonbons.

It's a cute idea to have platters for readers to snack on as they get lost in the pages of a book and require sustenance for the big plot twist coming. It's as though I've pulled back the curtain and found Narnia in this quaint and quirky bookshop. I imagine friends converging here after work, ordering a cocktail while they lament over the ending of a love affair, the pain of a broken heart...

The bookshop itself is chaotic: shelves of indiscriminate height and colour are squashed wherever they fit, making the space feel like a maze, which is rather charming, as if you're following the yellow brick road on a quest to the Emerald city. I choose a path to wander, edging around piles of books stacked in towers on the wooden floor. Shelves are bowed with the weight of so many novels, all jumbled together. I take my phone from my handbag and snap photos to show Eloise. She'll love this little labyrinth of a place.

I smile when I find a romantic comedy I edited a year ago, written by Sally, one of my favourite authors. The bookshop owner must have good taste! I go to take a picture to send to her and then think better of it. Unfortunately, Sally is one of the authors who no longer speaks to me, and that still hurts.

I thumb through a stack of novels. They're a motley mix of old and new in various languages. The arrangement in the bookshop is unusual, as if there's no classification system in place at all. Not alphabetised, not sorted into genre, colour, height order. Not even into languages. It's as though stock is placed wherever there's a gap on the shelves, but then how do they ever find anything? This avant-garde sort of muddled bookshop aesthetic is very on trend at the moment, but it makes me itch and I fight the urge to neaten up the shelves.

The path loops around and I come back out in front of the bar once more.

A woman of about sixty with long grey curls wearing a flamboyant yellow ruched dress catches my eye and lets out a gasp before dashing over to me. She double blinks and then expels a breath, as if I've surprised her somehow. Did she not hear me come in?

When she composes herself, she says, '*Ma chérie*, for a moment I thought you were someone else!' A fleeting almost unfathomable look dashes across her face – pain, maybe, before she masks it with a welcoming smile. 'I'm Valérie and I've got a potion and passage for you. Sit, sit.' She taps the seat of a stool and speaks as if we've made this appointment ahead of time, and not that I'm a tumbleweed who just blew in off the street.

'Bonjour, Valérie. Ah, I'm Coco,' I say, in case she truly is mixing me up with someone else. I'm a rule follower, so I duly do as I'm told and sit at the bar, intrigued by what a potion and passage might be. Something magical? Witchy? If only I *could* incant a spell that would fix my life.

'You're right on time, Coco.'

'I'm...?' The rest of my sentence is lost as Valérie makes a racket with a cocktail shaker as she energetically mixes vibrant-coloured spritzers and syrups. I'm not quite sure what she's making but it's rather labour intensive. She pulls open drawers and cupboards and bangs them closed, all while humming '*La vie en rose*'.

'Is that your daughter?' She points to the screensaver on my phone. 'You're very similar.'

I smile at the thought. '*Oui*, Eloise. She's thirteen going on thirty.'

'Ah, I bet she keeps you on your toes. She's got moxie, *non*?'

'Moxie, that's one way to put it, *oui*.' It's such an American word, but it rings true for Eloise.

'Are you ready?' Valérie asks and turns holding a test tube that produces a mist as if it really is a potion.

I've stepped into a real-life fairytale.

Valérie places the tube onto a wooden rack while it does the 'bubble, bubble, toil and trouble' thing and then hands me another small bottle topped off with a cork. It holds a tiny rolled-up scroll, complete with a little wax seal. It's adorable and I can't help but be swept away by the theatre of it all.

'A bespoke potion,' she says, pointing to the test tube with the steaming vapour. I'm Alice in Wonderland, fallen down the rabbit hole into this strange, new world. '*L'editeur, non*?'

The editor. I startle, snapping my gaze back to the woman. Do we know each other, and I've forgotten? Although it's not like me to forget a face. Is that why she did a double take when I walked in? I'm positive I've never met her before; she doesn't look familiar at all. So how does she know I'm an editor? Is it just a lucky guess? *Merde*, surely bad news can't travel this fast. 'Erm – it's...'

She cuts me off. '...The name of your very own potion, which I'll make exclusively for you when you visit. It suits you. Colourful and pretty. Sweet and sunshiny.'

Is she just intuitive? Common sense prevails. I'm in a whimsical bookshop. Editing is not exclusive to me. All her potions are probably literary themed. It's just a coincidence that I happen to be in that field.

'Oh, erm, *merci*.' I take a sip of the tiny drink, hoping it's not exorbitantly priced. It's sugary, citrusy, perfectly refreshing for these early spring days. '*Exquis*.'

Valérie waves me away. 'I suppose you're wondering about

the scroll? Well, wonder no more. Take it out, read it. Memorise it. Say it every day, like a mantra. In time, it will cure all that ails in your life. I promise you that. All you have to do is... believe.'

I upend the tube and somewhat reluctantly break the cute wax seal as I unfurl the delicate scroll. It reads: *A person often meets his destiny on the road he took to avoid it.* Jean de la Fontaine, French fabulist and seventeenth-century poet.

Whatever Valérie's game is, she's very good at it. The quote lifts my spirits. What if the mistakes that led me here *aren't* my undoing, but rather the path that will lead to my redemption? My own heroine moment. The idea appeals that this fork in the road could lead to bigger, better things for me and Eloise.

Obviously, this is a performance, a unique selling point for customers, not an actual panacea for my troubles, but it's still fun to pretend. Valérie has oodles of charisma and I bet she's popular here in Paris, because who *wouldn't* buy into this charm, this amusement?

It's hard not to be carried away when I'm surrounded by a mishmash of enchanting novels and an eccentric bookseller who makes me feel relaxed, like she truly has cast a spell over me. Whatever the case may be, I like Valérie's energy and I look forward to spending more time in this fascinating little bookshop bar.

'*Merci*, Valérie. It's an inspiring quote. It gives me much to consider.'

Valérie studies me while she polishes a glass. 'I'm always right, *ma chérie*. You'll soon learn.'

I raise a brow as I sip my drink. Do bookworms enjoy meeting here, exclaiming over their potions and passages or sprawling on one of the many plush chairs scattered about? Even with the disarray...

The door creaks as another customer enters. Sunlight pools

in, casting a diaphanous glow over the books. Dust motes dance, sparkling like glitter, which only adds to the magical feel of the special bookshop, so I refrain from mentioning it might be best to run a feather duster along the shelves once or twice a day; often my practical suggestions aren't received well. I suppose most people don't want solutions, they want sympathy, and I find that sort of thing hard to differentiate.

Valérie gives a fluttery wave and excuses herself to welcome the newcomer. I glance over my shoulder to see if she repeats the same performance or changes it up for everyone. She greets the man effusively and gives him hug, as if she knows him well. 'Your usual?'

The man says, '*Oui, merci.*' The bright light behind him makes it impossible to discern his features and I don't want to be caught being nosy, so I face the bar while he shuffles off towards a wrinkly leather chair at the back of the bookshop. The chair sighs in an almost humanly way as he sinks into it, as if welcoming his heft. I'm about to remark on the oddity of such a thing when I lock eyes with the man and let out a groan. It's my 'rescuer'. They do say bad things come in threes, and here he is in the flesh. *Again.*

From Valérie's familiarity with him, I guess he's a *habitué* here, which means *I* won't be able to use this place as a refuge, which is a shame as I don't often feel so comfortable in my surrounds like I do here already.

'It's *you*,' he says, narrowing his eyes like the egotistical male he is...

5

Honestly, he's acting like I dog eared a page of his favourite book. I guess it's going to have to be me who brings him back to reality where this alpha hero gets brought down a peg or two.

Before I can school him about the polite way to talk to the opposite sex, he blurts, 'Did you follow me here?'

The audacity. '*Excusez moi*? I was here first.'

Valérie swings her gaze between us.

'First?' he says. 'Didn't you only return to Paris a week ago?'

Why did I tell him that! I suppress an eyeroll. 'I meant I was here first. In the bookshop. *Today.*' Once again, I feel like I'm on the backfoot with him because he somehow manages to get the better of me by twisting what I say. Gaslighting at its finest. Doesn't surprise me one little bit.

'Coco, meet Henri.' Valérie gives me a bright smile, as if flashing her pearly whites will be enough to distract me from the fact this man is a bully.

'*Enchanté*,' I lie and lob a bit of sarcasm back his way. After the Alexander debacle, I will not let a man get the better of me.

Henri gives me a smile as fake as his personality. 'Likewise.'

'Ah – how do you two...?' Valérie's eyebrows pull together.

My brain fogs with anger as I recall him by the Eiffel Tower walking away as he muttered under his breath. I point an accusatory finger at him. 'This man called me a banana!'

Valérie's eyebrows shoot up, but a grin plays at her lips. 'Did you, Henri?'

'Guilty as charged.' He holds his palms up as if he's won a point. 'You must admit you acted foolishly.'

Not this again! 'You're a horrible troll of a man.'

He steeples his fingers in that way supercilious people do when they're about to impart their brand of wisdom, but unfortunately for him, I don't believe he's wise at all. 'And *you* need some hard lessons about how to live safely in Paris.'

I hold up a hand. 'Enough "lessons" for one day, Henri. You're not the be all and end all, not even close.'

'Is that so? Without me, you'd be at the gendarmerie right now.'

Valérie gasps. 'The gendarmerie? Why?'

I turn away from the pig-headed imbecile and say, 'Henri saved me from a trio of pickpockets who'd managed to get into my handbag and grab my purse and phone.'

He folds his arms across his muscular chest. I hadn't noticed his athletic physique before. 'Oh, so you *do* admit I saved you now?'

I give him a long look. 'You stopped some pickpockets, you didn't accomplish world peace.'

Valérie's head is on a swivel and each time she goes to speak, one of us cuts her off. She finally manages to intervene, and with a clap of her hands she says, 'This all makes perfect sense! If I remember correctly, Henri, your passage was: *Whatever souls are made from, his and mine are the same. Emily Brontë.*' Valérie gives us such a hopeful smile that I wonder if she believes the schtick she's selling. Whatever she's on about, I need to nip this in the bud before it blooms into trouble, but she quickly adds, '*Love!* The most glorious part of life.'

Surely she's not insinuating Henri and I are a good match? This horrible hottie of a man and *moi*?

'Love can be glorious; well, at least in romance novels, Valérie, and I'm sure there's a perfect soul out there for Henri, a woman who adores swollen-headed, conceited, toxic masculinity types. He shouldn't give up his hope that such a woman exists, but I'm afraid that woman is not me. We are *terrifically* unsuited. One of us would end up dead and the other in jail and while I do love a good challenge, a jail cell holds no appeal.'

My words flutter into the ether unheard. I've lost Valérie to a daydream; her eyes are glassy as she skips off to fantasyland.

'Why would you be the one in jail?' Henri reels back, as if actually offended that in my own fantasy I'm the one who gets the better deal.

'Well, I wouldn't be the *dead* one, would I?' I mean, is he even *listening*? Another handy facet of being an editor is that I've been exposed to many a good crime novel and have the inside scoop on poisons that are almost undetectable in an autopsy, like aconite, for example. While I'd never poison anyone on principle, even I have my limits, my breaking point, if you will, so I've cannily stored many a helpful nugget of homicide knowledge away just in case. Preparation is key.

'I can see it now,' Valérie says in an awed hush. 'A summery wedding, pretty flower girls, vows so beautiful there won't be a dry eye in the house... Oh, what fun!'

How strange this bookseller is, plotting a fictional summery French wedding while I'm plotting a fictional murder. The seesaw of life and death.

Surreptitiously, I gaze at Henri to see what he's making of these outrageous imaginings. Does Valérie often get swept away on flights of fancy like this? By the horror written all over his face, I guess not. Forget Alice in Wonderland, this is a whole other fairytale. A dark Grimms' fairytale.

Valérie is someplace else, where rainbows and butterflies abound. 'Actually, it can be a *literary*-themed wedding! Wouldn't that be *très chic*? So fitting for you both. An editor and a journalist. A match made in heaven.'

'A match made in hell more like,' Henri says under his breath.

'A two-tiered book cake! No, *three!*' Valérie says. 'With fondant spines of your favourite novels. Soulmates who buddy read from now until all eternity...'

A sense of panic twists inside me. Probably because of the appeal of men who grimace and scowl, and strut and saunter, who wear too-tight clothing that accentuates their muscles and have an arty but mysterious tattoo. And now I'm being fantasy-married off to a guy just like that. My brain screams, *RUN!*

'Oh, would you look at the time!' I hold up a bare wrist. 'I best be off. The day has gotten away from me. Uh... *L'addition, s'il vous plaît?*' Pay and dash. It's as good a plan as any.

'Ah, *oui*, I too better go. I've got that... thing.'

Henri throws some crumpled euros on the bar and leaves in a hurry, as if the idea of one day marrying me is so abhorrent he'd rather run into oncoming traffic. And truthfully, I feel the same, except I'd rather not get hit by a car in my efforts to escape.

'That went well,' I say faux brightly, my cheeks aflame that Henri finds me entirely detestable. 'How much do I owe you?' I take my purse from my bag, a vintage bejewelled thing I got from Saint Ouen flea market a decade ago that has stood the test of time, lasting me longer than the loves of my life combined, which says it all really.

'It's your first visit,' Valérie says. 'Therefore, you don't owe anything.'

I frown, waiting for the punchline. What kind of money-making gimmick is this if she doesn't charge for the service? I go to protest, because even though it's all a magic trick, it has been fun to suspend reality for a while. Up until we got to the Henri-is-my-soulmate part, that is.

'But...'

'*Non*,' she says, a sparkle in her eye as if she's still dreaming of my upcoming imaginary literary wedding. 'I'll see you soon, Coco. It's been a pleasure.'

I nod my thanks and turn to go, but a question stops me in my tracks. 'Why did you name this place The Paris Bookshop for the Broken Hearted?'

Her smile turns bittersweet. 'Coco, you know how books find us at the very right time, right when our souls are yearning for a fix that we cannot name?' I nod. Bookworms know this to be true. 'The same goes for The Paris Bookshop for the Broken Hearted. The lost, the lonely, heartsick, heartsore find their way here. Find sanctuary.' She holds up a hand as if sensing I'm going to scoff at such a frank admission. Which I sort of am. It's preposterous. 'I'll admit it seems outlandish, a weird sort of sorcery, but this wizardry goes beyond me,' Valérie says. 'One day, the first broken heart came, and then a flood of them. I curated the business around it. You see the theatrics as a ploy, a con, but it's not. This place fixes those who are mired in grief and the cure is different for everyone, as is the time it takes to work.'

Convenient. 'Books *are* a salve, so I presume that's what you mean.' Books are wonderful friends and a place to go when the world turns dark.

'*Non*, Coco. The books help, but that's not only where the magic lies.'

Now I've heard it all. What else is there to say? I don't want to hurt the woman's feelings but what she's claiming is outside the realms of possibility. Then I remember the dust motes dancing, the chair making an almost human sigh. Of course, the bookshop is not magical, not really alive, but there's just enough of a hint that it is to enchant you into believing there's something special inside these walls. 'I see,' I eventually manage.

'Take you, for example,' Valérie says.

'Me?'

'You, Coco. You're suffering with a broken heart. It's written in every line and plane of your face. It's obvious in the set of your jaw, as if you're holding on to your pain with your teeth alone.' OK, she's nailed that one. 'It's evident in your soulful sad eyes. And you found your way here...'

The sceptic in me wants to voice my disbelief, but it wouldn't be polite. I do admire her business acumen, even if there is no classification system in place for the books. Her guesses are strangely accurate too; perhaps she's learned to read body language. That's all it is.

'Well?' she prods. 'Am I right? You've recently suffered a broken heart?' The smile she gives me is so winsome I can't help but return it. Maybe Valérie really does believe in this woo-woo, so I let it be.

'*Oui*, I'm recently single.' And in retrospect, probably sadder about losing our publishing house now that I know what kind of man he was. OK, I'm devastated by the betrayal, but I'm an expert in compartmentalising and will myself not to let that hurt rise. 'However,' I rush to add, 'that doesn't mean I'm looking for love, especially not with a man like Henri.'

'*Fait accompli*. I cannot change what's written in the stars, *ma chérie,*' she says firmly as if it's decided. 'Here.' She hands me a business card. *My* business card. 'You dropped this before.'

There is one secret solved. Coco Chevallier. Editorial Director.

6

A week later, I face another slew of job application rejections and suffer through a range of aborted phone calls to connections in the industry who were suddenly 'late for a meeting' they'd forgotten about. I'm no expert on human behaviour, but even I gathered they couldn't *all* be late for a meeting. This brush off is mortifying. Humiliating. I curse Alexander. He's probably living his best life on some deserted beach, mai tai in hand, while I white-knuckle my way through the mire.

I clench a balled-up tissue as I doomscroll job ads, searching for a pathway that will tide me over, but I can't find anything that suits my background, not with people I *don't* know, at any rate. Publishing is a small world and like any meaty scandal, this has spread far and wide. I'm too scared to look on Twitter in case I stumble on a hashtag of my name trending for all the wrong reasons.

Hitting the pavement to visit bookshops in the local vicinity with my CV is the next best course of action to apply for a job in person. Surely the gossip hasn't made it to bookshops. While it's not editorial, my first love, it's still in the book world, and right now an income is the priority.

I stand and stretch, my shoulders stiff after stooping over the laptop. A walk will reinvigorate me before I pick up my daughter. I'm hoping to take Eloise to the Bibliothèque Rainer-Maria Rilke on boulevard de Port-Royal and sign her up for a library card. By Parisian standards it's a small library, but it's teen friendly and will be a peaceful place for Eloise to study as I slowly let her have more freedom now that she's made a few friends. Before I head out, I fill up a water bottle, as my budget is now strictly for necessities. I've put an amount aside for a celebratory dinner once I do find employment. Positive thinking and all that.

After dropping my CV into various places, I lose track of exactly where I am – which doesn't often happen. This new scatterbrained version of me is rather alarming at times and I only hope the change isn't permanent. When I turn to double back, I'm surprised to find myself by the laneway of The Paris Bookshop for the Broken Hearted.

Did my broken heart lead me here? I have a stern talk with myself. It's one thing to briefly lose my navigational skills, but quite another believing broken hearts magically find their way to a bookshop for a potion and a passage and a cure!

The only reasonable cure for a broken heart is time, and depending on the severity of the break, that pain may never fully disappear. I'm reminded of the Japanese art of Kintsugi, the centuries-old tradition of fixing broken pottery with golden seams. The pottery is more beautiful for these so-called 'flaws' when fixed with golden threads to bind the pieces back together. I love the thought that those scars are emphasised rather than camouflaged. If I were to follow the philosophy of Kintsugi, what are the golden threads that patch a broken heart

back together? Time? Patience. A holiday? They don't seem
golden enough somehow.

Maybe as always, I'm overthinking it. It's meant to be
metaphorical.

What else cures a pain such as this? A pain I rarely admit
I'm feeling because I'm the adult. I'm the one guiding this ship.
Maybe Valérie is on to something and the remedy is different
for everyone. If so, what are my golden threads made up of?

A new romance? *Real* love. I swipe the thought away before
it takes hold. Love is *not* the answer.

I'm brought back to the present when the ornate bookshop
door swings open as a tour group leave carrying bags of books.
As I move to let them pass, a sign in the window catches my
attention: *Bookseller wanted. Apply within.*

How can this be? A perfect solution that is... *too* perfect. I
think back to my previous visit. I didn't confide in Valérie about
my lack of employment so it's not as though she could orches-
trate this just for my benefit, could she? All part of her plan to
fix the broken part of me. It's clearly just a coincidence she's
looking for staff and one I should take advantage of since I'm
also looking for work.

Henri's smug face comes to mind. Could I work in a place
he frequents?

What am I even saying? There's no guarantee I'll get the job.
Anyway, the bigger problem would be working in a place where
books aren't in any discernible order. Though I am adept at
assimilating in the most hostile of environments, which this is
not, so it should be achievable no matter how disorganised it is.
The methodical part of my brain will have to deal with it.

Which brings me to the next problem: do I tell Valérie
about my vast experience in the book world? If she searches my
name on the internet, she'll soon stumble on one of the many

articles written about London Field Publishing, the company that had my name on the masthead right beside Alexander's. My beloved boutique publishing house that is now no longer a going concern, leaving a staggering heap of betrayed authors in its wake. If I don't tell her and she finds out, that'll be infinitely worse. A lie by omission is still a lie. It's hard to know – will she judge me on sight?

Even my biggest supporters, my best friends in the world of publishing, struggled to understand how I remained blithely unaware, or they suspected that I turned a blind eye and enjoyed the spoils, when I did no such thing. The only thing I'm guilty of is trusting Alexander and believing the systems in place would keep my investment safe.

It came crashing down when I overheard my editorial assistant Molly-Mae on her mobile phone one afternoon. She was whispering about an author with missing royalties. How the heck Molly-Mae knew about this and I didn't was the first shock. Soon enough, the terrible truth came to light and the world as I knew it came crashing down...

7

THEN

Co-work Office of London Field Publishing

Alexander swaggers into the office with a wide smile on his face as he winks at my editorial assistant Molly-Mae. That wink goes against our safe workplace practices, which he should very well know, having signed off on the handbook I created. Next he brings out the finger guns, *pew, pew, pew*, in her direction. Is this some kind of farce? When did he become Mr Winky Finger-Gun-Shooter Guy?

It's creepy, not to mention the fact that I, his long-term partner, am sitting at the long boardroom-like table we all share and don't quite know how to react, except to blow out my cheeks in frustration.

Alexander's flirtatious manner should be the least of my problems, but it bothers me, as if cracks are appearing that will soon splinter into a crater that we'll all disappear down. It's anxiety making me think this way and yet I can't get a handle on it, not at this moment at any rate. It doesn't help that the smiling buffoon is winking and pretending to be a gun slinger, of all things.

My sense of unease is only heightened by his faux grin, his jocular energy. It's out of character. At work he's usually broody, prickly, exudes an air of being wildly busy, probably so no one disturbs him, and they come to me for help instead. I'm learning too late that I might have been duped by this act, and it doesn't feel good. My stomach twists like I'm suffering a bout of seasickness; the very ground beneath feels unstable, like I'm going to fall through a trapdoor I didn't know was there.

I stand up and motion Alexander to the shared lounge area a few steps away. It's thankfully empty of sprawling bodies so we should be able to speak in relative privacy.

Alexander grins as he spins on a chair and leaps off as if he's a child. Does he not comprehend the serious amount of trouble we're in because of him? Is this carefree persona some kind of act – *nothing to see here, folks* – purely for the benefit of our employees?

'Good morning, darling.' He dives onto the sofa.

I do my best to keep on an even keel; after all, we have an audience and this is all rather sensitive information. 'It's 11.51, not exactly morning any more, Alex. Where have you been?'

He lifts a shoulder, *laissez-faire*, as if it doesn't matter that he's hours late to work on one of the most important days in our history.

We've been in a committed relationship for the last five years. Soon after we fell in love, we decided to quit our jobs at a big London publisher and build this company together. It took a fair amount of cajoling on his part to convince me, what with me being risk averse and feeling like it was all very rushed, but eventually I conceded. My parents' entrepreneurial spirit must be alive and well in me too, although I think it was more my love of words and being in control of choosing those stories that spoke to me most.

While we're (were?) in love, we keep separate apartments. I'd always imagined once our relationship solidified he'd move in with us, but it hasn't happened. And now I have an inkling as to why. You should never trust a man that doesn't keep his promises, and I for one should have held fast to that rule. Stupid, *stupid* me.

'Stop jiggling your leg like that,' I say, my voice calm, despite my inner turmoil.

He tuts. 'Did you get out of the wrong side of bed today, Coco?'

'That's obnoxious.' Is he purposely pushing my buttons to distract me? It's not working. I need answers so I can figure out a solution.

'How so?'

'Alexander, why are you acting like this is just any other day?' I'm hyperaware our staff are too close and stealing quick glances our way. I'm sure they're curious as to why the atmosphere has changed. I keep my voice low and my expression neutral when all I really want to do is yell at him to stop this performance for one bloody minute.

'It *is* any other day.' The jiggling of his foot belies his relaxed demeanour.

I lower my voice to a whisper. 'This place is about to collapse like a house of cards.' A sob in the back of my throat catches me unawares. I fight to keep my composure. 'Janae's independent auditor came back with the findings and I'd like an explanation. There are monies missing from every single edition she's published with us.' Small enough amounts, so the system didn't alert me. Cleverly done.

Janae is one of our most prolific cosy crime authors who has been with us from day one. She's published twenty-two books over that time and has gone from strength to strength in sales.'

'Oh...?' He tugs at his tie as if it's too tight.

'You were cc'd in the email this morning, so don't pretend you haven't seen it.'

A muscle in his jaw works. 'So? There was a slight... glitch with her royalties. Mistakes happen, I'm only human.'

My heart bongoes painfully against my ribs. Deception is written all over his face. I'm stuck, not sure how to get him to confess. Worse, I can't use my voice loud enough to emphasise the urgency of getting these discrepancies explained. *If* there's a reasonable explanation. It won't be hard to find the truth – just follow the money – but I haven't had time yet.

'There's already chatter on the London Field author Facebook group. A lot of them are now wondering if they're missing money too. I'd like to reassure the group that's not the case because now they're all threatening to get audits done. If they go down that road, what will they find?' I hold my breath, hoping for a reason, a *genuine* reason, that won't close our doors.

His Adam's apple bobs up and down. Not a good sign. It's like he's attempting to swallow his lies before they can slip from his mouth.

'*Alex?*'

In a flash, he drops the convivial act and his eyes darken, turn hard. 'Bloody Janae should have left well enough alone.' He lets out an expletive under his breath. 'It's the cost of doing business, Coco. Which you know nothing about as you sit in your ivory tower pandering to them all, obsessing over syntax and similes. Yeah, so what if I skimmed a bit from each author? That's what it takes to get them to the top.'

From *each* author?

My chest tightens, compressing my lungs. Ivory tower! The man is maddening, but if he means he's skimmed a bit for *their* benefit, does that mean it's been used for the greater good?

'Did you use those skimmed funds for promotion?' Maybe he paid some book influencers under the table? 'If so, then we can at least account for it. It's not ideal but we can show it hasn't been...' The word sits heavy on my tongue. '*Stolen.*'

I'm in charge of the small editorial department and Alexander handles the accounts and oversees marketing, and although we have dedicated staff exclusively for promotion, he still guides them. It's always been this way. From our monthly profit and loss reports, I've never had any reason to doubt him or the trajectory of income, which has been steadily increasing. Now I don't know which way is up and what exactly I'm dealing with here. Have my failsafes... failed?

'No, it wasn't used for promotion. I've moved heaven and earth for our authors. A handful of those have hit the number one chart position. *Number one!* Not bad for a five-year-old boutique publishing house. They won't begrudge us for taking a sweetener, surely?'

He's talking in riddles. My low-level headache ramps into a blinder and whatever control I had over myself vanishes. I bellow, 'What do you mean "*us*"? There is no us in this equation. *You* took it. Where is the money, Alexander?'

We're doomed. The business we built from the ground up is going to crumble, author by author, book by book. And for what?

There's a coldness to him that sends a shiver up my spine. I don't recognise this man before me. 'Fine. *I* got some of them to dizzying heights and *I* took payment for that.'

I scrub my face as tears threaten. This is worse than I'd expected. Much worse. 'But what for?' We pay ourselves decent enough salaries. The first few years were so lean that I used the remaining funds of my inheritance from my aunt to get by. Once we'd built the business up enough, our profits allowed us an increase in our own salaries. Every start up is the same – owners reap the rewards last. We pay ourselves an amount generous enough that I can afford a humble two-bedroom apartment in North London and he's on the same amount as me.

'It's gone.'

'*Where?* If you've taken "sweeteners" from every author, for every edition, we're talking about a lot of money here.' Deep down, I suspected as much. Small amounts are easier to miss in this context. It's only that I gave Janae exact sales figures in real time for her last novel and she noticed the difference on her royalty statement.

Alexander has the grace to blush. Then the puzzle pieces slide into place. 'You've been seeing someone else.' When we first started dating, he was grandiose: flowers, chocolates, first edition books. Fancy dinners in Michelin-starred establishments. When we started the company, I told him that while I appreciated those gestures, our money was best spent investing in the future. Still, he spent lavishly on himself, and I just put it down to our different personality types. It should be no surprise I'm a saver who once had a healthy emergency fund, until I used it all to make this place work.

Has he stolen the money to squander on another woman? The wink he gave to Molly-Mae unsettled me. It seemed so natural, so well practised. The more I consider there's another woman, perhaps multiple women, the more it all makes sense. It explains why he hasn't wanted to move in with us, why he often cancels last minute. Why he has been uncontactable some weekends. I'm a big fan of solitude, so my suspicions weren't aroused. I'd figured we had a healthy relationship built on trust and mutual understanding, and I enjoy schlepping around with Eloise on Saturdays as we explore London.

'I never said we were exclusive, Coco.' The betrayal feels like a gut punch. As though my entire London life has been a lie. He sounds like one of those god-awful men from *Sex and the City*.

My headache blooms into a migraine. '*You* talked about marriage. Babies!' I thank my lucky stars that I dodged that bullet. Apparently my workaholic sensibilities were a worry and he wasn't sure my *ambition* wouldn't get in the way of me having a second child. How did I let that comment go?

I have been such a fool for love. I want to crumble on to the rug.

'So you've spent all of the stolen money?' I fight the urge to pull my hair out because we're still being watched by office staff, including our new intern who has her mobile phone angled towards us. Great. This is probably being live streamed on TikTok as we speak.

'It's gone. It's all gone. I spent it on my happiness, and I expected our authors to be grateful since I got some of them, *especially* Janae, to the top of the bestseller charts, a feat, I might remind you, that she had not been able to achieve at any other publishing house.'

'Well, Alexander, you might feel that your marketing prowess helped, and I'm sure it did. But this is a business. You can't steal money from people because you think you deserve it. I mean, I can't even believe I have to spell this out to you.' The rage I feel is enough to make my hands quake and my legs buckle. He's abused his position of power and – worse – is going to take me down with him. The stab of pain that we were never exclusive is sidelined as I panic about the future of the business, which has the domino effect of interfering with my daughter's future. 'Janae is talking about getting the authorities involved.'

His lips move but no sound comes out. This piece of intel *finally* gets his attention. When his brain catches up with his mouth, he blurts, 'There's no need for the authorities to be involved, is there? We can doctor up some promotional invoices, explain it away.'

I feel a sort of loss, an ache in my heart, staring at this complete stranger opposite me. Like I'm skittering, skating atop that trapdoor, as it sneakily creaks open to swallow me whole. How did I not notice this unscrupulous side of him? How did I not see he's a lying, cheating snake? *Has* my ambition blinded me? No, I will not blame my ambition, or myself. All I'd yearned for was security for my daughter's future, and I worked hard to make that happen.

'We're not doctoring anything. We'll put this to rights. We'll pay them all back, every single penny of it, and just hope to God they don't press charges. Our names are going to be mud in the industry. Publishing is a small world and once this gets out to the masses, which it will, that's it for us. How could you do this, Alexander…?' All the pent-up energy I had leaves my body in a whoosh and I slump on the sofa. My mind turns to my daughter. Is this situation salvageable? What happens if I *do* lose everything?

'Let's not be hasty. I'll convene a meeting and tell them there's been a little hiccough with the accounting software. How about that?'

'What aren't you getting, Alexander? You can't lie!' How could I have loved this man? Dreamed of a future together. Hoped like some lovelorn idiot that we'd *eventually* move in together and live in blissful harmony. He was good with Eloise, not in the sense of participating in any parenting but goofing around to make her laugh and often included her in planning activities for weekends and the like.

He's been in her life for five years now; will this sudden breakup hurt her too? Another worry to add to the list.

'Well, on that note, I've got some calls to make.' He leans forward to kiss me on the cheek. The hide of the guy. I slide out of range.

'Like that, is it?' His lip curls.

His dark change in demeanour produces an involuntary shiver, but I will not be cowed by him. 'I'll organise a Teams meeting with our authors this afternoon. You'll own up to what you've done and promise to make amends as fast as possible. Then you'll hand in your resignation, and we'll figure out what comes next for London Field Publishing.'

'I'll take a leave of absence, let the furore die down, eh? People have short memories.'

I'm only half listening, sick of the sight of the guy while my mind spins with scenarios about how I can salvage the business and save my own skin.

Will there still *be* a business once we tell our authors what he's done? From the chatter I've witnessed on the Facebook group, there's much talk about abandoning ship, and I don't blame them. The trust is gone.

It's best if the thief himself owns up to his mistakes. Then I'll sweep in and reassure them I'm going to investigate the matter and make restitution. 'I'll arrange the meeting for 2 p.m. Please prepare what you're going to say. Be *contrite*, at least.'

'Two o'clock, yeah, sure, sure,' he says breezily. He salutes me as if I'm some sort of dictator and instead of getting to work, he makes a beeline for Molly-Mae. He whispers something in her ear, and she darts a nervous glance my way. What is that all about then? Just as I'm about to jump up to protect her, he makes a drinking gesture with his hand, as if he's off to get a coffee when there's a perfectly acceptable pod machine here. There's a shiftiness about him as he power-walks away. Call me crazy, but I have a premonition he won't be back.

* * *

After hosting the author Teams meeting solo – *no surprise there* – exhaustion gets the better of me. With a fixed smile in place, I let the staff know they can leave early today. They've now overheard what's going on, but I don't have the energy to tackle a talk with them right now.

When I'm finally alone, I lean my head on my desk and battle the urge to cry. While our staff have left, there's still a lot of people in the co-working space and the last thing I need is someone asking me if I'm OK; that will send me over the edge.

Our stable of authors are collectively seeking legal advice about cancelling their contracts. According to author Janae, who discovered the thefts, they're well within their rights to do this as per a specific clause in their contracts, which I do vaguely recollect.

Even romcom writer Sally has abandoned ship. My very first acquisition as editorial director in my own biz and the author I've grown the closest with. Editors shouldn't have favourites, but it's impossible not to, especially after five years, over many video chats and many manuscripts.

Sally sends her messy first drafts in a mad panic after churning out the bones of the story while learning about her heroine on the go.

When I take delivery, her first draft is riddled with errors, random gobbledygook notes in the margin and highlighted sections she's still to research. I roll my sleeves up and wade into the manuscript, enjoying the idea of being able to offer another set of fresh eyes, a different perspective. Round two is where the magic happens for Sally – taking her rough diamond and polishing it to a shine.

Conversely, there's Gillian, who meticulously plots her books, including down to the type of shoe her protagonist wears. Gillian is *always* affronted when I send structural edits – as if I'm ripping her work to shreds with my gentle suggestions about how to make the manuscript stronger. I wait a few days, and then call her to massage her delicate writer's ego hidden behind a rather brash exterior. A week later, having had time to consider the edit suggestions, she'll come back to me with a clearer mind and the knowledge that I *am* on her side. I'm her co-captain, happy to get muddy with her in the trenches to make her book the best it can be. And so she uncoils her shoulders and gets to work. I understand Gillian. She's much like me in terms of needing structure and a plan.

And I can't forget cantankerous Phillip, a retired DS who pens intricately layered police procedurals. The gruff man will not, under any circumstances, chat about his manuscript until he's first shared a litany of complaints about the state of the publishing industry. He particularly likes to grumble about crime author colleagues who write about policing matters incorrectly, which he sees as a slight against him personally and the entire UK police force.

Every author is different, nuanced, has their own quirks, strengths and weaknesses. Their own *rhythms*. I have developed a sort of innate author operating manual so that I'm able to play to those strengths and help coax the best story *from* authors *for* readers. Their behaviours are often driven by self-doubt, so it's a matter of recognising what they're afraid of and reassuring them that between us, we can make it work.

Inevitably, I grow close to my authors. It's a relationship built on trust and one I've tried to always protect. There's a real vulnerability when an author sends a manuscript to me, so I strive to make them feel they're in safe hands, and I'm not only their editor but their cheerleader too.

Perhaps I should speak in past tense though because the way the video call went, I sense they're not going to *be* my authors any more.

And already, I'm grieving the loss of these author–editor relationships. It'll be yet another breakup in a way, and I'm sad to even think of such an eventuality.

However, I can't pine now; time is of the essence, so I pull myself together and make a call to my lawyer to see what can be done to mitigate the damage and where I stand. My priority is our authors, and then I'll work out what's left to salvage. I only hope what Alexander stole doesn't have too many zeroes attached.

8

NOW

Bookseller wanted. Apply within.

I can't stop dithering outside the bookshop. Is it nerves? Maybe. I send up a silent prayer to the book gods that Valérie will hire me on the spot as I push open the heavy door to find the bookshop is busier today. She's serving customers at the bar. While I wait, I scour the bookshelves, righting fallen tomes and *accidentally* putting them in height order.

Henri is in his usual chair at the back, so I quickly avert my gaze but not before I catch the determined set of his jaw. The man always looks at odds with the world. It doesn't matter to me anyway. The only men in my life from here on out are my book boyfriends. And even those I'm going to keep a beady eye on in case they step out of line.

'Bonjour, Coco.' Valérie regally swishes over. Today she's wearing an oversized navy pinstriped suit with gold buttons, giving a nautical vibe. She's quite the fashionista and I suddenly feel drab in comparison. 'You're here about the job, I take it?'

How does she know these things? Confusion must flash

across my face because she laughs and says, 'You were staring at the "Bookseller Wanted" sign outside for a good fifteen minutes, as if you couldn't quite make up your mind.'

'Right. I was busy taking a trip down memory lane.' The reminder of where I've come from only fuels the fact that I need this job.

'Memory lane can be a blessing and a curse, and by the look on your face, it's the latter.'

'*Oui*, it's definitely the latter. Has the bookseller position been filled yet?'

Valérie motions for me to follow her to the quieter end of the bar away from a small tour group delighting over their potions and passages. I prop myself up on a stool and take great pains to not look in Henri's direction. The more I try not to, the harder it gets, probably because I can *feel* his laser-like eyes on me. No doubt the guy is itching for another round, but I am above all that pettiness and if I want this job, I'll have to play nice with him.

Valérie plonks a martini glass filled with a vibrant chartreuse concoction on the bar in front of me.

'Oh, *merci*, but it's a little early for a cocktail. I've got—'

'*Ma chérie*, it's a green goddess *mock*tail to perk you up. Normally I'd make your potion again, but something tells me you need an energy boost, and that will provide it. Get some colour in your cheeks. You're wearing a frown so big it threatens to swallow you up.'

I relax into a smile, hoping it eases my pinched expression, or next, I'll be adding premature ageing to the list of things to worry about. Eloise has already highlighted the fact I don't take care of my skin properly, and by that she means spending a fortune on serums and retinols and all sorts recommended on TikTok.

'Is it the lack of work that's bothering you?'

Do I play down my desperate need for a job or go for honesty? I sense Valérie will see through any half-truths. And so what if I'm desperate? I'm sure most of us have been in a similar bind before. '*Oui*, I need a job as a matter of urgency. Things haven't quite gone according to plan lately and, well, my daughter and I, we're starting over.'

Valérie gives me a solemn nod. 'Drink up, *ma chérie*, and I'll tell you about your new job.'

'My new— But aren't you going to interview me? Don't you want to know about my experience? What I might be able to offer you? What my best traits are? My worst?'

Valérie wrinkles her nose. 'How utterly boring. Words are just words, in some cases. You're not exactly applying for a role in the French Secret Service, Coco. You'll be required to make drinks, assemble our bookish charcuterie boards. Potions and passages are my domain, but perhaps that can come later. Sell books. Stack books. And run the book club because all the members do is argue and I've had it up to my eyeballs. They need a moderator who can guide them, be *en garde*, so to speak. Can you handle a bunch of unruly readers, Coco?' She waggles a brow in a way that suggests these readers are not your average bibliophiles.

I consider it. How boisterous can they be? I've found that, bookworms are usually accepting, sensitive types because reading expands their minds and deepens their empathy.

'I've had experience handling writers, so I'm sure I can handle a book club, no matter how boisterous they might be.' I sense Valérie is exaggerating. Book club discussions might become a little intense if they disagree over a book every now and then, but that's to be expected. Reading is subjective and no two people read a book the same way or take the same message from it. I'm sure I can steer them right. Keep things in order. Or is that the desperation speaking?

'Writers have nothing on these particular bookworms, but if you're up for the challenge, I'd love to have you, Coco. Staff come and go here in quick succession; it's to be expected. The days are hectic. Cleaning and restocking in the lulls becomes tedious. For transparency, I've had all manner of employees assure me they're here for the long haul and they don't last the week.'

Nothing can get in the way of saving for our own place. 'I appreciate the fair warning, but I'm sure I can handle it.'

'Then we have a deal.'

I swear I light up from the inside, and I'm not prone to such impractical concepts.

We chat about salary and work hours and the fact that there are very few rules when it comes to putting stock away. 'Books go wherever *feels* right,' Valérie says.

I suffer an involuntary eye twitch. 'I understand. The system is: there is no system.' In a way, that *is* a system. Can I live with it? That's the question. It's not my place to make a semblance of order when Valérie has intentionally made the bookshop disorderly; it's part of the appeal. Unless you like order in a disorderly world, like me.

'There's no computer system to input inventory in either, because I don't have enough years left on this earth for such mind-numbing jobs, so I just price them up when they arrive and *voilà*.'

'Enough years left? You're not exactly doddery, Valérie.' I guess she's around sixty years old but it's hard to tell because she's always well made up and immaculately groomed and has the energy of much younger person.

'This place keeps me young, but I feel doddery on the *inside*, so I'd rather spend my remaining decades avoiding inputting tiny little numbers onto a tiny little screen.'

'Makes sense,' I lie as part of me dies inside. How does she keep track of inventory, profit and loss? The answer is, clearly she doesn't. This will be an experiment – to see how I cope with someone who is the very opposite of me in terms of organisation.

I am concerned how I'll be able to recommend books if I can't look them up on a computer and find them easily on the shelves. Especially since there's such an eclectic mix of old and new, that will be a challenge, but also fun to explore each nook and cranny and discover what books we do have. I'm a master at creating mental maps, and if needed I can use a spreadsheet to keep track.

'When can you start?' We agree on four days per week as Valérie already has casual staff for the weekends and the bookshop is closed on Mondays.

'Is tomorrow too soon?'

'*Non*, tomorrow is perfect.'

'*Merci*, Valérie. I really appreciate this. I won't let you down.'

She waves me away as if no thanks are needed. 'You're on the path you're meant to be. It was always going to happen.' I'm coming to learn that Valérie often throws out sentences like positive affirmations. I'm not sure if it's because she's in the business of mending broken hearts thus is always trying to boost a mood, or if that's just a quirk of hers.

I say my au revoirs and go to leave, catching Henri surveying me with a look that implies he heard most of our conversation and is mulling it over. Who cares if he overhead that I'm a struggling solo mother who is starting over? OK, I care. I'm the type who prefers to keep my private life just that – private. It can't be helped, and not even Henri eavesdropping is going to dampen my mood. I did it! I am now gainfully employed!

Later that afternoon, with a spring in my step, I make the trek to Eloise's school. I'm excited to share the good news and show her the library as promised too. Perhaps we can take my parents to La Coupole for dinner. It's my dad's favourite brasserie especially when there's a special occasion to celebrate. It's a stunning landmark of the *belle époque* era with its art deco décor and gorgeous domed ceiling. It's rumoured to be British chef Rick Stein's preferred place to dine in Paris. Not that my dad cares about any of that, but he will like being spoiled with all the fresh seafood on offer, and it will go a small way in showing my gratitude to them for all they continue to do for us.

9

Eloise's expression is taut as she trudges towards me. *Merde.* Even from this distance I recognise the signs of mutiny; shoulders stiff and high, lips pressed hard into a straight line, eyes dark and fiery. This equation means she's suffered an upset and is only *just* holding herself together for the sake of appearances. I've learned to read the signals, so that I'm best equipped to deal with these moods. My heart lurches. What could've happened?

I muster a welcoming smile as I shrivel up inside. That mother guilt is a wily beast, always lying in wait. The pendulum of raising a teenager swings from high to low.

If I ask her what the issue is, she'll likely shut me down. The minefield of adolescence. Raising teens is like a game of chess, and it takes some careful consideration to decide which move to make.

First, I lead with the distraction technique in case it's just a crabby mood. 'Bonjour. Let's go the *bibliothèque* and get you a library card.'

She grunts in response and kicks at the pavement.

I'm not daunted though; I press on. 'I have the *most* wonderful news. I landed a job today! At a place called The Paris Bookshop for the Broken Hearted. I start tomorrow.'

'*Felicitations,* Mum,' she mumbles, glancing over her shoulder. Is she missing her friends? The trio of girls aren't hanging in a cluster by the steps as usual. Could that be why she's morose? She can't find them and feels left out?

'*Merci,* darling. It's a fascinating little place – quirky, full of all sorts of bookish curiosities. I'd love to take you there at the weekend and treat you to a book and you can meet the lovely owner, Valérie.'

'I don't feel up to it.' Her bottom lip wobbles slightly. There are times when she wants a shoulder to lean on, and other times she snaps at me for coddling her too much.

'It's only Wednesday, you might feel up to it at the weekend. We can wait and see. How was school? Are you keeping up with the workload OK?' Could it be a problem with a subject? She's always struggled with maths. 'Are your teachers nice? The students?'

'I hate all of it. The work, the teachers, the students. I hate Paris.'

We had just over two blissful weeks where she really seemed to be settling in aside from a few teary evenings after speaking to her BFFs in London. Perhaps the honeymoon period is waning. The swing of that pendulum is gnarly; you never quite know when it's on the way back until it's too late. 'Did something happen?' I guide her away from the school gates in the direction of the library.

She heaves a sigh as if she's carrying the weight of the world on her stiffened shoulders. Without her usual haughty mask in place, she looks so young, so childlike, as though her transition into confident teenager is really all smoke and mirrors. Why can't kids just stay kids? Adulthood comes soon enough. 'It's a long story.'

I give her hand a comforting squeeze. 'We've got time, darling, and this sounds important.' It must be serious, whatever's bothering her, because she doesn't shake my hand away and we're still near school where it's expressly *verboten* to show any displays of affection towards her.

'OK. But you have to promise you're not going to get involved.'

'Well that depends on...'

'*Promise.*'

I sigh. 'Fine. I promise under the condition that it's nothing serious.'

Eloise nods; the deal is made. 'Léa's been, like, off with me.' From what I've gathered, it seems as though Léa is the leader of the pack. That kind of dynamic always bothers me but I keep my opinions to myself for now.

'How so?'

'It started with some jokes about me being different coming from London, as if it's the Wild West or something.'

'Not very funny, I agree, but go on.'

'I kind of laughed them off because what else can you say without it turning into an argument? Or they'll tease me about being a snowflake, like I'm too sensitive or something?'

From the many self-help books I've read about rearing teenagers, I know this is *not* the time to give her a ten-point plan with various strategies. I'm supposed to *listen* to her as she shares her feelings, and once she's opened up I can then offer practical solutions. It all makes sense on paper, but in the real world, it's bloody hard not to demand she ditches these so-called friends. Growing up is just plain hard work without adding this kind of thing into the mix.

'I understand. You laughed it off in the hopes it would end there and obviously it hasn't?'

She pulls her lips to one side. 'No, it hasn't. Léa kept going on about stupid things, like how weird my shoes are.'

I drop my gaze to her shoes. Simple leather Mary Janes, a staple school shoe. I cannot envisage how one could label them weird.

We leave the busy street and head down Rue Madame. 'What shoes does Léa wear?' Not that I want Eloise to compare, or worse, cave in and buy the same shoe, but I'm genuinely curious.

Eloise makes a bitter sound: half grunt, half scoff. 'Louis Vuitton platform loafers. They're, like, really *nice*.'

'They're just a platform loafer. They go on your feet.' I can imagine just how much those loafers cost. Too much.

Eloise gives me one of those drawn-out sighs that reflects, I presume, that I'm missing the point. 'You're all about practicalities, but fashion is important too.' It's not that I don't care for fashion, I am half French after all, it's more that I don't agree with buying a brand name purely because everyone else is. Our wardrobes are full of good-quality fabrics rather than focusing on the brand itself, some we invested in new, others we found by scouring London thrift shops.

I fight the urge to lecture her about luxury items providing a faux sense of self-worth because that's not what she wants to hear, but it spills out anyway. 'Fashion is personal. You can still be *trés chic* without wearing designer clothes where you're effectively paying exorbitantly to advertise their brand for them.' She rolls her eyes. 'However,' I quickly add, 'this isn't about designer footwear versus mid-tier brands, this is about another teenager making you feel bad because of your adequate and sensible shoe choice, no?'

'It's a miracle!' she says, fist to the sky. 'You're getting it!'

'Well, I *am* very intelligent and I was once your age, Eloise. Despite what you think, things haven't changed that much.'

'That's depressing.'

'*Oui*. Most of us have suffered the same fate – not having the latest fashion, gadget, holiday that the upper echelon had. It's not new.'

'Well, it gets worse. After telling everyone about my weird babyish shoes, she started on my clothing choices.'

Now I'm confused. 'How, when you all wear the very same uniform?' I got Eloise's school uniform second-hand but made sure each piece was in good condition.

'Insta.'

'Instagram?' She shoots me a look. 'This is not a criticism. OK, it is, but can you use full words when you're in my company? I like words to be the regimented length.'

'Oh, Mum. *Seriously*.'

'So Léa looked at your Instagram page and decided your clothing isn't acceptable by Parisian standards...?' I'm beginning to dislike this Léa child.

She gives me a decisive nod. 'And... she me called me cheugy, which is a massive insult.'

That's a new word for the collection. I try to unscramble what it could possibly mean and come up blank. 'Cheugy? It's not a French word?'

Eloise shakes her head. 'No, it's English, but they use the same expression here. Blame social media.'

'There's no way of translating it. What does it mean?'

She flicks a silky strand of hair back. 'It's someone who is, like, mega off trend. Wears skinny jeans and sheepskin boots, has a side part, watches Friends reruns. Exudes that girl boss, hustle culture energy. Posts Insta pics that say, *Rosé all day!* Basically someone stuck in the early 2010s.'

'And that's a bad thing? It sounds suspiciously like me.'

She grins. '*Exactly!* Just like you! You have that cheugy Millennial vibe.'

I take a moment to determine whether I'm offended or not. Gen Z speak is meant to be mostly tongue-in-cheek; sass. But seriously, what's wrong with skinny jeans?

'In that case, you clearly don't fit the criteria for cheugy.'

She makes a face. 'I know, but my Insta goes back a long time when I did sort of look a *bit* cheugy.'

'You started your Instagram account at age thirteen, the minimum age requirement for the platform, the age you are *now*.'

'Right. A lot can change.'

'In *nine* months?'

'That's almost a *year*.' The passage of time must go much slower for teenagers. I regularly monitor her social media, and I haven't noticed any drastic cheugy-like change from the Eloise nine months ago to now. 'I wasn't, like, wearing sheepskin boots but I did make some questionable fashion choices. The sequined headband with a side part for example.'

I smile. 'Aw! I still love that headband! It's bedazzling, bright, sparkly...'

'*Babyish*.' I let the comment slide away. It's so strange how a child can pivot from sparkly headbands one day to coveting designer label shoes the next. 'Then the other two girls joined in, pointing out other posts, not just what I wore but also my captions. The rest of the class overheard and laughed too.'

This is why I didn't want her using social media. She

pushed from age eleven for it because 'everyone else uses it', but I wouldn't be swayed. She didn't meet the minimum age requirements, simple as that. I'd have held out forever if I'd had my way. 'That's not nice of her, Eloise. Did you tell her to stop being so rude?'

I'm not great with confrontations, who is really, and I sense my daughter is the same, especially being the new kid at school and not wanting to make waves. She blows out a frustrated breath. 'No, I just kept this dumbstruck smile on my face as if it was funny. *Urgh*, and then Léa asked me why I had Rapunzel hair. Was I hoping for a boy to come and rescue me from my bad fashion choices?'

My heart plummets. These girls *are* bullying her – for what reason?

'Eloise, you know this behaviour is not acceptable, don't you?'

She pulls a face. 'Yeah, I guess, but what if I *am* cheugy, and my hair *is* so 2010? Maybe it's time to cut it all off?'

What! Her hair is her crowning glory, long luscious locks that are naturally wavy. 'They all have those jellyfish cuts or wear coastal cowgirl pigtails with bows.'

The – what? Not even hair is simple to understand any more. 'So? Who cares what they have?'

'*I* care, because I want to fit in. Not stand out.'

Why are teens like this? These children are obviously trying to bring my daughter down a peg but how to get Eloise to understand this and to rail against it?

'I get that you're trying to fit in but changing who you are isn't the way to go about it. A *real* friend will love you no matter what clothes you wear, or how you style your hair. They won't stalk your social media posts to make fun of you, especially in front of others.'

'You don't know what it's *like*.'

'My first real friends were *fictional*, Eloise, and that made me a target because I had no desire to be included, so I do know what it's like. With us moving so often for my parents' business ventures I was the new kid far too many times to count and I learned fast it was always best to stay true to myself, no matter whether I fit in or not.'

Eloise gives me a long look as if she's debating arguing the point. 'Yeah, but Mum, it wouldn't bother you if you had no friends, as long as you had a book to read.'

'That's not entirely true. I'd get lonely just the same as you. But reading is a refuge when life gets tough. Instead of dwelling on my sadness, I escape into other worlds. It's the best form of therapy there is.'

'Yeah, but I don't want to escape into a book. I want to go back to London where my *real* friends are and I know that's not an option, so I guess I'm stuck with Léa and the gang.'

Ah! If all else fails, turn to her idol. 'Ask yourself, what would Taylor Swift do? She wouldn't kowtow to these girls. She wouldn't change her style, her hair. One thing I love about her is she stays true to herself. You don't see her rushing off for one of those starfish cuts...'

'Jellyfish.'

'...One of those jellyfish cuts, or some oddly named pigtails. Taylor would write a song about them and find nicer students to be friends with.'

'Hmm. Before this started, I really liked them, Léa especially. Now I don't know what to think. What if it's just that Léa is having a bad week? Should I give her another chance?'

'That's up to you, but if it were me, I'd distance myself from them for a bit.'

She expels a pent-up breath. 'Maybe.'

It's rare that my daughter is this vulnerable with me. I'm glad she's sharing these big feelings, even though I can't do much to help at this stage, except to monitor the situation and keep the lines of communication open. The tiger mum in me wants to march down to the school and demand justice. But that won't work. It'll only make it worse; been there done that got the silent treatment.

'Is that why we're here in Paris? So that you can distance yourself from Alexander?'

Eloise knows a pared-down version about what happened with Alexander. She's at the age I felt she was mature enough to handle the truth, or at least parts of it. After all, the man had been in her life for a long time.

A tricky part of parenting is knowing how much to share. Enough so they understand, not too much so they aren't burdened by it. 'No, I'm not keeping my distance from him, it's probably the other way around. We came back to Paris in large part because I needed the kind of support only my parents could give. Not just giving us a roof over our heads, but emotional support too. I needed home. I needed to lick my wounds and let them heal.'

'Because of the thefts?'

I frown. 'How do...?'

She shakes her head at me as if I'm dense. 'Google, mum. *Google*. You're not exactly a spontaneous person, and you're all jittery when you're pretending everything is fine.'

'I am?' My acting abilities are second to none; that faux brightness requires a lot of energy to keep up. Hadn't I nailed my role?

'You are. You speak in this high voice, and you paste on a terrifying smile that gives me nightmares.'

I guess my lockjaw was obvious to one and all. 'I'm sure it's not that bad!' She mimics it. 'OK, that is terrifying.'

'When you said you'd quit your job, I knew that couldn't be right. You'd never just leave your authors like that, especially not Sally and Janae.' They've grown close to Eloise over the years too, sending her birthday cards and small gifts at Christmas.

'I – uh.' Am flummoxed. I didn't want to tell her about the business, not yet anyway. It felt like too much on top of Alexander's disappearing act. The man didn't even have it in his heart to say goodbye to Eloise, and that bothered me. I'd have kept my cool in front of her, he knows that.

'So I researched online about what happened to you. How Alexander vanished. I'm glad your lawyer proved you weren't involved in the thefts.' Her voice turns hard. 'I'm mad that he got away with it. I really thought he was a great almost dad.'

Almost dad. God, it makes me want to wail. She deserves so much better. 'I'm mad too. I'm mad at myself for not setting up the system well enough to catch this type of betrayal. And mad that I couldn't salvage what was left and turn it around in my favour. Most of all, I'm sorry I had to uproot your life.'

'He has to answer for it, eventually, right?'

'I'm sure he will one day.' How to tell her that I, her organised mother who makes lists and covers every scenario, doesn't know how to fix this mess and get what's owed?

'You should get your authors back. Start again. Alone.'

I nod as if it's a wonderful idea. My daughter doesn't need an account of just how upset our authors were and the clause in their contracts that freed them to find new publishers. It strikes me that running a business was never my dream, and the loss of it all proves it. My love was always centred around editing and my passion for the stories themselves and the relationship with my authors as together we bring a new book into the world.

We get to the library and head upstairs. It's a bright colourful place for Eloise to study. We wander around perusing the shelves, but my mind is on Eloise and the fact she knows more than I thought about the fallout of the business. It is a modern world and she's a smart cookie.

She taps my shoulder, pulling me from my thoughts. 'So, is the search on for a new prince charming?'

'No! I've closed the book on men for the foreseeable.'

She runs her finger along a collection of classics with leather-bound spines. 'Why? Soon I'll be grown up and gone. You can't be alone forever or you'll end up best friends with *Alexa*, your virtual assistant.' She shudders. 'You'll live on wheels of brie and barrels of red wine...'

I tilt my head. '*Voilà*, the perfect life!'

'Come on, that's just sad!'

'Not really. I'll dive into my gothic romance reads era and have a slew of gothic book boyfriends to choose from. I can do sudoku and crochet and be blissfully happy.'

She laughs, the most beautiful melody in the moment. 'It sounds, erm... cosy. And probably for the best. You wouldn't want to fall in love in Paris in case we move back to London. Long-distance relationships never work.' Said with all the experience of a thirteen-year-old.

Do I temper her expectations by reminding her there will be no returning to London?

I'm saved from deciding when she says, 'So, where are we going tonight for our celebratory dinner?'

'We're taking your grandparents out for dinner to La Coupole to say thanks for all they've done for us.'

'*Parfait*.'

We spend the next hour sorting a library card and checking out the facilities at Bibliothèque Rainer-Maria Rilke, Eloise decreeing it perfect for her needs. I'm a little hesitant now because, when I agreed she could study at the library, it was with the thought that there'd be three or four of them walking here together. I keep my worries to myself for the moment though, not wanting to spoil the good mood between us.

10

There's a sense of excitement as I get ready for my first day at the Paris Bookshop for the Broken Hearted. It'll be fun to be on the other side of publishing, helping readers find the perfect novel. *If* I can find them in the jumble, that is.

If I don't get a move on though, I'm going to be late, which is *not* like me. The bedroom resembles the scene of a crime; clothes are discarded on every available surface. Nothing seems to fit properly or is either too dressy, or too casual. Why did I leave it until this morning to figure out my work attire? I'm slightly out of breath as I slip on a pair of distressed denim skinny jeans – just call me cheugy – and a navy and white striped tee and some ballet flats. At least I don't need to wear heels, and that *is* a bonus. I apply light make-up and spritz on a floral perfume. It will have to do.

'I'm off, Dad,' I say as I check my handbag, sunglasses, phone, purse before leaning over to kiss him on the cheek. It's jarring to feel so scattered and unprepared, but I really haven't been my methodical self since I left London. Part of me wonders if my efforts to compartmentalise all the hurt I feel isn't quite working...

'Wait, what about *petit dejeuner*?' Dad says with a yawn. 'I went to the *boulangerie* this morning and got a baguette for you and a *pain au chocolat* for Eloise.'

'*Merci, merci*. I'll have to eat quick.' He's gone to so much trouble, but I need to catch the bus and I'm not exactly sure which one. We had a late night and got carried away celebrating at our family dinner, and after a few glasses of wine I slept deeply for the first time in weeks, missing my alarm this morning and only waking when Maman gave my shoulder a quick squeeze reminding me I had to be up, before she headed off for an early work meeting.

While Dad plates up breakfast, I search online for the bus timetable to find the quickest route. In future, I'll walk, but there's no time this morning for that.

'Café crème?'

'*Oui, merci.*'

Dad bustles around the kitchen whistling a tune while he makes us coffee on the new-fangled machine that Eloise and I gifted them last Christmas. At first they were averse to using such a modern piece of technology, preferring to stick to their traditional French press. But over the holidays, Eloise showed them how to use it properly and now they're hooked.

He places down our coffees and takes a seat opposite me and shakes out his Le Monde newspaper. Dad is old school like that and won't hear of reading it on a device.

'I'll walk Eloise this morning and Maman will pick her up after school. She's planning on taking her to Le Bon Georges for their famous *mousse au chocolat*.'

Ooh la la, Paris and its gastronomic delights. This bistro Le Bon Georges is authentically French and uses only high-quality ingredients. They're famous for their gourmet mousse made with the very best chocolate, resulting in a rich intense flavour. Quite frankly, I'm jealous of their téte-à téte and am grateful to Maman for planning it. The more we show Eloise how wonderful Paris is, the quicker she'll settle in. Well, in theory.

'*Merci*. Eloise will love that. When you walk her to school, don't be offended if she asks you to leave her the block before.'

He laughs. 'Teenagers. You were the same. Go,' he says as I ignore the breakfast on my plate, my stomach somersaulting with first-day nerves and my lack of preparation. 'Get yourself in the right frame of mind so you're ready for the day. They're going to love you.'

My dad knows me so well. I kiss his cheek. And down the hall I yell through the bathroom door to Eloise, who is *still* taking a shower. Her muffled reply comes, something about cutting the cord. She often calls me a helicopter mother because I'm always hovering. If only she knew I was wearing skinny jeans today... I take a quick snap and send it to her to make her laugh.

'*Je t'aime*, Eloise.'

'*Oui*.' How humbling it is to be a mum of a teen. The shower shuts off. 'Have fun.'

I pause for a moment. Do I mention Léa and the gang again? Remind her to be strong and walk away even if it means sitting alone for a while? She seems jovial enough, so I decide against it, not wanting her to spend her morning worrying.

11

The morning at the bookshop flies by as I rush to serve customers and help tidy up glassware from the bar area. There's a lot more foot traffic than on my previous visits and I'm quite frazzled by it all even though Valérie did warn me about such a thing. 'Are mornings always this busy?' I ask as I blow back an escaped strand of hair, sure I'm looking bedraggled after running about to and fro. The thing is, while there's a lot of bodies in the bookshop, they don't seem to convert to many book sales. Perhaps the bar is where Valérie recoups costs? It's busy as patrons get behind the spirit of getting their own potions and passages. It's only my first day though so perhaps it's too early to judge whether the bookshop can stand on its own.

'*Oui*, it ebbs and flows. It's always busier closer to the weekend.'

I'm about to ask about bookshop sales when a seventy-something woman wearing a conservative beige pantsuit approaches the bar and takes up a stool, letting out a long sigh as if the day is already letting her down. 'Bonjour, Valérie.' She acknowledges her with a nod. 'We have a new recruit, I see.' She speaks in American-accented French and motions in my direction.

'I'm Coco,' I say, giving her a wide smile. 'It's lovely to meet you...?' I hold out a hand, which she takes in hers and shakes with a firm grip.

'Agnes.' I mentally dub her as American Agnes, so I can try and keep track of regular customers' names.

'Coco's going to run the book club,' Valérie says, waggling her eyebrows.

Agnes lets out a chortle. 'All I can say is *bonne chance*, Coco. *Bonne chance*. The central issue is that they don't read anything of any *literary* value. They're easily manipulated by mainstream media. All it takes is a fleeting glance at a colourful ad on social media or some such and they'll traipse in here to buy the book without questioning if it's right for them, or if the book has any merit. They get sucked in by clever covers and snazzy marketing campaigns.'

I'm taken aback by Agnes's judgemental views and try to quickly process an appropriate reaction. Literary snobbery is rife in Literati-Land and it's one of my biggest pet peeves. 'Ah – isn't it just common sense to have an attention-grabbing tagline on the cover that appeals to readers? Good cover art conveys the genre and style and is a quick and effective first impression that readers will recognise on the spot, without having to read a single word of the blurb. All in all, it's done in an effort to get exposure for a book in a very crowded marketplace.' I can't lie, I take umbrage to what Agnes thinks, but perhaps that's because I know how hard it is to get a book to stand out when there's so much competition.

Valérie supresses a smile while Agnes continues her tirade, ignoring my soliloquy. I ramble longer than I meant to; perhaps

I need to remember that I'm not in the publishing business any more and most people aren't interested in the hows and whys.

'Honestly, if our book club members stopped and *listened* once in a while I could expand their minds with recommendations for the greatest literature ever written. DH Lawrence, for example, but no, they want the latest *bonk*buster, or ice hockey romance – *Mon Dieu*! Or they like...'

Bonkbuster? Who even calls it that these days? 'Ah well, there's always an explosion of popularity for certain genres, it's just the way...' The words dry on my tongue as Agnes speaks over the top of me. I'm translating that as she's not interested in my opinion and only wants to share hers.

'*Someone* has to help educate them, and if not me, then who? They clearly need to broaden their range by reading authors with real literary merit, but will they? *Non, non, non*. All they want to read is a bestselling – and let's face it, probably ghostwritten – thriller with twists that are far too outlandish to be believable, or some dark *romantasy*, which is really thinly disguised pornographic nonsense, with no need of a plot.'

I double blink. Agnes has a lot to say and does a lot of emphasising to get her rather narrow viewpoint across. Is this why the book club is quote-unquote 'unruly'? Imagine if they're *all* like her? 'Do you read romantasy then?' I ask, puzzled by this opinionated woman.

Agnes reels back with her hand on her chest. '*Absolutely not!* I wouldn't give that sort of... *pornography* the time of day.'

It doesn't compute. She doth protest too much. 'How do you know they are pornographic if you haven't read them?' Am I coming across as combative? I hope not. But I'm truly curious how she can dismiss certain genres if she hasn't picked up a copy. And she does seem to know a lot of the popular genres and tropes – how, if she's not that way inclined?

'Coco, I keep abreast with the literary climate by chatting with likeminded individuals who share the same beliefs as me – we keep each other aware of what to avoid, although it's not hard to tell, is it? The covers give it away, with those infantile cartoon characters splashed across the front. I mean, it's absurd.' I can't help but bristle. I love the progression of cover art through the years and I'm sure most readers would agree. 'Knowing literature as well as I do, I've tried to educate the book club.'

I raise my eyebrows so high I'm sure they're now part of my hairline. 'And how did *that* go?'

'Badly. They weren't even *thankful*. They continue to brush my concerns away and tease me about being a prude. If they had their way, books would soon be a series of emojis. *Eggplant* emojis. That's what the world is coming to.'

For a seventy-something, Agnes seems to have a handle on what's popular with the younger generation. There's clearly more to her than just her literary bias, but it's all rather extreme.

'I'm not quite sure how to react to that.' As much as I'd like to drop a truth bomb into the conversation, I sense my first day on the job is not the right time. Not everyone wants to hear the truth, Agnes is the prime example of this. She wants to be heard but doesn't want to *listen*.

Do the other members find this sort of condescension offensive? Or do they really just laugh it off and call her prudish? I'm sure her literary put-downs grate after a while.

Still, this is my job now, so it's probably sensible to start managing her literary bigotry gently when we're alone, rather than in front of the group. 'Being open to new genres is one of the functions of a good book club, don't you agree?'

'Yes, *wholeheartedly!*' she says. Have I changed her mind so easily? 'So, you'll tell them that our first book club pick will be a literary classic and insist they actually *read* it?' Her voice is eager.

OK, that backfired.

I inhale as I organise a response that will gently get my point across. 'What makes book clubs great is having the ability to keep an open mind and respect everyone's right to read whatever genre they choose, even if those choices are eyebrow-raising to you. While you enjoy literary fiction, others may enjoy spicy romantasy and that's perfectly acceptable. You won't be forced to read a book that you find personally offensive, as they won't be forced to read a classic if that's not their speed.'

'I'm not sure you *understand* the depths of their salaciousness, Coco, but you'll soon learn. Books like *that* are a crime against literature!'

Spicy, smutty books are de rigeur these days, becoming popular again, being shared on sites like TikTok, but it's not as if the genre is new; it's simply been renamed from erotica. 'I, uh... see.' My algorithm breaks. I'm not sure how to defend these books and not get the woman offside.

Agnes sighs when she doesn't get the reaction she wants from me and turns to Valérie. 'Next Coco will suggest we choose an *obscene* book! One of those domestic noir types, where the heroine falls for the abusive hero who is somehow a molecular scientist with anger management issues, yet they push all of that to one side for the graphic sex scenes! When will this madness *end*?'

What? The plot she mentions is very familiar to me. How can she possibly know such detail without reading the book? 'Are you getting this information from... book reviews?'

Agnes gives me an impatient huff. 'No, it's simply that those novels are all the same...'

But they're clearly not! 'I – but – I...' I'm saved from stuttering a response when Valérie cuts in.

'If Coco *did* choose a spicy novel, you'd read it, wouldn't you, if only for the sake of providing educated discourse for the novel?' Valérie stirs the pot, with a cheeky twinkle in her eye.

'Absolutely *not*! I wouldn't read such filth.' Her lips curl in distaste.

I frown, frustrated – gah! 'How can you call it filth if you haven't read it, though? Shouldn't you give it a chance, as you want them to give your genre a chance?'

Agnes shakes her head as if disappointed in me. 'Seriously? Explicit sexual content has no business in literature, period.'

Her argument has no merit, and if only I was braver I'd tell her straight. Ah, but there might be a way... 'You mentioned DH Lawrence as one of the literary greats.' Agnes gives me a curt nod. 'If I recall correctly, *Lady Chatterley's Lover* has graphic sexual depictions? So much so that it was banned from sale in many countries?'

Her lip quivers as she battles to retort. 'That's an *entirely* different beast. It's fine if it's not, if it's not... *gratuitous*, isn't it?'

I hide a smile at winning a point. 'Are all spicy books now gratuitous?'

She nods vehemently this time. '*All* of them, yes. I'm rarely satisfied with the book club choices, Coco, so I'm not expecting much. It's more of a social club for me. I'm certainly not going to meet my literary equivalent here and I've come to terms with that.'

'Right. It's just I find that by embracing all kinds of stories I learn so much about others, and about myself along the way.' She gives me a puzzled frown, as if I'm not making sense. I let it go for now. Agnes is certainly going to make book club interesting. I'm keen to see how the other members handle her archaic literary views. 'Can I get you a drink?'

'I'll have an iced coffee, thanks, and don't skimp on the whipped cream. I'll take my table by the leaning wall of books.'

'Sure.' After she saunters away, I face Valérie, so many questions prickling the tip of my tongue, but the one that wins out is not about Agnes – well, not first at any rate. 'The leaning wall of books?'

'Ah, I forgot to show you the courtyard. Just outside we have a book wall made with damaged novels that were destined for the rubbish pile. I couldn't abide by such a waste of those precious tomes. I made a pile of them outside in the undercover area, and soon that pile grew. In the end, I had so many books that the wall sort of grew itself... if that makes sense? Once the wall was built, people kept donating books, so I made steps out of them and now there's an entire book garden. My engineering skills are basic, hence it's called the leaning wall of books. But don't worry, it's reinforced so it won't topple on unsuspecting bookworms.'

'Wow. I need to see this book garden.'

'I'll make Agnes's iced coffee and we can take it out to her and have a peep. The book garden is very popular with tourists who come to take photos on the steps with the leaning book wall in the background.'

'You're very clever getting to the heart of a bookworm.' The potions and passages and now a book garden!

'Bookworms aren't so hard to understand.'

'Speaking of bookworms...' I glance over my shoulder to make sure Agnes is not lurking within hearing distance. 'How do the book club members get along with Agnes?' I'm hoping in the heat of the moment I have the courage to keep order.

Valérie grins while she mixes milk into a shot of coffee and

adds ice cubes and generously layers it with cream and a
dusting of cocoa powder. 'They call her the literary snob, but it's
all in good fun. They're not always patient when she goes off on
a rant but I'm sure she enjoys the debate.'

'Why is she so adamant?'

With a shrug she says, 'A generational hangup? A sort of
inherent pretension about books, probably from the way she
grew up. In her world, seventy-five-year-old women don't read
literature as "low brow" as sports romance, or at least that's
what she *wants* you to believe. Or maybe... Agnes is also
suffering a broken heart and she comes here to fix it, but rather
than admitting that, she defaults to book talk, the only way she
knows how.'

I swallow back a scoff. Agnes does not resemble someone
suffering a broken heart. Not in the least. 'Well, how will she
fix this *alleged* broken heart then...? What will you do to help
her?'

'That's a secret, Coco. But let me just say that soon Agnes
will see the way forward, but hers is a slow recovery because
what ails her is so ingrained.'

Now she's speaking in riddles, surely?

Valérie surveys me, clearly spotting the doubt that flashes
across my features. 'Not everyone wears a broken heart the
same way, Coco. Some of us hide it better.'

I contemplate it, finding the truth in her words. I'm quite
proficient at hiding my heartbreak from the world; it's only
Valérie who has been savvy enough to pick up on it. And why
do I feel the need to pretend Alexander didn't hurt me but hurt
only the business? I suppose I don't want to come across as
naïve, vulnerable, but it's more, isn't it? It's that I don't want to
admit, even to myself, I'm absolutely gutted that what we had
wasn't real, at least not for him. I'd really, genuinely, fell head

over heels for him, and that love only continued to grow over the five years we were together.

Instead of admitting to myself, my daughter, the world around me that I am suffering, I paste on a smile and pretend. I turn to books to find solace.

Valérie slides the iced coffee on a tray and hands it to me. 'Follow me through the book tunnel.'

'There's a book tunnel?'

Valérie's eyes shine as if she's getting a kick out of showing me the bookish architecture around the shop. 'Let me show you.'

With tray in hand, drink sloshing precariously, I take care as I follow Valérie through the rabbit warren of a bookshop. Next to the chair where Henri usually sits there's an archway, and painted above in French cursive is the phrase 'Reading is a portal into another world'.

The tunnel is just that – an arched hallway with books stacked as if they are bricks themselves that go all the way around, transforming a passageway into a literary burrow. String lights are looped in a zigzag, producing a warm shimmery glow that gives the tunnel a cosy feel and allows enough illumination to read the spines on display. 'How do they stay upright?' I ask, sweeping my gaze from left to right, noticing small gaps because the books are different sizes.

'They're secured from behind and pinned together. These beauties were all bound for landfill and now they live on.'

We walk through the book tunnel, which is surprisingly long and rich with the scent of old books. I can't wait to show Eloise. 'I'm glad these books have been saved and made into art.'

'*Oui*, me too. There is always a way to repurpose books if they can no longer be read. And that's the only the time you'll find me destroying a book, if it cannot be fixed by the book doctor.'

'Of course there's a book doctor.' Nothing surprises me here any more.

Valérie grins. 'Isidore is actually a book binder, but that title doesn't do her justice, because she does so much more than that. She's of the opinion that every book should be saved, if at all possible, whether it's a prized valuable first edition or a mass market paperback. There's no money in those, but she saves as many as she can. She's a petite French woman with a boisterous laugh and a predilection for travel and is gifted with strikingly tiny hands perfect for such delicate fine work.'

The plot thickens. 'I can't wait to meet Isidore. I don't think I've ever come face to face with a book doctor before.'

'You'll meet her soon enough. She's a member of the book club.'

'What kind of novels does she like?' What if she's a literary snob too and my role in the book club becomes more of a referee than moderator?

Valérie takes a second before saying, 'Isidore reads anything and everything. She's probably so open with her reading because she deals in life and death every day.'

'Life and death?'

'Of the *books*, Coco. The books' lives are in her *tiny* hands. It's a big responsibility to shoulder, a significant burden, so she comes here to decompress.'

'And she's heartbroken too?'

'Very. Think of all the novels she can't fix. Depressing, *non*?'

Wow, OK, I've never heard of anything quite like this before. A book doctor who grieves for those which she cannot save. It's sweet that Isidore cares for all books in such a way, and not only those with a big price tag attached.

I'm keen to meet this tiny-handed woman. While it's understandable that she's sad about the books that are not salvageable, is there more to it? 'Is she also part of the heartbreak club? Like the rest of us?' I'm not sure why I pry, but I still find this whole broken heart cure mumbo jumbo fairly wacky. And surely I'm not the only one who is dubious?

Valérie flashes me a frown. 'Nice try, Coco. In this instance, think of *me* like a doctor. I cannot share such privileged information! It goes against my very principles.'

I'm in a parallel universe where nothing makes sense, yet everything makes *perfect* sense. Still, I push. 'How do I help them if I don't know what's wrong?'

'Your job is to find them books to read that help along their journey of healing. Books *are* like medicine, in cases like this, so ply them with uplifting reads which in conjunction with my assistance will get our special customers back on the path to happiness.'

'I'll do my best.'

We come to the end of the tunnel into the muted sunlight of the book garden, which is shaded by a pergola where purple and white wisteria blooms hang. Agnes holds a copy of Victor Hugo's *Les Misérables* in her hand with the leaning wall of books a stunning backdrop behind her. It's a showstopper, all those colourful spines on display like a Lego world made from books. There's also a thick notebook on the table. A diary?

I place down Agnes's drink, and she gives me a curt smile. '*Merci*, Coco.' Her expression is softer in the gauzy sunlight, as if some of the fire inside her has been extinguished. While I place a napkin down, I take a moment to surreptitiously survey her. There is an air of dejection about her when she's sitting alone like this; she seems smaller, less sure somehow. Perhaps I'm not the only one hiding the broken parts. The thought gives me pause.

'Enjoy your drink, Agnes. Let me know if you need anything else.'

I follow Valérie back through the tunnel to the bookshop. 'Are there any more surprises around here?' Book architecture, broken hearts, book doctors. What else can there be!

Valérie takes a moment to consider it. 'Ah! You haven't seen the book loft upstairs. It's a relaxation zone with hammocks, daybeds, beanbags. A mishmash of seating areas for customers to laze or sprawl on when they read.' Valérie points to a black wrought-iron staircase on the far side of the bookshop. I noticed the stairs earlier but haven't had time to think much of it. 'You can explore upstairs tomorrow. Let's have lunch. I'll show you how I assemble a charcuterie board, and we can share the spoils.'

My stomach rumbles at the thought of lunch after only taking a few bites at breakfast, but I'm intrigued about the book loft upstairs. The idea of a bookish contemplative quiet zone appeals, and I wonder if there's anything this wily bookseller hasn't thought of...

12

The next day, I get to the bookshop early so I can scope out the book loft before the day gets underway.

'You're not going to make this a habit, are you?' Valérie says from behind the coffee machine. 'I'm not used to punctual staff. If you're going to be reliable, it's going to be hard for me to cope when you leave.'

My chest tightens. 'Why would I leave?'

She ushers me inside. 'Ah, my dearest Coco. This, as we both know, is a stopgap in your new life. So don't ruin me by being too good or I'll come to expect it from future employees.'

Is it a stopgap? Old me would have a spreadsheet of goals and aspirations, but I'm still too heartsick to think ahead. My grand ten-year plan for London Field is literally just a worthless piece of paper now. All that planning for zip. My dreams up in smoke. It's still hard to believe that it's all gone.

It might be pure cowardice but I'm happy cooling my heels at the bookshop hiding from the publishing industry. I'm not sure it's a stopgap so much as a lifeline.

'You have a very odd way of looking at the world,' I say. 'And

I like it. I promise to be a less reliable employee if that's what you really want?' While we're joking, I do question how she copes if she's got a revolving door of staff. It must be hard on her if she can't count on anyone long term.

'*Merci.* Café crème?'

'*Oui.* I'm going to have a look up there.' I point. 'Before we're officially open.'

'Ah, now your early arrival makes sense. Do that and I'll put together a breakfast tray for us.' More food. Valérie has a really soft maternal side to her, or she just likes feeding me up.

I take the stairs two at a time. The wooden floors creak as I step around colourful oversized beanbags and hammocks that swing softly in the breeze from an open window. In each corner is a daybed, like the ones you find on tropical holidays. They're dressed with stylish European cushions and navy linen throw rugs. From the rear window there's a beautiful view of the River Seine and the Eiffel Tower. It's breathtaking, and I can only imagine bibliophiles nabbing a spot and whiling away the day reading in supreme comfort. Readers always talk about finding a bookish paradise, the perfect place to read... and it's been right here in Paris all along.

Next to each perch point, there are tables with drink and charcuterie menus and a cute little bell that says 'Ring for service'. I take a punt and ring the bell and Valérie shouts, 'Don't think I'm running up all those stairs for you, Coco.' And I laugh. Do customers even know this area exists? I didn't hear anyone ring the bell yesterday and didn't notice anyone venture up these stairs either. Maybe it's my job to tell them this space exists.

There is a stacked bookshelf full of colourful spines with a plaque that reads:

Bibliothéque Madeline. Feel free to read and return these
books as you wish.

Has Valérie named this library after a character from a
book? While it's not a children's area, I'm reminded of the kids'
book series *Madeline* set in a boarding school in Paris. It's still
popular to this day and has even been adapted into TV and
film.

I go downstairs to ask about the book loft area, but there are
already customers milling about and a few at the bar perusing
the drinks menu. 'Drink your café crème while it's hot, Coco,
and I'll take care of this. Have your breakfast.'

'It's OK, let me help and then we can both sit down to eat.'

I approach a man with a camera slung around his neck.
'Bonjour.'

'Hello,' he says in an Australian accent, so I switch to
English.

'Are you looking for any book in particular?' I'm still not
quite sure how to best assist customers in finding books
because they're not easy to find. I'm learning the lay of the land
the more times I approach customers and rifle through shelves,
and it's only day two, so I suppose it'll take a bit of time. He
regards me cooly as if deciding whether I'm up to the job. 'Do
you work here?'

Is that a trick question? 'Yes? Can I help you find a book?'

'OK, I'm looking for something to read while I'm at a café. A
classic. Think Tolstoy but make it fun.'

'That is quite the ask.' *Impossible!* Russian classics aren't
exactly known for their humour.

'Between us, I'm trying to impress a woman, so it'll be more
like a prop than a book I intend on reading.'

Now I've heard it all. 'And you think that will work?'

'Yes, I'm certain it'll show my keen intellect.'

I take a moment to consider whether it'll be easier to help this man with the truth, or to just find a book by a Russian author. He must sense my quandary because he says, 'Is it not hot? Me reading a Tolstoy equivalent?'

I grimace. 'Not in the slightest, especially if it's all fake.'

'That's why I came here; the bookshop name intrigued me.' He shuffles closer and whispers, 'I'm suffering through a bout of...' Now I'm intrigued! Why do men always stop at the good bits? He drops his head and rubs at his temples, as if truly suffering a malady of some sort. '*Unrequited love.*'

When he lifts his head once more, his eyes are full of anguish. Oh, he's got it bad. Does the bookshop draw lonely people too? People who want to love but are stuck? What am I even saying? It's not real! It's just a name. A very savvy business name that gives people hope who are in need of some.

'I see. Look, I'm not a doctor but this is a clear case of lovesickness.'

'Yes. Yes, that's exactly what it is. Worse, I'm going back to Sydney soon. If I don't make my feelings known I'll spend the rest of my life wondering what if.'

'We can't have that.'

'It would be torture. The woman I've got my heart set on is well read – I've seen her with classics, memoirs, historical fiction and all sorts. I want to get her attention with what I'm reading and be awed by my choice.'

'What do you like reading?'

'Anything and everything, but this has to be right. Has to be the perfect novel.'

It's sweet really. 'OK, well, have you ever considered a book of poetry?'

'What, like Rupi Kaur, Neil Hilborn and such?'

'Yes, like them. I've just found the most beautiful book of poems in here somewhere. Let me find it. We have it in English and French...'

'OK.'

I motion for the customer to follow me as I find the small hardback book in a stack by the till. Either Valérie really likes poetry, or these were discounted because she has boxes of them, and lots of copies scattered around the bookshop. 'Here it is.'

He takes the proffered book. 'But... poetry? Isn't that a bit obvious?'

'Not this kind of poetry. It's the type that makes you think. How well do you know this woman?'

'We frequent the same café, usually taking a table beside one another, and aside from a few stolen glances we have shared not a single word. When I go to speak, I freeze. She's French and my language skills are rudimentary at best.'

'Well then, this book might be just the talking point you need. Perhaps you could buy a copy in French and ask for her help translating?'

A warm smile spreads across his face. 'You are a genius.'

'I've read a lot of romance novels.'

I ring up his purchases and he promises to return and let me know about the mysterious French woman who's stolen his heart.

13

'Fixing broken hearts already, I see.' Valérie lifts a brow as she watches the guy leave the bookshop, happier than when he arrived.

I jump at the sound of her voice behind me. 'Not exactly broken, it's more of an unrequited conundrum. He's in love with a French woman but they have never spoken and he's returning to Australia soon.'

She holds a hand to her heart. '*La douleur exquise.*'

Translated, it's 'the exquisite pain', but the meaning is much deeper than that. It's the heartrending hurt that goes with a love not reciprocated. '*Oui.* Poor man.'

'Isn't it strange that...?' Her voice peters off as she waits for me to connect the dots.

'Just say it, Valérie.'

She polishes her specs as she draws it out. 'Isn't unrequited love *just* as heartbreaking as any other type? And he managed to find his way here.'

I shake my head. 'Because he was looking for a book and this is a *book*shop.'

'And yet you discussed a real-life romance plot in detail with the stranger.'

'You eavesdropper.'

'*Oui*, of course. I was curious to see you in action. You handled it well. Not only does the bookshop cater for those with a broken heart, but also for lonely hearts, lost souls, the grief stricken, the star crossed. There's a remedy for everyone.'

'You really believe it, don't you?'

'You will too, Coco. Eventually. You're just a little more stubborn than most.'

'*Moi*? Hardly.'

She grins. 'You, *ma chérie*, are going to learn that not everything has a rational explanation. Sometimes there's a certain magic in Parisian air that we have no control over. That coupled with a potion, a passage, the comfort of a good book, and strangers suffering the same or similar fate are the ingredients to mend a broken heart. There, I've told you the science behind it.'

A scoff escapes. 'That's the *science* behind it?' I can't hide the scepticism from my voice.

Valérie gives me a slow nod.

'There's a mystical magical breeze that blows in and fixes people?'

'You're simplifying it.'

The notion of such a premise is difficult for me to swallow, but Valérie means well. 'It's... hard for me to reconcile, is all.'

'You need to open your heart *and* your mind.'

'Is that a requirement of the job?'

A guffaw of laughter escapes. 'Put away reason for a minute. What if the bookshop really did have the ability to help people who suffered alone for so long? Wouldn't that be special?'

'Of course. But you can't make promises that you can't keep, because one day it might come back to bite you.' What if a customer fully expects to be 'cured' of their heartbreak and it fails?

'Why can't I keep my promises?'

'Because you can't cure a broken heart. It's not *scientifically* possible. And by then the damage is done.'

'In *A Farewell to Arms*, Hemingway talks about how life damages most of us in one way or another and that those broken parts of us become stronger for it.'

'Wouldn't it be *weaker*? The broken parts forever altered; delicate, prone to breaking again?' I picture the pottery of Kintsugi, those beautiful golden seams, that patch up breaks.

'*Non*, Coco! Haven't you ever had a scar on your body? They're thick, tough and strong, as if a reminder to us that all is not lost; we're resilient, as goes with the wounds on a heart.'

Are the golden seams *tougher* than the pottery itself? Or am I missing the point? It's not about the fix itself, it's about healing. Being made whole again, albeit slightly different than before. 'Maybe.'

'Maybe? I'll get you to believe eventually. Out of interest, what book did you suggest for the Australian man?'

'*Un Baiser D'adieu.*' A Kiss Goodbye. 'We have so many copies. I read one of the poems and I felt so *moved* by it.'

'The perfect choice.'

'Do you love poetry? Is that why there are so many copies of it around the bookshop?'

She takes a moment to consider it. '*Oui*. Good poetry should be heartbreaking, and all at once uplifting, and that's what I feel when I read those poems.'

'Ah, you chose it because it deals with heartbreak. And might help customers?'

'It's what the people need, *non*?' Valérie is called to back to the bar.

A young man approaches me with a skittish look on his face. 'Where are the puppies?' he says in broken English. He has a hint of an accent. German, maybe.

'Books about dogs?'

His eyebrows knit as he shakes his head. 'Not books. Puppies.'

This is an easy query to solve. 'Sorry, this is a bookshop.'

He checks his watch as if he's got somewhere to be. 'The... *puppies*. Where are they?'

'We sell *books*, not puppies. There are no puppies here.'

'Benjamin told me pick up the puppies. Here.'

I gasp. 'Is this some kind of drug deal?' The word 'drug' echoes around the bookshop, bringing, of all people, Henri by my side. Great, the old hero-to-the-rescue routine I'll have to suffer through once more.

'What's going on?' he demands as if he's the gendarmerie. The young guy is acting fishy, so it's best I share my suspicions in case there *is* a haul of illicit drugs secreted among these unsuspecting innocent novels, even if the person I share it with is Henri. 'Are you OK?'

'I'm fairly certain this young man, who, I might add, has his whole life ahead of him and should be making better choices, might be involved in some sort of nefarious drug deal, and they've organised the exchange to take place here! I've edited many a crime novel and I know a code word when I hear one. *Puppies*. I mean, it's blatantly obvious.'

Henri's expression darkens as he waits for an explanation from the young man, who scratches the back of his neck as if he's not quite sure what he's walked into. Am I reading this all wrong? It's just the way he's acting so sketchy and whispering about puppies.

'The puppies?' he says and lifts his palms up. 'I'm here to pick them up.'

'Oh,' Henri says with an understanding nod. 'Outside to the left, about five doors up. The dog groomer.'

'Oh. Of course.' I want to curl up and die. 'I misunderstood.'

Henri leads the guy to the front door and shows him the way, leaving me, thankfully, alone with my mortification. It *could* have been a drug exchange; I'm only protecting our customers by being observant and keeping my wits about me.

He's not going to let it go though, being Henri. Far too soon he returns, his lips pressed tight together while he holds up a hand implying I should wait. I'm sensing he's about to laugh uproariously or self-combust – maybe both?

'Before you start, you didn't see how dodgy he was acting, and I've learned from recent experiences to be on guard a little more than strictly necessary.'

My explanation doesn't work. Laughter explodes from Henri, so loud it's like a sonic boom. I soon throw my hands over my ears and say, 'Are you *quite* finished?' Alas, the fool can't hear me over the sounds erupting from his own body. After a full minute, having drawn a crowd of customers, he finally manages to regain some composure.

I apologise profusely. 'Sorry, he's got a medical condition. He can't control it.' That just makes him laugh more.

'Oh, Coco. I don't quite know how to take you.'

Story of my life.

'I'm really not sure what I was thinking. It all happened so fast and I was in the moment with no time to process it. I mean, you hear about these things all the time, don't you?'

'True. And absolutely nothing surprises me any more in this

bookshop, so you were right to be suspicious. Can I buy you a coffee? It looks like you could use the jolt of caffeine.'

'Thanks, but I've got one going cold behind the bar already.' While Valérie is fairly lax as a boss, I don't want to take advantage, even if a coffee break with Henri would be just the thing after this morning.

'OK, another time.'

I nod and he goes to his chair at the back. Why the abrupt change in Henri? He went from laughing jester to caring about me.

There's no time to contemplate it as the bookshop fills up once more with the before-lunch crowd. Valérie said it ebbs and flows, but I decide to see if there's a pattern to it, certain times that are clearly busier, that way I can be prepared for the busy spells. I feel a spreadsheet might be in order, just for fun. Valérie would clutch her heart if I got scientific about it.

14

Tuesday rolls around and that means I'm back to the bookshop after a weekend that didn't quite go according to plan. Eloise is really driving the point home about returning to London and it makes my heart ache each time I have to tell her no. I thought I'd enjoy having a three-day weekend, since the bookshop is closed on Mondays, but in actual fact, I found myself a little unmoored yesterday while Eloise was at school and my parents at work. It's a relief to get back to the bookshop.

'Bonjour.' I welcome happy faces as I pick up novels from the floor and reshelve displaced tomes. It's just after lunch and my entire body aches. Now all of Valérie's warnings make perfect sense. This job is not for the faint-hearted. Or it's a matter of fitness and building my stamina.

I mention the library upstairs to customers who look like they're in no rush and it soon fills. The table service bells sound off for the rest of the interminable day and I rue the fact I'm such a conscientious employee. The Devil's Loft, I've renamed it, due to the countless times I've run up and down the stairs. It's almost a full-time job on its own. *This* is why Valérie doesn't mention the space to anyone. I'm going to have legs of steel and will be asleep standing up if it doesn't abate soon.

There's a heavy knock on the service door. 'Delivery!' a voice calls out. I go to the door to find it locked.

'Just looking for the key, won't be long.'

Valérie is nowhere to be found, so I open drawers and cupboards. I finally see a set of keys on a hook by the bar. The delivery driver has gone but a towering pile of boxes sit on the pebbled ground. And just my luck, the bright spring day darkens as fat raindrops fall.

I cart one of the smaller boxes inside and it's shockingly heavy; that or my muscles have given up for the day. I call out again for Valérie. Nothing. Where is she? There are a handful of customers milling about, but I'm not sure what the protocol is on leaving customers unattended. I don't want boxes of new books to be drenched in the rain either. This is why employee manuals come in very useful. Would Valérie consider one if I do the hard work? It would help in situations like this, to have a clear plan in place. Let's face it, she would hate the idea, but I might push for it anyway, since she admitted she does have a revolving door when it comes to staff.

'Valérie!' I call one more time, but I'm met with no response; instead, I come face to face with Henri.

'She's not here,' he says.

'Do you know where she is?'

He lifts a casual shoulder. 'What do you need?'

I have an internal debate about asking him for help, but as the rain comes down harder, the decision is made for me. 'We've had a delivery of books that are currently getting soaked but I don't want to leave the bookshop floor if she's not around to keep an eye out.'

'I'll bring them in, you watch the bookshop.'

Before I can thank him, he disappears. Does Henri often help around the bookshop? He knows the layout and the processes. I help a few customers with queries before Henri comes back. 'I put them in the storage room for you.'

'*Merci*. Where *is* the storage room?' The bookshop is like a labyrinth, with hidden spaces and small rooms and doors. A surprise at every turn. Restocking is one of the most important aspects of the job, and so far Valérie has just left boxes stacked by the bar in the mornings ready for me to unpack whenever there's been a lull, so I don't know where to find them when she's not here.

'The green door, just off the kitchen. It's a jumble, and there's almost no room to manoeuvre, so if you need a hand getting the boxes out later, let me know.' I'm about to thank him, enjoying our newfound connection, when he says, 'I can't see you being able to lift those boxes somehow.' *And* he's ruined it.

'Why? Because I'm a woman?'

His face colours. 'No, not because of that. They're heavy, is all. Like, seriously heavy. I'm sure half the boxes in the stock-room have been abandoned because they're back-spasm inducing.'

I slip my hands in my jean pockets. 'Wouldn't a rather easy solution be to simply open the box and remove the books by hand?'

'Now you mention it.' A grin splits his face. 'You're going to be good for this place, Coco.'

He stands close enough that I can smell soap on his skin, an appley cinnamon scent which seems at odds with the gruff macho man persona he's got going on.

'Why does that sound insincere coming from you?'

'*Moi?*' He does his best impersonation of an innocent person as he takes a seat in his usual leather chair.

'*Oui.* You often come across hot and cold. Is that on purpose?'

He cocks his head as if genuinely surprised by my comment.

'Do I? I'm sorry if I've upset you, Coco. Lately I've viewed the world through a much harsher lens. Not an excuse, but there it is anyway.'

Is Henri another victim of heartbreak? How does Valérie determine such a thing? She said something about how it was written in every line and plane of my face. In the way I held myself. I survey Henri's features, searching for telltale markings of heartbreak, but all I see is a very good-looking man. If I were pushed, I could admit maybe his eyes hold a touch of sadness, but I couldn't say for sure. I'm overthinking the whole thing! Valérie is simply a marketing genius and has constructed the perfect business to woo bookworms and the lost and lonely among us, and even Henri has been swept up in the hype. I remain dubious.

Why is Henri here every day then? When Valérie planned our upcoming imaginary wedding, she mentioned he is a journalist. Does he use this space to write? He does have a laptop but he mostly stares through it.

Ah, maybe it's nothing to do with his heart and he's suffering a case of writer's block! For some reason, I don't feel on an even enough keel to ask him.

'I get it,' I say. 'I feel a little like that too at the moment, and so far men are mostly copping it.' Where did that come from? I don't share my feelings, I push them into a box and lock it and throw away the key.

'Now it makes sense. You have a broken heart just like the rest.'

'Don't tell me you believe in all that?'

'Don't you?' he asks.

'No, I don't.'

'Is it your broken heart that makes you so hostile to the idea?'

'*Excusez moi?*'

'Sorry, there I go again. I told... someone... about our confrontation by the Eiffel Tower and she told me in no uncertain terms that I'd behaved very badly indeed. In fact, she accused me of victim blaming and gender assumptions. Told me I was not to use problematic phrases like "asking for trouble". You were right; apparently I *am* a dinosaur. So, with that in mind, I promise to do better.'

Who is this woman he's referring to? Has she waved a magic wand and fixed the mansplainer? Whoever she is, she deserves a medal.

'You're... *apologising*?'

Henri hesitates for a fraction too long.

I narrow my eyes. He narrows his.

It should surprise absolutely no one that the transformation is only skin deep!

He wiggles in his chair as if suddenly uncomfortable in his own skin. 'I will apologise if you think I need to, but there's also the matter of the lack of thanks that we haven't resolved. You've never thanked me for stepping up and *saving* you from the pickpockets. Wouldn't it be sensible if we agreed we *both* weren't at our best that day and move on? We can shake on it.'

'What a load of word salad! Shake on it? What are we, making a bet?'

'Word salad?'

'Word salad,' I confirm in a clear, strong voice.

'I don't think you're hearing me.'

I huff. 'Because I'm a *banane*?'

I get a little thrill when his cheeks pinken.

Henri rakes a hand through his hair. 'You're not going to move past this unless I apologise, are you? I understand, I do. But you must admit that you were annoyed too. *Oui*, I shouldn't have called you a banana. There are many other fitting words I could have used.'

Is he for real? 'You are the limit. I hope you replay *this* conversation with the woman who tried to guide you. If you do, I expect we'll meet again here tomorrow, and you can apologise to me *twice*.'

I walk to the bar area and serve a customer asking for a bottle of sparkling water. My mind is still on gruff Henri though. He doesn't seem the type to get bent and twisted over love. It would probably break his steely heart if he didn't get the last word in. That's more his speed.

Henri saunters casually over to me as if we didn't just come to loggerheads – another red flag. Why *do* hot men saunter like that? How do they even *know* how to? It must come naturally, or it's their big ego energy that has them swaggering as if they're king of the world.

Well, Henri *is* the king – the king of idiots, that is.

'You'll get used to it,' Henri says, placing his empty coffee cup on the bar. I'm about to tell him I will do no such thing when he says, 'Valérie disappears a lot.'

I should ignore him but I'm worried that if the place gets really busy again, I'll be out of my depth, and I may actually need to call on him. 'She does this often then?' My pulse speeds up at the idea I'm in charge when I really don't know the first thing about cocktails, and certainly nothing about potions and passages.

'*Oui*. Perhaps she needs a time out. Like we all do occasionally.'

'Some more than others.' I shoot him a laser-like glare, implying that I need time out from him when he goes off on one of his I-didn't-thank-him-for-rescuing-me tangents. He's the one who needs the time out from saying all the wrong things, of that I'm certain, but in light of this new development I let it go for now and focus on the important question.

'Where does she go?' It seems an odd way to run a business, but so far nothing in the bookshop has been done in the usual way.

'She never says.'

I unpack the boxes of books Henri carted out to the storage room for me and decide to make a display featuring them. They're all spring romances with gorgeous sun-drenched sea vista covers which should sell well if customers can find them more easily. I search the bookshop floor for a table I can use. I find one tucked down a pathway stacked with dusty guidebooks. I move them to a shelf closer to the front door, where they'll be easily seen. And then I navigate the table through the tight pathway, trying not to knock books as I go. I set it up close to the bar area where there's more foot traffic. By the time I've organised a spring display, complete with cocktail glasses and drink umbrellas, I turn to find that Henri has gone but that he's left some euros for his coffee. Not even an au revoir. It shouldn't bother me; he leaves at the same time every day, which I couldn't help but notice, only because I'm keeping a record of the bursts and lulls and not for any other reason.

There are only a few customers perusing the shelves so while it's quiet, I take Valérie's laptop and design some flyers about the upcoming book club meeting. I print a stack to leave on tables around the bookshop and bar and hang some outside in the book garden by the leaning tower of books. The more members we can get to join, the more chance we have of selling them the monthly book club pick.

An hour later, Valérie waltzes back in with no explanation about where she's been. There's something different about her, a quietness that I interpret to mean now is not the time to quiz her about the absence. Instead, I show her that I've moved the guidebooks to a more prominent position in case she needs to find them and tell her about the new stock that Henri helped bring in, which I've displayed on a table in the hopes they'll be snapped up quickly.

As usual, Valérie glides straight past any business talk. 'Isn't Henri a gem? Such devilish good looks too.'

'Devilish good looks are one thing, a modern-day sensitive man with a good heart is where it's at, and sadly, Henri fails at the start line.'

'Ah.' Her face falls. 'Why don't you take off for the day? You've done a great job while it's been so hectic and I know you must be feeling it after running up those steps to the book loft.'

I glance at my watch. I'm too late to pick up Eloise from school but if I leave now I should get home in time to make dinner so Maman doesn't have to. '*Merci*. I'll see you tomorrow.'

We kiss cheeks and I leave the bookshop, but I can still smell it – the lemony vanilla scent that clings to my clothes, my hair, the pads of my fingers. I take a moment to reflect on the day and sense there was a shift in Valérie, something that stole the edge of her smile. Or I'm seeing things that aren't there? Maybe like me, her feet are sore and her face is aching from all the smiling; plus, she has the added pressure of performing that *joie de vivre* for her potions and passages customers...

15

When Saturday rolls around, I fight the urge to stay cocooned in bed. It's been a long, busy week, as my body adjusts to a job where I'm on my feet all day and then coming home to my daughter who doesn't seem to be settling in no matter what I try. I'm determined to have a good weekend together and show her just how great Paris can be. I'm finding it a bit of a revelation not running my own business any more and the extra work that goes with it. Maybe it's also the change in outlook and being in my hometown once more.

The bookshop job is much more physical than I'm used to with editing, where I'd be mostly at my desk all day or reading a manuscript on my kindle in a comfy chair. Running up and down the stairs to the book loft is the shock my body needs. It feels almost as if it's bringing me back to life, like hitting the reset button.

It's fun chatting to customers and figuring out ways to display books to get more eyes on them. Valérie has given me carte blanche to do what I want to help sell more books, so I'm relishing the freedom to do just that. So far, it seems that the bar is her main source of income and the bookshop an afterthought where customers are concerned. I'd like to balance those scales if I can, so I'm happy to have the weekend to ponder ways in which to do so. Retail is a whole new beast, after all.

First, I'm meeting with my friend Anais for a bite to eat and a walk. We haven't seen each other for a year or so. Once upon a time, I was her editor when I worked for a bigger publisher, and we became great friends. She's been living in Paris for a long time now and recently renovated a boutique hotel by the Luxembourg Gardens. From what I've seen online, she's turned it into a bookish literary haven.

Being a fellow publishing industry pal, Anais will no doubt have heard of any gossip still circulating about me or if the rumour mill has mercifully moved onto someone else. I hate admitting it, even to myself, but I'm sort of hoping Alexander has had his comeuppance and it didn't all blow over for him while he was hiding out. I need to figure out a plan for him and what he owes me personally after the fallout, but my heart isn't in it yet. Most days, it's easier to just get on with this new life and pretend London never happened. It's self-preservation, I guess.

'Eloise?' I knock on the bathroom door. 'Are you almost done?' Why do teenagers take the longest showers? She has absolutely no care or concern for water restrictions or the fact that three other family members need to share the amenities.

'*Non*. I'm washing my hair.'

'Wash it faster.'

'How? The conditioner needs to soak in for at least five minutes!'

'According to the manufacturer's instructions, one to three minutes is advised.'

There's a garbled sound and then, 'You've read the instructions on this exact bottle of conditioner?'

Honestly, at times I despair. 'Yes, otherwise how else would I know the recommended time to leave the conditioner in my hair?'

A full fifteen minutes later, my daughter finally exits the bathroom, enveloped in a cloud of steam. We do the switching-places tango. 'Chill, Mum! Jeez.'

Easy for her to say. 'Eloise, you need to keep in mind there are other...'

She gives me a cool stare that quite stops me in my tracks. Where do they learn these intimidation tactics? Teenagers are really a different breed. 'Weren't you in a hurry to shower, not lecture me?'

Do I push the point or let it go for the sake of, well, peace? She's not going to care one iota about my lecture anyway. 'Be mindful of others, is all. It's not too much to ask.'

'OK, Boomer.'

I hold in a sigh as she stalks off. So that went well.

* * *

I shower, which is a quick torturous affair because Eloise hasn't read the simple instructions on a conditioner bottle and has used all the hot water.

In the bedroom, I get myself dressed and ready, looking forward to getting out for the day.

The room is a mess of clothes, as if she couldn't decide what to wear and pulled every item from the drawers. 'Eloise! Hang up your towel and put all this away please.'

'Urgh.' She returns and leans against the door jamb. 'How long until we leave? I want my own room.'

'Not long, darling.' It's best to keep the timeframe vague when it comes to teenagers; I've learned that over the last little while. I'd like to get a place soon too, but I need a healthy savings buffer to cover costs and any contingencies that may arise. 'I'll meet you in front of Montparnasse Tower on Avenue du Maine in a few hours?' The tower is close to my parents' apartment and a good place to meet. 'We can visit the observation deck if you like?' It's one of the best places to view the Eiffel Tower and marvel at the panoramic sprawl of the city, but it's overlooked by many tourists as it's not as well-known as, say, the Place du Trocadero, or Sacré Coeur in Montmartre.

'Can we not? How many times do I *need* to see the Eiffel Tower?'

'You'll lose your French citizenship if you say that out loud.'

'Ha, good then we can go back to London.'

'Very funny. I'll text you when I'm on my way.'

I head out into the warm spring day and make my way to the Metro to get a train to the 6th arrondissement to meet Anais.

* * *

When I arrive at La Palette, I scour the pretty floral-filled terrace for my friend. The brasserie is a left bank institution. It's said the artist Picasso and musician Jim Morrison used to be frequent guests. Jim Morrison is actually buried in Père-Lachaise cemetery. His grave is the most visited out of all the famous people resting in peace there. The necropolis might just be quirky enough for Eloise's tastes, so I make a mental note to ask her if she wants to visit soon.

Anais waves me over to a table in a strip of sunlight. 'Bonjour, Coco! It's been too long.' We kiss cheeks.

'Bonjour, Anais. It has.' I take a seat as a waiter appears. We order a bottle of Sancerre and steak frites, a typical Parisian lunch offering. 'How is it going at the hotel?' There's a radiance to her face that was missing the last time I saw her at a literary festival.

'The hotel is going from strength to strength thanks to my cousin, Manon. I get to enjoy the perks of living there and writing romance novels, which thankfully, I've grown to love again. For a while there I felt like I'd lost my mojo. The words wouldn't come, or if they did they were about my heroine massacring cheating lying men two at a time. Not exactly on brand for me.' I laugh at the thought. Anais writes sweet romantic comedies so there's no way she'd get away with a vengeful protagonist killing off her heroes.

'I'm glad we got you back from the dark side.'

'*Oui.* It's strange to say, but the divorce was the best thing that ever happened to me. What I didn't know then is that it's a grieving process. I wish I'd known that earlier and saved myself the angst.'

'That's an interesting take.' Will I feel the same soon enough?

She nods. 'Time dulls down all the hurt, the humiliation, but more than that...' She makes a contemplative face. 'I came to understand that I'd been so desperate to find love at the time that I overlooked all the ways in which it wasn't working and I settled for that, because I didn't want to be alone, when in reality, I was *still* alone. The marriage only had one participant who was playing by the rules – *moi*. Even now, I reflect and wonder why I wasn't honest with myself about it.'

The waiter returns with the wine and pours us each a glass before bustling off to another table.

Anais' frank admission gives me pause. Have I done the very

same thing with Alexander? Overlooked all those red flags because it was easier to pretend the relationship was on the right trajectory? Clearly so.

'Why do we blame ourselves though?' I say. 'That's the question we should be asking.'

She holds her wine glass up and we clink before each taking a sip. 'You know, that's true too. It must be a default setting where we look internally and subconsciously direct the blame back our way. The thing is, I don't think Francois-Xavier ever loved me. I'm sure now that I was an easy mark for him.'

'No, Anais. Surely he couldn't be that cold and calculating?'

'He is, but something tells me he might behave better in future.'

'I won't ask.'

She lets out an evil little cackle. 'Best not.'

'Before *I* was the main topic of chat in the publishing world, I heard Margaret pulled the pin and went out on her own?' Margaret is a legend in the industry and is Anais' literary agent. She doesn't mince words and has her finger on the pulse of publishing. I'm slightly terrified of her intimidating ways, but she's mostly harmless, just of old school ilk where she doesn't sugarcoat a damn thing.

'*Oui*, it's been a fabulous fresh start for Margaret and for the authors who followed her. Margaret finally had enough of the power dynamics and not being heard in a company that was successful largely because of her. When she made that leap, as scary as it was, it gave her the freedom to do it her way. And she's doing incredibly well. Of course, I've heard all about your predicament. You can't let him win, Coco. You're an amazing editor. Are you going to go back to it? I can't help but think you need to follow Margaret's lead and start your own firm. Alone.'

My anxiety ramps up. I fight the urge to nervously scratch at my skin. I'm not sure why I'm still so ashamed, as if I'm the one who had sticky fingers and not Alexander. I'd been hoping to ask Anais about the gossip, but now that I'm face to face with her it's awkward delving into it. There's no accounting for how stupid I feel, still. 'Well...' I best rip the plaster off because we're going to get there no matter how I dance around the subject. 'I couldn't get an editorial job for love nor money and I have zero capital to start over. I don't even have enough to rent an apartment yet. How dire does all that sound?'

'It sounds grossly unfair to me.' She reaches across the table and places her hand atop mine.

I give her a small smile. 'I'm working in a bookshop and saving for an apartment. How the mighty fall, eh?' I go on to summarise my version of events, aware that I'm probably coming across robotic and detached. It's easier that way, to stand back from it as if I'm recounting someone else's woes.

By the time I'm finished telling her the whole sorry story, Anais' shoulders are up around her ears. 'And you never found the money?'

'He said it was gone.'

She tuts. 'I'm so sorry this happened. And for him to rub salt in the wounds with your editorial assistant. I wonder if she was in on it?'

'Editorial assistant?' I ask with a frown.

Anais' face twists. '*Merde*, you didn't see the post on Instagram?'

I shake my head as the pieces suddenly click into place. That wink; it still makes me shudder. 'Can you show me the post?' Some broken hearts might find comfort (or pain) in scrolling through their lost love's social media accounts, ruminating about what could have been or keeping watch. Not me. I blocked Alexander so I'd never have to see his mug again.

There will be no stumbling on memories that catch me unaware. It's easier that way, to forget he ever existed. But if my suspicions are correct about that creepy wink he gave Molly-Mae, then I've been played a fool *twice*.

Anais swipes open her phone and scrolls with a look of intense concentration on her face. When she finds the post, she asks, 'Isn't this your editorial assistant?' When she turns her phone around, there's a photo of Molly-Mae, my *former* highly ambitious editorial assistant, kissing Alexander's cheek. The caption says: *Hard launching this beauty. In my darkest times, I found the light. Molly-Mae helped dust me off and made me whole again. Love conquers all.*

My bruised heart stutters to a stop. I put a hand to my chest to stop the pain.

This betrayal is one too many. My face crumples as I finally let tears fall. The motherboard inside me misfires for all the world to see. How could they? I'd been so supportive of Molly-Mae, seeing a lot of my younger self in her, her drive, the way she had her eye on the future, when the whole time she had her eye on Alexander. Now it makes sense why she was trying to cover up the fact that Janae had raised concerns and didn't feed that back to me. Were they in on it together? Was it a way to get me out of the picture?

I hastily swipe at my tears and try to get a handle on my emotions. 'Sorry, Anais. I don't know what came over me. I feel so utterly, *utterly* stupid. And like second best.'

Anais' eyes are full of concern as I pass her the phone back. 'I'm so sorry, Coco. I shouldn't have shown you that post!'

I wave her concerns away. 'I'm glad you did. I can't get over how brazen he is, acting like what happened wasn't his fault!' My blood boils at the thought of him vanishing with the stolen funds and happily starting over after I sorted the mess out, losing everything in the process. 'What did his caption say again?' I bite down on my lip.

For some reason, the idiocy of what he wrote makes me laugh. It seems so at odds to how he usually speaks. Anais bites down on her lip too and soon we fall about laughing.

When I finally gather myself, I sputter, 'Hard launching.' And it starts us off again. At some point, the waiter returns with our meals and gives us a strange look as we dissolve into laughter once more.

Anais says, 'Love conquers all!' My stomach muscles seize up from so much chortling.

'They deserve one another. Although I always liked Molly-Mae.' And I don't know for sure, they could have become an item *after* I left, but still, it goes against the girl code. We eat companionably for a minute. The steak is tender and covered with lashings of buttery bearnaise sauce. The frites are crispy and crunchy.

'Do you want me to tell you what I've heard bandied about?'

In the long run it's probably preferable to have all the facts at hand, and surely there's no more shocks like that one. 'May as well.'

Anais swipes mascara smudges from under her eyes. 'My agent Margaret mentioned that there were all these positive articles about Alexander popping up on industry websites and the like. For example, there was one about his history of giving back to those in the literary world from less fortunate backgrounds. How he was set on helping them get a foot in the door of the publishing industry.'

'That's a blatant lie. He hasn't helped anyone.'

'Right. Margaret believes it's the work of a PR firm.'

I cup my head in my hands. 'Molly-Mae worked at a PR firm before switching to editorial.'

'There you go, they're working together on a campaign to make him out to be this literary philanthropist.'

'And me hightailing it out of London must make me seem like the guilty party.'

She makes a moue with her mouth. 'Maybe not. Don't forget it's a terrifically small industry and a lot of us have dealt with Alexander over the years. It's obvious he's in damage control mode, whereas you did the right thing and then moved back home.'

'I hope it comes across that way. Still, the question remains: why? Why did he forgo his stake in a successful business, lose a steady income that was pretty much guaranteed, to skim off the top like that?'

'Because he's got a massive ego, Coco, and he thought he'd never get caught.'

Ah. *Of course.* He didn't think he was risking anything. He knew the systems I'd installed wouldn't alert. He just didn't factor in that I'd share author sales in real time with Janae and then have her question those amounts later.

I slide my fingers over my temples as a headache blooms. The knife in my back twists once more. 'When this exploded, one of my main concerns was finding replacement jobs for our staff, and Molly-Mae told me not to worry, that the enforced break would do her good.' I let out a bitter laugh.

'An enforced break paid for with stolen funds.'

'And holed up with Alexander.' There was clearly some scheming between the two, and I didn't see it.

'They deserve each other.'

After I'd tied up all the loose ends, I left quickly, mortified that my life had changed so dramatically almost overnight. I've never suffered that intense public shame before and all I wanted to do was hide. Now I see it for what it is, and my desire to fight returns. 'Why should *I* lose it all? I don't allow people to manipulate me. I'm not a pushover.' It dawns on me I've simply given myself the space to grieve these losses before I rise up and get back what's mine. And that's a sensible approach. I've been in a fog, still unable to see clearly and make rational choices when it comes to Alexander.

'What will you do?'

'Therein lies the problem. My savvy but expensive lawyer made an agreement with our authors that the authorities wouldn't be involved, mostly for *my* benefit, as long as we paid them back within a certain timeframe, which I managed to do by liquidating everything, and a payment plan is still in place while we wait for royalties from retailers like Amazon and the like.' I toy with my napkin while Anais pours us two generous glasses of wine because we've obviously scared the waiter off with our hysterical laughter. 'By then I'd already spent an exorbitant amount of money on a forensic accountant to trace it all. If I go down the legal route again, a civil suit against Alexander, I dread to think how much more it will cost. According to my lawyer, it'll be more than what I originally invested in the company, so is it worth doing? I mean, if I won then everyone in the industry would hear about it and know for sure that I wasn't involved, but that will come at a financial cost to me.' Not to mention the time and effort involved, dredging up the whole mess again, bringing the scandal back to the fore, requiring another level of energy that I don't have.

'I know how prohibitive legal fees can be and I see your point. It's a tough decision but probably worth pursuing if you want to continue to work in publishing.' She takes a delicate sip of wine and says, 'There should be consequences for what he did.'

'There must be another way to hold him accountable that won't cost me more in legal fees.'

'You're as clever as they come, Coco. You'll figure out the path forward. Eventually you'll realise that Alexander did you a favour.'

While it sounds strange, it's true. This faux relationship could have lasted forever without me being aware of the seedy underbelly. '*Merci,* Anais.'

'Next, you need to find love again.'

I laugh, half choking on a wedge of crusty bread. 'I don't think so somehow.'

'You know, that's exactly what I thought after my divorce. But the best cure for heartbreak *is* love!'

I narrow my eyes. 'How can you be so sure?' Everyone seems to have a remedy for heartbreak but I remain unconvinced.

'A new romance helps put all the pieces back together.'

Henri's face flashes in my mind, and I mentally swipe the image away. 'I do love a good romance, a bad boy, but the safe sort, under the cover of a book. Speaking of, you'll have to visit me at The Paris Bookshop for the Broken Hearted. Valérie has a range of your backlist in stock, and they sell out almost as quickly as she can order them in.'

'Ooh, I've heard about that place! Potions and passages for those suffering from a broken heart? One of my friends went there and *voilà*, found love the very next day. She claims the place is magical, wondrous, and the owner has some special power to see into people and fix them up. Is it true?'

My eyebrows pull together. 'How can it be?'

Anais surveys me for a beat. '*Oui*, it's peculiar, but what if she really does have a gift? Has she tried it on you?'

'Yes, she's already planning my upcoming literary wedding to journalist Henri.'

Anais raises a brow. 'And who is this Henri then? Is he gorgeous? I bet he's gorgeous.'

I wave her away. 'Jude Law circa 1990 sort of looks.'

'Well, stop right there. That isn't just gorgeous, that's rip-your-clothes-off hot.'

I laugh, imagining such a thing. 'You'd think so, but he's got this saviour complex.' I fill her in on our first run-in, when I literally ended up in his arms, then the pickpocket incident and later him arriving at the bookshop claiming I followed him.

'So three times Lady Love put this hot guy who already wants to *protect* you in your direct line of sight and you don't think it's meant to be?'

I scoff. 'Well, if you believe in all that nonsense, maybe, but I don't. He's at the bookshop every day, writing I guess, although I don't see much finger-on-keyboard action. He's...' What is he? The more time I spend with Henri, the more I sense that he's a little lost himself. '...An enigma. Besides, I don't trust my judgement with men any more, but I concede he's rather nice to look at.'

'I'll have to pop into the bookshop for a visit, and I'd love you to see the hotel too, when you're free.' Anais holds her glass aloft. 'Here's to endless possibilities and the courage to take risks for the brightest, shiniest of futures.'

We clink glasses. Anais is the inspiring kind of friend who is good for the soul. Her words are more meaningful because she's walked the same path and come out the other side. She has a hotel that gave up its secrets in a strange bit of happenstance, she's madly in love, and she's thriving in her writing career. There's hope for me yet.

It's time to control the narrative of my own life.

16

Later that day, I have to physically drag Eloise from The Paris Bookshop for the Broken Hearted, pushing her along as if she's a lame donkey. 'Au revoir, Valérie!' she calls out, her usual cool demeanour replaced by an effusiveness I haven't seen in a long time.

'Au revoir, Eloise.'

She loops her arm through her overfull tote. 'That's it, I'm forgoing the library and I'll study upstairs in the book loft.'

'Even with your "cringe" mum working there?' I can't help but tease. A few weeks ago she wouldn't have been seen dead in the same vicinity as me.

'Why do Boomers always try and speak Gen Z?'

I gasp. 'I am *not* a Boomer, I'm a very proud Millennial, I'll have you know.' I'm happy that Eloise wants to make use of the bookshop, but it's too far from school for her to walk alone so unless she's with friends I'm not going to be comfortable with it. I don't mention it now; as is the way with contrary teens, she may forget all about it by next week.

'I *love* Valérie. Do you think she's a white witch?'

I wrinkle my nose. 'White witch indeed! No, I think she's a very smart businessperson who instinctively understands bookworms and has catered to their every desire.'

Eloise rolls her eyes as if I just don't get it. 'You make it sound so basic, as if she's only there to make money.'

I frown. 'That's exactly what she's there for. It's a simple case of economics.'

'You're so left-brained, Mum. Valérie clearly doesn't care about the money side of things. I saw her give away potions and passages to a few people today, and she watched that woman put a book in her ratty knapsack and turned the other way.'

'What woman?'

'The one with the red T-shirt, hair sort of a bird's nest.'

Come to think of it, I did see that woman too. 'Valérie might be lax at times, but I can't see her being comfortable letting shoplifters snatch a book.' Since there's no employee manual, once again I'm left to decipher this on my own, and surely rule number one of retail is don't let people steal?

I don't hear the *duh* but it's written all over Eloise's face. 'The woman had a hungry look about her. I'm guessing Valérie turned a blind eye so the woman would at least have the comfort of a book to make her happy.'

I mull it over. How is this thirteen-year-old so aware? I chide myself for not seeing that same plaintive need in the young woman with the unkempt hair. 'I'll keep an eye out for her in future. Valérie believes the broken hearted find their way to the bookshop to be healed, and at first I assumed she meant from love gone wrong, but it's broader than that.' It's all a farce but Eloise loves this sort of stuff.

'Really? So that woman with the red T-shirt found her way there by magic for a cure?'

'If you believe Valérie, then yes.'

'Wow, she never told me *that*.'

'Maybe because you're not heartbroken.'

'Mum, come on. All teenagers are heartbroken. Especially me. I've got an iPhone that belongs in the Jurassic period. That makes me sad at least ten times a day.'

'Oh poor you, an iPhone that works perfectly fine. First world problems, Eloise.'

'I don't even have to use filters because the camera is so grainy. It's like something from the eighties. Like a Polaroid, for crying out loud.'

We share a laugh. Eloise would love the latest tech gadgets but knows it's not going to happen. Now, buying the latest books, well, that's another thing entirely and I'll always support that.

'I bet Valérie's potions and passages will help that woman. I'm certain of it. Speaking of which, has she cured *your* broken heart yet, or are you still writing down all the pros and cons of your new Parisian life before you allow her to work her magic on you?' She shoots me a cheeky grin.

Times like this, all the worry I feel about my daughter evaporates. While she might be a hormonal grenade to be handled with extreme care at times, underneath that behaviour lies an empathetic soul. 'There's nothing wrong with writing out the pros and cons for every situation if you're unsure.'

'But did she help you yet or not?'

I shake my head. 'Valérie's got it in her head that Henri is the one for me.'

'Ooh, that old Jude Law guy?'

I bristle in Henri's defence. 'He's not old!'

'He's like, what... thirty or *forty*?'

'Yes, you're right, he's well on his way to being decrepit.' I shake my head. Teenagers are hilarious.

Eloise is practically skipping with joy, probably the after-glow of a successful bookshop haul, and it's good to see a radiance about her again. The last month or so has been tricky. 'Why don't you like this Henri guy then? Is there no chemistry?'

How does she even *know* about chemistry? 'He's just...' How to explain it to a thirteen-year-old? '...Rather irritating.'

'How?'

'He just is.'

'Yeah, but how? Does he laugh too loud, or—'

'Yes!' I grab hold of the excuse – any excuse. 'He laughed so hard the other day he frightened customers. Who behaves like that, especially in a bookshop? He's *strange*.'

'*Mum.*'

'What?'

'You don't really think he's strange, do you? It's more that you're feeling strange in his presence. When you say stuff like that I know you're lying. You like the guy!'

'I do not like him!' I say with all the bluster of a child.

'I mean like as a *friend*. You always get a bit antsy when you hope that person will like you back. You act sort of... scattered when it happens.'

'Oh, not this again. I'm a very regimented disciplined person. I wouldn't describe myself as scattered at all.'

'OK.'

'OK?'

'You can be both, all at once.'

'Impossible.'

'So you don't think he's cute?'

I fumble with an answer. 'No... Yes... Well, I haven't noticed.'

She lets out an impatient sigh. 'More lies! I thought we weren't *supposed* to lie to each other. Why can't you admit you like him and you do think he's got that mad rizz?'

'Mad rizz?'

'Charisma.'

She's got me there with the lie agreement we made. I huff. 'Fine. By society's standards he may be considered handsome, and I would agree. However, his personality leaves a lot to be desired.'

'That feels like more lies smothered in a lot of unnecessary words.'

'Fine. Fine. He's ridiculously attractive and I do like the man one minute and then despise him the next so I'm really not sure what that's all about. Valérie sings his praises and it all feels a bit forced. I know virtually nothing about him, even though he's at the bookshop most days.'

I feel an uncomfortable flush when Henri's face flashes in my mind and would much prefer to drop this subject.

'You would look cute together, but it's probably not the right time and timing is *everything*.'

I don't bother asking how she knows this to be true. The internet has a lot to answer for. 'So,' I say while she's in an expansive mood. 'How were Léa and the other girls yesterday?' Eloise had kept her distance during the school week but couldn't avoid them for a group project for art.

She waves a hand in a so-so motion. 'They couldn't say much because we were in class doing that stupid project together with a teacher close by, but there were still little comments here and there.'

'What kind of comments?'

'About my hair, mostly, why I insist on the Rapunzel look. They also joked about me living with my grandparents in a small apartment in Montparnasse, as if the arrondissement proves I'm not one of them, who all live fancy apartments in the 7th with views over the Eiffel Tower or something.'

Bullying hasn't changed through the ages. 'That must be upsetting, to have them judge you for things that are out of your control.' The tiger mum in me roars at such an injustice done to my daughter. Belittling her for living in a humbler abode. It's so out of line. But I keep my thoughts private.

Eloise drops her head as if the memory is heavy. 'Yeah, it's sort of embarrassing because they make sure they're just loud enough for those around us to hear, but not loud enough to catch the attention of the teacher.'

Tiny monsters at thirteen. 'You're handling it really well, but I can step in if needed and I promise I won't make a scene. I can keep it confidential and ask them to keep an eye out so it's not as if you told on the girls.'

She guffaws. 'Not risking it. It's OK, I'm just going to ignore it. It's weird though, I sort of feel sorry for Léa.'

'What, why?' Is Eloise buying into the manipulation from these girls?

She wrinkles her brow. 'This boy in my maths class told me her *maman* died last year. It all happened suddenly and after that she changed. Turned nasty.'

Losing her *maman* at the age of twelve is awful to contemplate. 'Ooh, that's terrible news. A traumatic experience I'm sure, but that doesn't give her the right to hurt others,' I say gently, wondering if I'm being callous. Perhaps this girl needs compassion more than anything, but it's hard to separate my protective instinct from the equation.

'*Oui*, I agree, but it does sort of explain it.'

'Perhaps it would be sensible to speak to a teacher on the quiet about what's going on. I wonder if this is a cry for help. She probably needs some support to deal with her ongoing grief and could connect with the school therapist about why she's lashing out. You'd be helping her, even if it didn't feel quite like that.'

'I'm sure she'd know it was me who spoke up though.'

'Hmm.' This is such a complicated time. 'Does that really matter in the scheme of things? What if her behaviour escalates? What if all she really needs is a shoulder to cry on, a trained professional to listen to her and give her strategies to cope rather than bully the new girl? It sounds like she's trying to hurt you because *she's* hurting.'

'*Oui*, I guess. It's just so awkward at lunchtimes. Everyone looks at me weirdly because I'm not sitting with Léa and rest of them now. I'm finding it hard to make friends because I'm sure they're all scared of her too, and I think they're worried if they sit with me, she might start on them.'

'What about the kids from your music class?' Don't musical kids stick together? Form bands and bonds?

She rolls her eyes. 'They hang out by the music room and mostly keep to themselves.'

'Can you hang out with them?'

She contemplates it. 'Maybe.'

We come to a row of bouquinistes, the booksellers on the bank of the Seine. Eloise stops to check out the Paris postcards. While she's flicking through them, I say, 'Just to confirm, I can't make one teeny call to the school and tell them to handle it sensitively?'

She waves to the stallholder and hands over some coins for a couple of postcards. 'No way. That will only make it worse, and besides, what can you say? They told me to cut my hair and wear different clothes? That they live in a more prestigious area? Léa will tell the teachers they were trying to *help* me fit in. She's got them all fooled.' We continue walking along the River Seine as boats chug along the waterway.

I exhale a long breath. I promised Eloise that I would never go behind her back in these matters as long as she is open and honest with me, but if I felt there was an urgent need to intervene, I'd tell her and that would be that. Teenagers need to learn the skills to stand up for themselves and navigate bullying, but only to a point before parent intervention is necessary. Unfortunately, my strong-willed daughter never quite sees it that way. 'OK, but promise me you will think of telling a teacher if it continues? You never know, Léa might need help and doesn't know how to ask for it. You could be doing her a favour.'

'I promise. Now, can we talk about *anything* else?'

'Sure.'

'Let's get some *canelés* at the patisserie for Mémère?' *Canelés* are a French pastry filled with rum and vanilla custard, drenched in a sugar syrup, giving it a caramelised taste. They're Maman's favourite.

I grin. 'We can. Let's take a little picnic to Jardin Atlantique and see if she'll join us for the afternoon?'

'*Parfait.*'

'I wish your grandad wasn't working.' He doesn't usually work weekends but they're looking at taking over another small laundry so he's going over their accounts to see if it's viable.

Eloise gives my shoulder a pat. 'Same, but he said if he gets this other business his plan is to merge with theirs and then eventually sell so they can retire.'

'They'll never retire. They like the hustle too much.' It's one of the things I love about them – they're always alive with ideas, and purpose. They enjoy working.

'Even though it's super lame an adult has to walk me to school, I do like spending time with him in the mornings. He's been telling me all about you as a teenager, and wow, I didn't know you were so wild, Mum! You used to sneak out?'

I laugh; me the rebel is not quite how it went. 'Did he tell you where I used to sneak out to?'

'No, where did you go?'

'The library! They always wanted me home early when they were working late, but I wanted to study in the library.'

She slaps her forehead. '*Really?* That is *so* lame.'

'Really. They wouldn't let me travel that far alone...'

'Sounds familiar!'

I grin. 'And I loved visiting libraries. No matter where we lived, I'd hunt them out and spend time in them all. It cemented my love of reading, of words. I didn't know if I'd be a writer, or a librarian, a bookseller, or an editor, I just knew I'd be in the industry someday. But my very staid and boring parents told me it would ease their minds if I just studied at home while they worked. So, to ease their minds, I did, until they worked late and then I'd go the library.'

'That's not exactly wild.'

'It was at thirteen.'

'I'm going to have to speak to Grandad about his story-telling. What an epic letdown.'

17

The following Tuesday, I'm back at The Bookshop for the Broken Hearted, taking a delivery of stock. The sun is shining and it's warmer than forecast, so I open the windows to let in the fresh, blossom-scented spring breeze. 'You can pop them by the door,' I say to the courier. 'I'll get them inside soon.' I'll cart them in one by one and put the stock away in the lulls, so the boxes don't get relegated to the storeroom and lost forever.

The weekend must have been a busy one as there are plenty of spaces on the shelves, and even some of the towering piles of books situated on the wooden floor are now gone entirely. It helps that Valérie prices second-hand books affordably. They start from one euro depending on age and condition.

'Coco,' Valérie calls out. 'Your café crème is on the bar.'

'*Merci*. I won't be long!' I heft one of the boxes to the main bookshop floor.

'Why are you carrying such a heavy box?' she remarks with a lift of her brow. 'You'll hurt your back doing that.'

'Well...'

She clucks her tongue. 'Use the trolley, *ma chérie*. That's what it's for.'

A trolley! 'The other day when I asked Henri for help with the stock he didn't mention that there's a trolley, and surely he must have seen it before, since he's here so often he's practically part of the furniture.'

'Because he's a *man*. They don't see what's right in front of them. That or he just wanted to haul heavy boxes in front of you to show off his big muscles.'

I blush. 'I'm sure he did no such thing.'

'You must admit he does have a nice physique.'

'It's... OK. Is this appropriate to talk about at work?'

'We're in the business of curing broken hearts so naturally talk about men will arise, *non*?'

It's hard to gauge the rules without an employee manual, but Valérie will not be convinced she needs one. 'Right, but are we allowed to *objectify* them like that?'

'Oh, Coco, you're a hoot. Of course we are! Henri is a handsome specimen of a man and there's no harm in looking at his muscles when he flexes them doing odd jobs around the bookshop, is there?'

Well... Before the words leave my lips, she shakes her head as if baffled by me. 'The book trolley is against the wall to the left of the kitchen, bright yellow, you can't miss it. But sit down, have your coffee first.'

I join Valérie at the bar as we chat away over coffee and fresh buttery croissants, spreading flaky pastry all over the place as we go. 'Your daughter is a delight. Beautiful and book smart.'

'*Merci*, Valérie. She's a little too smart at times.'

'Teenage daughters can humble you like no other.'

I laugh. 'Sounds like you're speaking from experience.' It

strikes me I don't know anything about Valérie's private life, probably because she's too busy digging into everyone else's.

She waves me away and reaches for a beignet, a French donut. 'Something like that. Now, tell me, how are you enjoying it here so far?'

'It's absolute mayhem. Chaos. It's dusty, musty, my legs ache at the end of the day running those stairs, and I have a multitude of small burns from using the coffee machine incorrectly. The customers are weird and wonderful and ask the strangest questions, and I honestly have never felt so *alive*.'

'*Bien*. And Henri, you're getting along now?'

'As much as we can when someone runs hot and cold like he does.'

There's a benevolence in her eyes. I wonder if she's asked Henri about me too, patiently waiting for us to stop banging heads.

'Once you get to know him better, you'll see him for what he really is. A warm, kind-hearted soul who's on his way out of a rough patch just like everyone here.'

'OK.' I don't delve any further into it because I'm sure she's just angling for me to admit I'm keen on the guy so she can plan our wedding. Sure, I'm intrigued by him, but I'm disillusioned by the opposite sex and wonder if that's going to be permanent.

'And you're all ready for the book club on Thursday?'

I nod. 'As ready as I can be. I've sorted the catering from the patisserie; they'll deliver on the day, along with your regular order for the charcuterie boards for the bookshop. I've had a number of enquiries—'

'Bonjour, Valérie!' A booming voice interrupts us, making me jump in fright. I'm surprised to see such volume come from a petite young woman with a pink pixie haircut. 'Who is this then?' She jerks a thumb in my direction.

'This is Coco,' Valérie says. 'Your new book club moderator.'

She gives me a slow once over that makes me shrink a little against such overt scrutiny. 'Are you sure she's up for the job? No offence, Coco, but by looks alone, I don't think you are.'

Is this about my skinny jeans again? Or my permanent pinched expression that is locked in place no matter how many breathing exercises I do? 'What makes you say that?' I ask, curious.

'There's a timidity to you, *non*? You're wringing your hands like you're nervous, you're wearing ballet flats like you're delicate, and is that a blouse with *frills*? It's very pirate chic, if that's the look you were going for.'

'It's librarian chic.' Also known as one of my seven work outfits. I'm not exactly a clotheshorse, but I have a capsule wardrobe I can rotate and mix and match so I don't have to think about it much. I'll probably lose my French citizenship mentioning that fashion doesn't inspire me, but honestly, who can pretend about these things? 'If I were to spoil myself it would be a book-buying spree, not a blouse with or without frills.'

'That makes sense. I'll reserve further judgement for a day or two.'

I hide a smile. 'Lucky me.'

First impressions are important and how I gauge most personalities. This pink-haired individual – with her wild outfit, wearing dramatic winged liner – appears to be a rather unique straight talker. I enjoy the forthrightness of people who don't mince words because I know where I stand with them. There are no surprises.

'So,' I say. 'I'm also intrigued by what you're wearing. Are you trying to blend in, or stand out?' I point to the juxtaposition of high visibility fluoro shorts with reflective stripes, coupled with a camouflage top, like she wants to be at one with the jungle. 'It's like a sartorial battle between being seen and being hidden.'

It takes her a moment to process what I'm asking. '*Oui,* that's me in a nutshell. A paradox! And I go by the name of Ziggy.'

'Nice to meet you, Ziggy. I'll reserve further judgement for a day or two.'

'Touché. So, this morning I was chatting online to my good friend Freya Cooper...'

I blanch. Does she mean the *author* Freya Cooper? The author Freya Cooper who was up until recently published with London Field Publishing? I gulp back worry.

'...And she was telling me all about her upcoming release. A summer book about second-chance love. I've been invited to the book launch in London. Isn't that *magnifique*?' My chest tightens at the thought. I edited that book myself and had to let it go, along with Freya. It's a wonderful escapist read that really tugs at the heartstrings.

How can this be, though? Just a coincidence?

'You must know her well?' I ask Ziggy.

'*Oui.* I'm friends with all the big-name authors. I'm a well-known book content creator. A hundred thousand on Insta.'

'Followers?'

'Well, it's not posts, is it?' She shriek-laughs. The grating sound is going to take some getting used to. My shoulders are up around my ears, but they slowly release once I realise that as a content creator, Ziggy must know lots of authors at a superficial level. There's nothing to be concerned about, and it's not like Freya would share the behind-the-scenes details about London Field Publishing crumbling with an online acquaintance. My secret is still safe.

Inside, I roil at the fact I'm keeping my old life hidden,

feeling that same sense of shame, but I can't seem to get past it. Knowing Valérie well enough now, I trust she'd believe my version of events, but I don't want to be seen as a patsy, or worse, be pitied. At lunch with Anais, I felt warrior like, ready to avenge my name, my pride, but that buzz soon ended when I got home and saw my bank balance. First, I must get my safety nets back in place before I make any rash decisions.

Ziggy is staring at me, waiting for a response about her Instagram. 'One hundred thousand followers is very impressive.' Book content creators are important members of the bookish community who read, review and support writers they love using all sorts of mediums for their content creation: videos, pictures, blogs, vlogs, in-person events. They're instrumental in helping spread the word about books and are an asset to the writing community. Creators and authors often grow close as they interact over the course of many books across social media. Ziggy might be close to my former author, but I'm sure it's only surface-level, because Freya is usually rather circumspect. Even doing a book launch is out of character. I guess she's muddling along with a new publisher and the launch is a result of that. Wanting to fit in, to do the right thing by her new team. My heart squeezes at the thought that book landed in someone else's lap.

Another woman wanders in, wearing a flowy organza dress. 'Bonjour. Oh – who are you? A new staff member?'

'I'm Coco.' Valérie gives her the same spiel about me running the book club.

'Coco is the same as you, Lucy, half-British, half-French, recently moved back from London.'

'Ooh nice! Welcome.' She gives me a wide smile. 'You're utterly perfect. Just the right amount of demureness, with that quiet intensity that you will need to keep control. I'll help you, if they get out of hand, don't worry.'

'Coco is sassy too,' Ziggy throws in for good measure.

'I'm well read, if that's of any importance?' I say, amused that they have sized me up to see if I'll fit here.

'And oh so humble.' Ziggy laughs.

'Isn't reading what it's all about though?' I ask. 'Being a book club and all.'

Lucy wrinkles her nose. 'We try not to judge others on their reading habits, you see, or we wouldn't *have* a book club. Some members speed read, and *is* that really reading? Well, let's not bring that up again. That debate went on through the night and we've now learned that some things are best left unsaid; but I digress. A few members don't ever read the assigned book club pick and that's OK too.' Lucy radiates calmness compared to the other book club members such as Agnes and Ziggy. I hope there are more like her with a Zen-like presence.

Ziggy rolls her eyes, clearly chomping at the bit to speak, but Lucy holds a hand up to stop her interrupting.

'Who are we to force them to read? Maybe their dog got sick, or they dropped their book in the bath. There are plenty of reasons why they might not get to it and it's best not to make an example of them,' Lucy says.

Ziggy huffs. 'I wholeheartedly disagree. Which is my right as a book club member. Why bother coming to book club if they're not going to read? We have to sit there and listen to them harp on about books from four thousand years ago while they trash-talk new styles and throw the word "woke" around in the wrong context. It's frustrating to say the least.'

'Some only read literary fiction and that's their prerogative. It's a judgement-free zone.'

They're obviously talking about American Agnes.

'Not for me, it's not. I'll judge them accordingly,' Ziggy says with a mischievous glint in her eyes. What have I got myself into?

'You will *not*, Ziggy.' Lucy flashes me a reassuring smile.

Ziggy falls onto a chair. 'Don't be alarmed, Coco. It's always fun, if not a little loud.'

'Yes,' confirms Lucy. 'We have a lot of drop-ins who treat it like wine club or maybe escape-the-controlling-husband club. Who knows their motivations, but everyone is welcome.'

Ziggy emphatically shakes her head. 'No, it's called a book club, Lucy. BOOK club.'

I double blink as they parry back and forth about the merits of a book club being solely for reading or not. Now the unruly part is making more sense. They dissolve into an argument about dog-earring pages of a book, of all things.

'Are they always like this?' I ask Valérie, who is paying not one bit of attention to them as she loads the dishwasher with cocktail glasses.

'Always, you learn to tune out and it becomes like white noise.'

Ziggy blows out a breath. 'Well, my good friend Freya Cooper would be very upset if the advance review copy she sent was treated in such a violent way.'

'Violent?' Lucy gasps. 'It's simply turning down the corner of a piece of paper!'

'It was once a living, breathing thing, a beautiful tree, and we must respect its past.'

Lucy lets out a frustrated sigh. 'Oh, here she goes. Holier than thou. Next she'll be name dropping all her eco warrior author friends. What she probably hasn't told you is that she slides into their DMs. Weasels her way into their very lives. That's why we call her Obsessive Fan Girl.'

Ziggy folds her arms defensively. '*So?* How else would I chat to them? I can't exactly slide into their *house*, can I? Although I have been to Stephen's house once. Well, technically an Airbnb, when he was in Paris for a literary event, but it was a chance meeting.'

Lucy guffaws.

Ziggy shoots her a glare and continues. 'There he was, head down as he chatted on the phone, and I was doing the same myself when he ran straight into me and knocked me flying. After I realised it was him, I really felt the sting of all those cuts and grazes. He was hurt too. Twisted his ankle. So there we were, a heap on the pavement right by the Arc De Triomphe—'

'Admit it, you Misery'd your way in. Just like the character Annie Wilkes.'

Ziggy's mouth falls open. 'I did no such thing! I was genuinely hurt. Legs akimbo, pride dented, and when I gazed into those deep azure eyes of his, I noticed the same sense of *longing* reflected back at me. But sadly, being a married man, he couldn't act on those feelings. And neither could I – I respect the sanctity of marriage.'

'Act on what feelings?' Lucy laughs. 'He called you an Uber, and that was it.'

'A *premier* Uber. And he gave me a signed copy of his latest book.'

'Was it the one with the twist – the wife was the serial killer and she set her husband up to take the fall because he was cheating on her with his masseuse and she swore revenge?'

Ziggy nods.

'Well, none of us have to read it now, do we?' Valérie says with a tut as she turns the dishwasher on and exits the bar and heads towards the book tunnel.

'You'll get used to Lucy,' Ziggy says. 'She cannot help herself. They call her Spoiler Alert.'

'They? More like *you*,' Lucy says. 'I don't mean to spoil the plot. It's hard to keep track of all those thrillers when they're named *The Wife's Killer*, or *The Locked Room*. It's impossible not to mix them all up so I have to sort of remind myself of the storyline to make sure we're discussing the same book. My nickname is rather uncalled for.'

Ziggy says, 'What about mine! You started the whole Obsessive Fan Girl thing, which is categorically untrue! I'm sure it's jealousy speaking because of my close friendship with so many authors. I can't help it if I've got a certain *je ne sais quoi* that these bestselling writers sense even over the internet.' She lifts her hands in surrender. 'Of course, no one in the book club can admit that it's my winning personality, my impressive bilingual skills and great way of articulating, that has aided in these author friendships, so they try to bring me down a peg.'

Lucy groans. 'That's not exactly true, Ziggy. Why don't you tell Coco how many times you walked up and down the pavement in front of Stephen's Airbnb until you "accidentally" bumped into him?' Lucy swings her gaze to me. 'So many that I'm sure she burned a hole in the pavement. Ziggy saw his post on Twitter, a picture of the Arc de Triomphe, taken from the window of his apartment. She figured out which building it was then walked up and down it until she could action her very own meet-cute, complete with the inevitable bumping of heads, the ubiquitous baguette flying into the air, while her tote bag falls to the floor and, *mon Dieu*, but which book should fall from its very clutches but *his*? A setup of the finest order... *Et voilà*, he's taken the bait and believes he's truly hurt this innocent French ingénue, whose humble baguette is now in three pieces. What a farce!'

Ziggy's mouth drops open. 'You should be a writer with that fantastical imagination of yours.' The apples of her cheeks pink while Lucy waits her out. I'm carried away by their bickering and invested in the story. 'Fine, so I might have orchestrated a meet-cute? Does that make me a bad person? *Non*, it does not.'

'It makes you a stalker. And what about the sanctity of marriage you respect so highly?'

'What if he had an open marriage, then what? Every good romcom starts with a meet-cute, and I decided my own grand passion would be the same. It's not illegal to walk up and down the pavement until an author you admire happens along.'

'Who is this Stephen? You don't mean Stephen King?'

'*Merde!*' Ziggy says. 'Stephen King is old enough to be my *grand-pere*!' Even Lucy looks a little green around the gills at that suggestion.

An awkward laugh escapes me. 'Sorry, I wasn't thinking.'

'She's obsessed with Stephen Silver.'

'Ooh, the American who writes pulse-racing thrillers?'

'*Oui*, and here comes the plot twist,' Ziggy says. 'Not long after we met, his wife died! *Tragique*.'

'Really?' I scramble to think of the wife in question and the tragic accident but can't place it.

Ziggy nods solemnly. 'A terrible, terrible accident. They were holidaying in a sleepy village in the UK and her hair dryer ended up in the bath when she was in it. Electrocuted.'

'That sounds – impossible. There are safety precautions these days, especially in hotels that prevent this sort of accident from happening.'

Ziggy waves me away. '*Oui*, she should have been more careful.'

Lucy's lip wobbles until she bursts out laughing. 'No one

died! This is just another of Ziggy's fantasies. He is still married to his lovely wife but Ziggy gets carried away to fantasyland.'

I'm going to have my hands full with this book club. Valérie was right to warn me.

'It could happen,' Ziggy protests.

I shake my head, still reeling.

'Sorry,' Ziggy laughs. 'You'll get used to my sense of humour. *Oui*, I stalked the guy but only to get his signature on my book and possibly an invitation to his summer home in Long Island. *But*... it didn't happen.'

'Ziggy's put love to one side after a terrible breakup.'

'Oh?' I say. 'I'm sorry to hear that.'

'That's how we became friends,' says Lucy. 'We both ended up here at the same time. Ziggy had been dumped by her online beau—'

'Online, *oui*, but it was real love.'

'He was an aspiring author, who *I feel* used her for her connections, but we often disagree on this.'

'That's terrible. I'm sorry, Ziggy.'

She lifts a shoulder. 'It's OK. Valérie sorted me out with a potion and passage and now I know true love is on its way; it's only a matter of being patient.'

'Oh?'

'*Oui. Ce qui sera sera.*' What will be, will be. How do they all just have blind faith? What the hell does Valérie put in those potions to make them trust her like that? Whatever it is, she clearly didn't put it in mine.

'And you, Lucy, were you suffering an upset too?'

A lot of broken-hearted souls do find their way to the book-shop, even I can't disagree with that. But how? Word of mouth about the eccentric bookseller?

'My cat died. Scout, named after the character from *To Kill a*

Mockingbird. She was a rescue, and my first ever pet.' Lucy shrugs as if it's just one of those things. 'Poor Scout had had a rough life. She was battle scarred and wary but she slowly began to trust me and then she suddenly died.'

'At least she found out what it meant to be loved and cared for in her final months,' Ziggy says, giving Lucy's hand a squeeze.

'*Oui.* Valérie did a potion and passage for me and it pointed me in the direction my life should take after that loss. Now I foster rescue cats until they find their forever home. It seems a fitting tribute to Scout.'

'That's a lovely thing to do.'

'And it led me to finding love with the vet from the rescue centre. I wasn't exactly looking for love, but it found me.' Lucy's expression brightens. 'Valérie told me I'd find my missing puzzle piece, and I did.'

'She did,' Ziggy confirms. 'He's a really nice guy even if he doesn't read fiction.'

Lucy gives me an apologetic smile. 'He's a nonfiction nerd. A history buff.'

'He sounds interesting.' But it's not as if Valérie had a hand in her meeting the vet at the rescue centre. It's just dumb luck.

'So... book club in two days,' Ziggy says. 'Finally, the gang are back together.'

'How many of you are there?' I'm not exactly sure who the core group is, except for American Agnes, Lucy, Ziggy and the book doctor Isidore, who I've yet to meet. Hopefully not Henri.

'There's six regulars and usually a handful of drop-ins.'

'Though, strangely enough, the drop-ins never seem to come back.' Lucy gives Ziggy a pointed look, which she ignores.

'Are there any men in the group?' I ask as subtly as anything.

'As much as we aim for diversity, we only have one,' Lucy says.

'The rest are probably intimidated by strong women.'

I laugh. One. Surely it's not him. 'What's his name?'

'Henri.'

La vache! 'And how does he behave in a group setting?'

Lucy cocks her head as if curious about my question. 'Behave! You make him sound like a naughty child!'

'*Everyone* loves Henri.' Ziggy rolls her eyes. 'It can be quite nauseating at times.'

I'm sure shock is evident in my eyes. 'They do? But isn't he belligerent and bossy, the very epitome of toxic masculinity?'

Lucy reels. 'What, no! Have you met Henri?'

We must be speaking of two different Henris! I point to his regular chair in the back. 'The Henri who sits there, mumbling and staring?'

'*Oui!* Far too handsome for his own good. But he's also sworn off love, the poor heartsick man.'

Ziggy lowers her voice to a whisper. 'His wife did a runner. Up and vanished one day leaving only a brief note. "This time I'm not coming back."'

'Cruel, vindictive woman, she was. Not a reader,' Lucy adds, as if that explains it.

'*Oui*, and therein lies the problem. How can anyone make a life with someone who doesn't worship books?'

Lucy nods her head in agreeance. 'It can never work.'

'Where did she go?' I survey my nails as if I'm only half listening.

'Ran off. She was always running off though. A month here and there. An aspiring actress who needed to be on the move for her career, but when it would inevitably fizzle out she'd come back to him. This time, Henri's put his foot down and divorced her. It's been well over a year. She's recently hooked up with some two-bit reality show celebrity who looks like he fell in a pot of orange paint. It's been all over the gossip sites, but we haven't shown Henri.'

'*Really?*' How awful for Henri. He must have really loved her to put up with that sort of thing.

'*Oui!*'

I turn to Henri's wrinkled leather chair at the back of the bookshop, away from most of the noise and the bright sunlight. These women see a different Henri to the man I've been getting to know. I recall our last conversation, where he mentioned a woman telling him the way he spoke to me by the Eiffel Tower that day was bang out of order; so if not his wife, who was that woman? And why do I care?

18

It's the day of the book club meet and instead of treating it as any other day, I drink too much caffeine so that I'm jittery as I sidestep customers in my efforts to get the space ready. I've set up in a quiet area at the back, near Henri's chair, much to his chagrin.

'Why are you setting up near me? I'm trying to work and you're making an awful racket.'

'It's quieter here. Customers are less likely to interrupt during the meeting, that's why.'

On Thursdays, Valérie keeps the bookshop open late, mostly for the bar, which has a gaggle of regulars who meet here for *après*-work drinks and for tourists meandering after dinner near the Eiffel Tower.

'But book club is always held at the front of the shop, by the windows. This is my space.'

'I'm sorry, I didn't realise you paid rent to work here.'

'I don't pay – oh. Very funny.'

'Henri, please, I've got a million things to cross off my list before this evening and I haven't scheduled listening to you complain.'

'Not this again.'

I slide an ottoman into the middle of a semi-circle of chairs. 'Not what again?' I'm only half listening as I mentally configure the space and where I'll put the finger food platters and the cups and drinks. Valérie supplies coffee, tea, juice and water, but apparently most members buy drinks from the bar – which tracks with most book clubs I've been to, where wine consumption is just as important as reading.

'You're acting like I'm a bully, when I'm no such thing.'

Hands on hips, I survey the placement of the ottoman. It's central enough, without being in the way. I lay a bunch of book club leaflets on it for customers who wander by today and might like to return and join in later.

'Well...?'

I stifle a sigh. 'Well, what?'

'We can be friends, you know.'

'I sense there's a but...'

His lips quirk into a half smile. 'And if there was?'

'Then I would be right about you. *Again.*'

He presses his lips together so hard the edges turn white. I can't help it; I laugh. 'So just to win the point, you will forgo the "but"?'

He remains mute but struggles against a smile.

'Fine.' I let out a breath. 'I will happily be your friend if you stop bossing me around. This might come as a shock to you, but you're not actually employed here, therefore, you cannot give me orders.'

'More's the pity.'

I tilt my head and give him a long look.

'What *do* you do here all day?' It feels more like his laptop is a prop. It's open but the screensaver jumps around while he stares off into space. There's no clacking of keys or sliding of the mouse. Is it his heartbreak that makes him so morose? For that, I can give him some grace. If the story about his wife is true, it would be a bitter pill to swallow.

'I write.'

'I'm no expert but usually words don't fall on a page by using the power of your mind alone, so are you actually working?' I mimic typing. 'I don't see a lot of this.'

He grins. 'So you spend all day watching me, do you?'

I blush. 'I'm very observant, that's all.'

'I do work.'

'You're not going to make this so-called friendship easy, are you, Henri?'

'Fine. I attempt to work.'

'On?'

'I'm currently trying to write about the upcoming Festival du Livre Paris that will be held at Grand Palais Éphémère, but I don't have the energy to string another tedious sentence together today.'

His shoulders sag as if the weight of his word count is a physical thing, pushing against his athletic frame. It's strange. I feel the press of sadness at the reminder of the literary festival too. This coming April, I was scheduled to attend the event. I'd hazard a guess that my invitation will be revoked and security told to not allow me entry in case I steal the silverware.

In the spirit of him opening up, I share a titbit. 'In my former life as an editor, I happen to know a few remedies for writer's block. Vacuuming or cleaning the bath are at the top of the list.'

He laughs. 'Is this a cunning ploy to get me to do the vacuuming around here?'

'That depends.' I grin. 'If you're amenable or not. I mean, it would be for the greater good, the sake of your article.'

His eyebrows pull together. 'So doing a chore more odious than the work itself is the way forward?'

I nod. 'Works every time. A reset. Or you could clean your apartment top to bottom. Walk around the Champ de Mars until your legs ache, and you'll be dreaming of this perfectly soft leathery chair to sink into, the excuse of work, as you pull your computer onto your lap.'

'But what if the well is dry? What if I have lost the spark forever?'

Dare I say it? 'Sex is third on the list.'

'Is sex so boring too that it'll drive me back to writing?'

I can feel my cheeks pink. Why does my mind suddenly picture Henri naked entwined in crisp white sheets! I blink and blink to remove the vision but it's stuck, frozen in place. A strange warmth races through me. Who turned the temperature up? Henri's frowning, probably because I'm glitching. I cough and clear my throat, scrambling for a response. 'I want it noted, I did not make the list.' I'm blushing furiously, and really, how does one blush furiously? It's nonsensical, and yet I can *feel* it, almost as if I'm radiating supreme pinkness. My writers always cackle about number three on "the list" and it's all in good fun, but Henri's blindsided me here. 'I suppose the, erm... intimacy is more a circuit breaker than a chore. But I wouldn't know.'

His eyes go wide. 'You've never had sex?'

My forehead wrinkles. 'No, I mean I've never had to use sex as a cure for writer's block because I'm not a writer!'

'Oh!' He laughs again, although I'm not sure what at. My body feels weighted. Woozy. It's all that coffee I practically inhaled.

'...Any other remedies?'

Thankfully, the other suggestions are not sexually oriented or I might pass out. 'Weeding the garden and having a closet clear out.'

'I'm beginning to see the appeal of writing.'

There's such a forlorn air about him at times. I dither with whether to pry. Knowing Henri, he'll probably take it as an affront. Curiosity gets the better of me and I blurt, 'How long have you been struggling with work?'

He runs a hand through his shock of dark blonde hair. 'A little over a year. I have good days and bad days. It's not so much a block as it's a total disregard for the job, which is more of a concern.'

The timeline fits with his wife leaving. Here we have it, another lost soul with a broken heart. 'What was the catalyst for it?' I'm *definitely* prying, but it's not for *my* sake – it's for the sake of his word count and because he's in a bind.

'I can't quite put my finger on a definite reason.' He surveys me with slight suspicion. 'There's a certain ennui when I go to type. I can still churn articles out, meet my quotas, but the excitement for it has gone.'

'Ah, it's more of a mid-life—'

'Don't you dare say it.'

'Confusion?' I quickly add with a smirk.

He shakes his head but a smile plays at his lips. '*Oui,* an existential... confusion. Life made so much sense until it didn't. And isn't that so depressing, to question the point of it all when you're my age?'

I take a moment to consider it. 'Wouldn't it be stranger if you didn't question it? You're obviously going through a time of uncertainty, and that has led you here. But nothing lasts, not even the bad times.'

'I'll have to remember that. *Not even the bad times.*' He scrubs his face with a hand as if wanting to wipe away all the angst, the heaviness of the conversation. 'Sorry, I'm not usually so morose.'

My eyebrows shoot up, provoking a gale of laughter from us. While he might not be morose all the time, he's not exactly the bubbly sort. Henri wears a sort of weariness in the set of his jaw, in the depths of his dark blue eyes, but the closer I look, the more I see his posturing as a *de*fence, rather than offence. Are we all the same here in The Bookshop for the Broken Hearted, putting on a front as we trudge along, hoping the pain, the sadness, the hurt subsides and a happier day dawns? God forbid that we open up and honestly share our troubles. Maybe Henri and I are more alike than I first thought.

An awkward silence hangs between us, so I say, 'I better get back to work.'

'Of course.' He glances at his watch and curses as if he's late for something. '*Merde!* I must go. See you at book club.' He closes the laptop and packs away his things in a courier bag and departs.

'Au revoir.' After he leaves, I check the time on my phone. As expected, Henri has a pattern of leaving the bookshop at the same time every day. Around 4 p.m., give or take a few minutes. Where does he go? Does he have to go to the office to file his stories? Or check-in, debrief?

I move his chair into the semi-circle, hoping I haven't broken some cardinal rule about moving it.

Valérie wanders over, feather duster in hand. 'Is Henri coming back to book club this evening?'

'*Oui.*'

Her forehead creases as if she's concerned about him. She has a pensive look in her eyes.

'What's the story with his wife?' Usually everyone's heartbreak stories are off limits, but I sense it's not the same with Henri. The book club girls have already opened up about it, so it can't exactly be top secret.

Valérie puckers her mouth in distaste. 'Horrible woman. Shrewd, cold and calculating. They were on-again, off-again for the longest time like a bad habit he couldn't quit. They were terribly unsuited. Coco, I'm breaking my privilege here so please keep that between us. He finally got rid of her and now we're left to help him pick up the pieces.'

'Lips are sealed.' Good for him. Who could put up with a fickle partner like that? 'It's just so at odds with the Henri I see. He's not the pushover, puppy dog type at all.'

'Love does strange things to people. Henri had his reasons for holding on.'

'What reasons?'

An illness? A promise? A family? Perhaps there are children involved. What else could it be? Maybe it's as simple as keeping his wedding vows sacrosanct.

'Oh, this and that.'

I hug myself tight, feeling strangely sad for Henri and his dysfunctional marriage. 'Will he eventually soften and take her back, do you think?' Not that it's any of my business, but it interests me from a human condition standpoint.

Valérie considers it for the longest time. 'Hard to say. They've divorced but she's the type that would love the show of marrying the same man twice. All we can do is hope the bookshop works its magic. He deserves the kind of love that's found in the books. He's a good man. And I can personally relate to what he's going through.'

Is her own broken heart the reason she set up the bookshop in the first place? Why she's prone to flights of fancy about potions and passages being the tonic?

'What do you relate to specifically?'

'Now, *ma chérie*, you've been here all of five minutes and you want me to give up all my secrets?'

'If you don't mind.'

Laughter burbles from her. 'And you've shared all of your secrets with me?' She arches a lofty brow.

'*Touché.*'

'All in good time.'

'That's not very specific.'

'Everyone has a history and Henri needs to close the book on his and start over. Just like *you're* starting over, Coco.'

I shake my head. 'You're not great at subtlety, Valérie.'

A guffaw escapes her. Am I missing something? 'Fine, I'll be brutally honest with you, if you think you can take it?'

'Sure.'

'I see the sparks between you and Henri. I can't help but feel that you'd be perfect for each other. I'm not a matchmaker, even though I can help mend broken hearts. And I'm telling you that if you let that guard down, you might be happily surprised at what comes your way.'

'Ah, not this again.'

Valérie sighs and continues. 'You're both stubborn and stuck in a rut. Without intervention, you'll spend the next few years bickering while quietly admiring one another from afar and get nowhere in the game of love.'

Does she not see that we're totally mismatched? That we can barely hold a conversation without it devolving into an argument? He might be able to hide his prickliness every now and then but that doesn't change the fact the guy is practically a cactus. If I'm honest with myself, Henri is quite the enigma and I find it hard not to be swept away by the idea of him, but that's exactly why I can't act on these burgeoning feelings. I cannot start up with another man who'll break my heart and my trust again. It's *way* too soon to open that Pandora's box. Besides, I barely know anything about him, other than he's almost too good looking and has a big chip on his shoulder. And I'm not going to share any of that with Valérie.

'I don't understand the science behind this? Just because we're both stubborn doesn't mean we're soulmates.' There's no hope for her; she's an incurable romantic and I fear that simply because we're single and in the same vicinity, it's enough for her to assume love will blossom. 'How do you calculate such a thing?' Next she'll be pulling out tarot cards or something. I get she wants her friend to find happiness, but at what cost?

'There's nothing so sterile as science involved. It's a sense, a premonition. A change in the atmosphere when you're together. Like the first day you walked in here, time froze like a caesura, and when I looked for the cause, there you were, sunlight streaming behind you, giving you an almost ethereal glow. Soon after, Henri wandered in and bang, I sensed the *coup de foudre*. An obvious sign that you two were meant to meet. I don't usually match people – it's not part of the service. But that day... it was fate showing me the way.'

I don't mention I also felt that way when I first laid eyes on Henri. It's out of the realms of reality and I blame it on my hasty escape from London. 'This is whimsical, even for you, Valérie.'

The word nerd in me likes the idea of a caesura to indicate a weighted pause so that even the most unaware would pick up on the special moment. I think back to that fateful day when I flew into his arms, as if Cupid shoved me fair in the back towards him. And then running into him again by the Eiffel Tower, I'd felt so *stupid*, having needed to be rescued.

'Lovebirds with damaged wings are *always* hesitant.' Why does she have to make so much sense sometimes? I'm damaged,

Henri is damaged. But that's the thing with love: every time you open your heart to a person, you're at risk for what inevitably comes next – the end. Another rivulet of golden threads. A smile that's a little wobblier. A sleep plagued with *If Onlys*. But it does go the distance for some lucky couples; my parents are a prime example of that. So why not me?

'It's not the right time for me.'

'"Under love's heavy burden do I sink."'

'Are you quoting Shakespeare to me now?'

'*Oui*, Romeo and Juliet. Don't let your past determine your future, Coco. You're much too special for that.'

I'm momentarily struck by it. Have I let the mistakes of the past change the course of my life because I've been so determined not to be made a fool of again? Not to be *abandoned*? Did I hit the pause button on my own private life after that first overwhelming upset when I was pregnant, until I finally let someone in, only for it to happen all over again? Even my daughter is worried I'll end up a lonely old woman, eating my body weight in *fromage* and glugging too much wine. What's the worst that could happen if I let go completely? What if I did fall in love again? Would that be so bad?

'I'm going to leave you to ponder that, Coco.'

'Book club preparations. I better get back to it.' While I finish prepping, sorting the catering, the drinks and accoutrements, my mind goes to Henri and all the ways I can talk myself out of the idea of him. He doesn't exactly seem interested in me; that long ago day when Valérie was imagining our wedding, he practically ran out of the bookshop, down the laneway and into oncoming traffic to get away.

I simply don't have enough data about Henri to formulate a conclusion either way. So the next plan of action is to get into the heart of Henri and see how it ticks.

19

I haven't even uttered my welcome spiel and already book club has dissolved into pandemonium. American Agnes is standing with a hand held up a mere whisper away from Ziggy's face after an argument about the most desirable length of a book. Lucy is trying to placate Agnes and keep Ziggy quiet, both of which are failing. Isidore is surveying her nails. I take a moment to inspect her hands and find that, as Valérie mentioned, they are indeed rather tiny and perfect for her specialised work. A drop-in named Allegra introduces herself as a speed reader. I hold my breath at the admission, knowing the group are strangely divided about such a thing, but it doesn't matter; no one is listening to the poor woman. 'I wish I could read fast,' I say. 'My TBR pile is out of control.'

She gives me a grateful smile. 'It just takes some practice, that's all.' The noise ramps up with no hope of abating.

I move to the front of the group. 'Can I have quiet, please.'

Valérie is busy at the bar, but a flash of worry crosses her face. As a moderator, I'm failing already. Do they think I'm too

mousy, a pushover? Well, while I might be circumspect, that
doesn't mean I don't have it in me to take control.

'Quiet, please!'

Isidore yawns.

Agnes removes her hand from Ziggy's personal space and
says in a shrill tone, 'You are misinformed just like always! The
best novels are always over one hundred thousand words and
that's all there is to it. I will not be drawn further.'

'Wait,' Lucy says. 'At our last meeting you were imploring us
to read Joseph Conrad's *Heart of Darkness* so we'd be "educated"
about the damage of Western colonialism and exploitation...'

'You actually listened?' Agnes rebuts. 'That's a first!'

Lucy rolls her eyes. 'Yes, I do listen, even though you're
mostly condescending. My point is that book was only just over
forty thousand words, and now you're saying the complete
opposite, that only a novel over 100k is worthy.'

Agnes sighs. 'If you listened with *both* ears, Lucy, you would
understand I'm talking about modern day books, the trashy
type that you and Ziggy are so fond of. Those ridiculous
romances where the plot is practically spelled out on the very
cover itself for the reader, like the tropes "one bed" or "forced
proximity". Can't we, as an intelligent species, read the blurb to
make an informed choice? There's no mystery, is there? We
already know it's going to end in a happy ever after. We're going
backwards here, or can't anyone see that?'

Silence falls but the atmosphere is taut, electric. Almost
blistering. If I don't step in there will be mutiny! '*Bonsoir,
bonsoir!*' I say, clipboard pressed against my chest. 'Welcome to
book club!'

'What have I missed?' a woman wearing double denim asks,
throwing herself on Henri's chair. Where is Henri?

'Nothing, nothing at all!' I say brightly, maybe too brightly because she narrows her eyes and waits me out. 'I'm Coco, welcome to book club.' I'm hoping to keep this modicum of control while I can. 'You are?'

'Nikolina.' She gives me a little wave and pulls a cushion onto her lap.

'Nikolina is our resident dog-earer, so whatever you do, don't lend her your books. She also reads paperbacks in the *bath*!' Agnes says.

Before it can descend in madness again, I say, 'Welcome, welcome. Now that I've got your, ahem, attention, just a bit of housekeeping. I'm your new moderator, Coco, former editor by trade, now enjoying my role as bookseller.'

'Former editor! From where?' Lucy asks. 'London?'

'Oh, well, yes, London.' I go for a girlish giggle but fail miserably. I've never been a girly girl who can giggle and hair flick; something to work on, I guess. 'Never mind all that! HA!' Oh God, kill me. My nerves are ratcheting up as they stare at me, so many eyeballs, so many different intensities. *Focus.* 'Drinks are on the table to your left, or you're welcome to visit Valérie behind the bar if you want wine or cocktails. Help yourself to the platters. I've been told you last read *And There Went the Stranger*, and I read it too so I'd be informed for this evening's chat. Shall we begin?'

'Let's begin.' Lucy gives me an encouraging thumbs-up.

'We should never have trusted Agnes with a book club pick,' Ziggy says. 'I'm sure the author just pulled out a dictionary and yanked out as many ten-letter words as he could and put them all together.'

Agnes gasps, 'That's sacrilege!'

I'm a little gobsmacked the group *let* Agnes choose the book, since they're so clearly at odds with her. Maybe they take it in turns? I kick myself for not checking with Valérie how they handle it, as I envisage carnage, trying to get them to agree on the next book club pick.

'I quite liked the book,' I say. 'The gentle, rhythmic prose was almost at odds with the laborious aspects of farm life and her daily toil. Her loneliness felt so real, the way she described the inky night, the stars her friends. When the stranger visits, I put myself in her place; what would I have done? Trusted him, or not?' I know full well I'd have locked every door and window and been cradling a baseball bat, demanding he get off my property, but I'm keen to hear their opinions.

Agnes sends me a warm smile. '*I* would have shot him point blank, but that's just me. I grew up on a farm in Iowa, but our protagonist, well, she is *lonely*...'

Isidore speaks up. 'The protagonist was naïve and vulnerable so I felt myself holding my breath, hoping she wouldn't be so trusting, but also wanting him to *be* trustworthy. It was a tense read. I loved it.'

'It creeped me right out,' Lucy says. 'Who lets a stranger in like that? Especially a big hulking presence like his. No, I hated it. It felt unnecessarily evil.'

'*Evil?* Did you read the ending?' Agnes asks.

Lucy shakes her head. 'No, I found it disturbing. Give me a sweet romcom over this any day.'

'And you, Ziggy?' I ask. 'Did you enjoy the book despite its use of formal vocabulary? Do you think the protagonist made the right choice?'

'Honestly, it was indescribably boring. Sure, I liked the idea of her having to decide – is he good or bad and is her loneliness worth the risk – but the pacing was so slow. We had an entire chapter of her opening the front door. Then a chapter on her closing the door. It could have been better edited.'

'You don't think that pacing device upped the tension?' I ask.

'*Non*, it felt like the author dragged every scene out. I hated it. Next!'

We go around the circle as a few more members come in late, and soon they're all talking over the top of each other again and arguing about their differing views on the novel. Agnes takes offence, as if she personally penned the novel, and raises her voice to be heard.

Henri approaches just as the conversation is reaching a fever pitch, voices crescendo-ing so that even patrons at the bar stop to stare.

I stand again and clap to get their attention. 'Stop. Please!' My blood pressure spikes. 'STOP!'

Henri moves close to say something to me, but it's lost in the cacophony. He scoots closer and whispers in my ear, his proximity sends a thrill down the length of me. When he places a finger to my chin to direct my gaze, my knees almost give out from under me. It's probably because I'm overstimulated by the intensity of book club. 'Would you like some help to save you the headache you're bound to have later?'

I appreciate he hasn't come in all guns blazing and taken over. He's actually asked me this time if I need saving, and the truth of the matter is, I bloody well do.

I mimic his movements, cupping his face and getting up close and personal even though it goes against my principles about personal space. He won't be able to hear me unless I'm practically on top of him. 'Yes please, for all that is holy, get them to be quiet.'

We're pressed up close and it sends a current through me. However, this is not the time to get woozy over a man, especially a man I don't know well enough. Is this some self-sabotage thing on my behalf? There are a lot of reasons I can't jump the gun, numero uno being I work here and if it all amounted to a fling, then that would make it awkward. And anyway, what am I even saying – it's book club and I've lost control of them again.

It feels all very *Lord of the Flies*, so there's nothing to do except lift my wine glass and take a few gulps.

Henri brackets his hands around his mouth and yells, 'Order! ORDER!' What is this, a court of law? I smother a grin.

They hush instantly and I find myself flummoxed. Yes, I wanted them to speak with their inside voices, but why did they listen to Henri and not me? Admittedly, he's a fine specimen of the opposite sex, but that is rather sexist of them, if so. Or is it because I'm new and they're testing me? The jury is still out.

Henri flashes me a triumphant smile. I *should* be happy. I *try* to be happy. He turns back to the group. 'I could hear you arguing from a block away! It's Coco's first book club and you're not being very hospitable.'

Ziggy hangs her head, as if ashamed. What kind of control does he have over them? This is – this is *worrying*. A man wanders in and all their verve, their moxie, dies. That can't be right! Are they *scared* of him?

'It's fine,' I say, taking charge once more. 'They're *animated*. As long as we can discuss books in a respectful way from now on. Thanks for your assistance but I've got this.'

A man cannot and will not hold the puppet strings of a mostly female group. Not on my watch.

'Anyway, it's time for the next book club selection! I'm not sure how you go about it so I've taken the liberty of picking a book I think you'll all enjoy...' I name the title and all hell breaks loose.

'We've read that!'

'You didn't read it.'

'I was going to.'

'I'm not buying a book by an author with a problematic past like she has.'

'Sounds *magnifique!*'

'Why not?'

'*Non, non, non, non.* Let us make our own suggestions. It's the diplomatic way.'

Patience taut, I say, 'OK, fine! Write down your choices and we'll pick at random.'

I hurry to the bar and ask for a repository of any description. 'What for?' Valérie asks, unable to hide her grin. 'You're doing great!' *As if!*

She's probably worried if she hands over a ceramic bowl, I'll whack someone over the head with it. And I just might if they start yelling again.

'For their book club suggestions.'

'OK.' She bustles about, hunting for a receptacle. Perhaps this interminable evening might be grating on me and I'm not my most patient self at present. Eventually, she hands me a small book tote. 'Use this.'

Back at the group, they're acting shady, keeping their suggestions close to the chest, or folded and in the palms of their hands. What an odd group! Why all the secrecy?

I go from each one and they post their suggestion in the tote bag, while I think of another book I can suggest since they clearly didn't like the first one I had in mind. I quickly scrawl another suggestion on a piece of paper and pop it in the tote with theirs.

I'm about to ask who wants to choose but common sense prevails and I save another argument. 'Ready?' I ask and hold the bag high as I use my other arm to root around and pick a piece of paper and unwrap it.

'Ooh,' I say when I see the title. It's my pick after all! My second suggestion, at any rate. I'm thrilled by this as not only do I want to read it, but Valérie has so many copies that it will help move them if they all purchase one. I'm also planning to do 'staff book reviews' that I can print and place near displays to help with visibility. 'The book of the month is *Un Baiser D'adieu* by Larivière.' A Kiss Goodbye. The poetry book I recommended to the Australian guy hoping to woo the French girl at the café.

Nikolina lets out a whoop. 'I've been looking forward to this one even though it's not my usual style...'

Ziggy claps. 'Everyone on TikTok is raving about this book. *Everyone.*' I almost fall over that we have a couple of enthusiasts. Could they finally be settling into the group with me at the helm?

'*Wonderful,* Ziggy,' Agnes says, her voice laced with sarcasm. 'You've just managed to turn my enthusiasm into exasperation. TikTok recommends it, therefore it must be a dud.'

Before it kicks off again, I cut in. 'Let's not allow that sort of judgement into the group. It doesn't matter where we heard about the book, whether it's from TikTok or a literary eMagazine. Can we agree there's no need to denigrate what platforms or media book club members use?'

I'm not sure if it's because it's getting late or the wine consumption, but the group have mellowed and make agreeable sounds.

'It's a great choice and there are plenty of copies available for those who'd like to buy one and help support the bookshop. I'm keen to read it myself having heard it's got a Rupi Kaur vibe with a French twist to it.'

'I've heard a lot about this one!' Lucy says. 'Don't shoot me but I've also seen it splashed across TikTok. You have to admit it's pretty cool that the younger generation champion books on the platform and make bestsellers out of a *broad* range of authors, and genres. It's not all hockey romance, Agnes.'

Agnes purses her lips. 'Thank God for small mercies.'

Isidore lifts her tiny hand. 'It's not just the younger generation championing books online either. Bibliophiles from all ages and walks of life do the same. I think we can agree that reading brings us all together, and it's about sharing the joy of a book that touched you.'

'Very true,' I say.

Agnes pushes her specs up the bridge of her nose. 'I'm sure being as literary minded as I am, I'll enjoy it. Poetry is for intellectuals, after all.'

Mon Dieu! 'And on that note, I'd like to thank you all for coming. Come and see me at the counter if you'd like to purchase a copy of *A Kiss Goodbye*, otherwise I'll see you all in a month!'

Lucy pulls back as if confused. 'A month for book club, yes, but we also meet informally in two weeks to read together.'

'Oh?' I say. 'How does that go?' For obvious reasons, I can't imagine the book club members reading together quietly.

'Really well,' Lucy says at the same time Ziggy blurts. 'As well as you'd expect.'

'Right, fabulous. OK, see you in two weeks.'

While everyone gathers their things and the evening wraps up, I go and find a stack of the poetry books and take them to the counter. Henri wanders over, a twinkle in his eye as if he's amused. It's nice to see he's lost that morose look he has during the day, as if his work, or lack thereof, gets him down.

'I am ready to sleep for a week,' I say.

'I bet. Did you have fun though?'

'There were moments. It's like being in control of a classroom full of kindergarten kids, all fighting to speak the loudest. Do you want to buy a copy?' I wave the slim volume.

'*Oui*. We have a lot of big personalities in the group. They're a boisterous bunch but their hearts are in the right place. You'll see, they can be the most stalwart friends in times of need. You'll get used to it.'

Now that is interesting. Has the group bonded over their shared heartbreak? Or have they just been supportive of Henri? Women are like that – protective.

I yawn, completely depleted. 'You have a lot of faith in me.'

He gives my upper arm a squeeze. 'Just learn to harness your savage side.'

I laugh as Henri taps his card to pay for the book. 'I like the sound of that.'

Valérie returns from the office with the empty bar till tray in her hand. 'Oh, *ma chérie*, you handled book club remarkably well.'

Another yawn gets the better of me. Is there a carbon monoxide leak I should be worrying about? How can I be so exhausted? 'You're lying so I don't quit, aren't you?'

'*Oui!* But something tells me you're not a quitter, Coco.'

She's right. I'm going to enjoy musing over how best to take control of the group. I've met a lot of dominant personalities in my life but not all in one space at the same time. I'll do some research and find a solution on how best to make the book club meetings harmonious. There must be a nonfiction tome about such a thing. '*Non*, I won't quit, but I probably will ask for raise.'

Soon, the others are lined up behind Henri to purchase the book. Lucy gives me a hug before she leaves and Valérie gives them all a peck on the cheek. After they leave, they huddle outside the bookshop as if not wanting the night to end. They're laughing and joking, and Ziggy has an arm around Agnes's shoulder. Huh? It doesn't make sense. Maybe they enjoy bickering over books? It's a mystery for another day.

'Why don't you head off, Coco?' Valérie says. 'I'll clean up.'

'*Non*, I—'

'Go.' She stares me down and I know I won't win this argument.

I gather up my things. 'Don't forget to take a copy of *Un Baiser D'adieu* for yourself, Coco. If you don't read it, you'll never hear the end of it from them.'

'*Merci.*'

'I'll drive you home,' Henri says.

I'm too tired to argue. '*Merci.*' Henri leads me out of the cute-as-a-button cobblestone laneway and onto the street where we find a beat-up little Peugeot. The body of the small vehicle is covered in dents, which I find slightly alarming. 'How long have you been driving?' I ask.

'Why?' he says with a questioning smile.

Is it rude to be so obvious about my doubt in his driving capabilities? It's just, I do have a daughter I'd like to get home to in one piece. 'Your car has more dimples than a golf ball.'

'Parking in Paris is a blood sport.'

20

On Saturday, Eloise and I are visiting the very macabre but interesting Catacombs. I've always wanted to visit the underground ossuary that is a resting place for over six million people. While it sounds creepy, it's a historical sight so well worth seeing and it's different enough to appeal to a teenager. I want to reconnect with her after a busy week, where we didn't see each other as much as usual because of my work commitments and her after school activities with my parents. We get tickets at the booth and join the queue that snakes around the attraction.

'We're going to be waiting *forever*.'

'The joy of living in Paris.' The queues for museums are even worse, particularly on the first Sunday of every month where entry is free. 'Did you get your art project finished last week?'

'We did. It's so lame though I doubt we'll get good marks for it, but I just wanted out of the group.'

We shuffle forward a few steps. 'So Léa's behaviour hasn't improved?'

'Nope.'

'And you didn't tell a teacher, or the school therapist?'

'No. I mean, I'm sure the teachers see it too, but they pretend they can't. If I say something, I'm likely to get blamed for bullying the girl who lost her mum, you know?'

It cannot be the case. I'm certain teachers wouldn't ignore bad behaviour, even if the child is grieving. They would be mindful of the circumstances, but they still have a duty of care to all students. 'Who are you sitting with at lunch then?'

She drops her gaze, skips ahead of me. 'Lots of kids.'

'*Eloise.*' My daughter is great at avoidance. 'We promised each other no lies.'

She turns on the spot. 'You say that and then *you* lie.'

'What lie?'

'Like you pretending you're *not* into that Jude Law guy.'

I guffaw. 'Lying about Henri being handsome-yet-infuriating isn't really a lie, it was more me avoiding an uncomfortable truth.'

'Oh?' Eloise is in a weird mood today. One minute she seems energetic and carefree, the next like she wants to argue. 'So you do like him? *Great!*' she screeches dramatically. 'Now we're going to be stuck here for the next *five* years.'

Does she think that's my limit for how long a man will love me? I remind myself not to rise to the bait, but it takes an extreme amount of willpower. 'Would it bother you if I dated then?' I have no plans to, but I'm curious how she'll answer. It's not as if I've paraded a lot of men around her. There's been one! Any casual dates before Alexander came along were kept away from home so as not to confuse Eloise.

'What about the whole leaving London thing because "our life there had run its course"? That was another lie. You lost your business, your partner, everything, and instead you made it seem like you'd had enough of the place.'

I let out a frustrated sigh. 'I'm the adult, Eloise, and I told you the bare bones of what happened, and I kept the worst of it from you for your own good.'

'So you're allowed to lie?'

I swallow down intense sadness. 'I wasn't lying, I was doing what I thought best while I was under a lot of pressure. You were already very distressed about leaving your friends; I didn't want to lump you with my issues. To be frank, I was bloody heartbroken myself, El, and it took a lot of effort to pretend I wasn't about to fall apart.'

'Why don't you ever tell me then?' She deflates like the wind has left her sails. 'You always act like nothing bothers you.'

'You're too young to be worrying about me.' I've already told her more than I should have, but I want her to understand that I haven't dragged her to Paris on a whim.

'I wish you'd stop treating me like an *enfant*.'

'What's really going on here? This isn't about me at all, is it?'

Her throat works as she fights off tears. I take her into my arms and hold her as she softly cries. This has been building for a while, disguised by hostility directed towards me.

'Tell me,' I say, speaking into her wavy locks as I hug her tight. 'What's making you so upset?'

'I miss my friends. Like, I really, really miss them. Daisy and Harriet video called me last night and...' Fresh sobs steal her voice.

'And?'

'And they were having a sleepover with a few girls from school and I felt so left out. Soon they'll forget all about me, and don't say it won't happen because it will. It was the same when

Bailey left.' Bailey had been her best friend since nursery. He and his family relocated to Edinburgh last spring. 'I haven't spoken to him for *months*.'

'That's not true! You chatted on an Instagram post about that fantasy series on Netflix.'

'Stalker, much?'

'Good parenting, *much*?' It should be no surprise that I monitor her social media, but I was upfront about parental controls and she is well aware of it. 'You know the "much" really doesn't—'

'Don't.'

'Fine. You still chat to Bailey fairly often and I'm sure it'll be the same with Daisy and Harriet.'

She pulls a lock of hair up and surveys the end in the way teenagers do. What are they looking for, split ends? The meaning of life? 'A few comments on Insta every now and then isn't the same. Daisy and Harriet are going to get closer while I'm stuck in Paris sitting with kids who don't even know my name. Can we go back to London? *Please*? I'll miss Mémère and Grandad, but I won't miss this place.'

Oof. How do you explain to a teenage girl in crisis like this? She doesn't understand the concept of giving it time because it feels so immediately awful, and in her mind there's a simple solution – returning to her oldest friends who'll welcome her with open arms. It hurts to see her tormented like this, but I know from personal experience of being the new kid far too many times that she will eventually find her way. I only hope it's sooner rather than later.

'I'm sorry, darling, I know this is a difficult period of adjustment for you, and actually for me too.' Maybe it is time I am more honest with her about my feelings. 'I hate to see you upset. But truthfully, I want you to know that we can't go back to London. This is home now. I know it's not what you want to hear. If you give it time it will get better, it will. You'll make new friends just as good as Daisy and—'

'No one will ever be as good as Daisy and Harriet. I *hate* my life!' She's too far gone to reason with now.

'Ooh look, we're getting closer.'

'Who cares. I *hate* this place.' Her face twists with rage; her eyes fill with tears. I don't think I've quite hated Alexander for causing this upheaval as much as I do right now. It's heart wrenching to see her struggling like this. How can I fix it? How *can* I be certain she will make friends as lovely as giggly Daisy and bookworm Harriet? They were three peas in a pod, and I ripped Eloise away. Her anguish is logical.

'You're right. This place is the worst, but we're here now so we might as well visit and then we can make a list of everything we hate about it.' There! Get on their level. Be supportive!

'Urgh, Mum! That's so lame.'

'You're right, that is lame. I've been reading books about navigating the teen years, but I swear their strategies only incite more venom from you. How could they get it so very wrong what with being child psychologists and all?'

Her face breaks into a smile that turns into a snort laugh. 'Oh, Mum! Tell me you're joking.'

'*I'm not.* I spent a fortune on those books!'

'The nerd in you is strong.'

'I always turn to books for answers, but perhaps I got it wrong this time.'

She bumps me with her hip. 'At least you tried. I'm a brat but one day I won't be.'

Out of the mouths of babes, eh? 'I can hang on until then.'

'Let's visit the underground caves. And then eat. I feel like crepes.'

I don't highlight her contrary nature, I just roll with it. 'Crepes it is.'

21

The following Tuesday, I'm late getting home having stopped off to my catch up with my publishing pal Fleur, who informed me her publishing director was now keen to interview me for an editorial job. It took me all of one minute to say thanks but no thanks. I'm not sure why I was so definite about it. I'm still processing the reason. Perhaps I'm learning to listen to my intuition rather than calculate all the pros and cons of any given situation. It didn't appeal any more, so I declined. Simple.

I only hope I don't regret that later. This new version of me enjoys working at the bookshop and that's enough for now.

With my key in the lock, I hear her before I see her.

Eloise is in floods of tears, leaning against my diminutive *maman* like her heart is truly breaking.

'*Bonsoir*,' Maman says. 'I've suggested Eloise take a nice warm bath.' She turns to my daughter. '*Oui?*'

Eloise nods and, without greeting me, she goes to the bathroom. 'Problems at school?' I ask.

Maman nods. 'Apparently she can handle it, though.'

'She clearly needs support. I'm going to have to intervene.'

'Can you call them without letting Eloise know? I'm not sure she can handle any more right now.'

We agreed never to lie, but in this case what choice do I have? If I tell her I plan on having a quiet word with the principal, she'll go mad. While I don't like breaking promises to my daughter, occasionally it must be done, otherwise I fear this situation will never be resolved.

After the bath, Eloise settles in the bedroom, noise cancelling headphones on. I give her a hug but he pushes me away. 'I want to be alone.'

'OK. If you change your mind let me know.'

When I return to the kitchen, Maman has made coffee. I sit opposite her and cradle my chin with a hand.

'You're doing the right thing,' she says softly. 'What if their behaviour gets worse?'

I gulp back the sour taste of duplicity. Being a mum is all about making those tough choices, and it's not easy.

'That's what I'm worried about. While her moods always fluctuate, this has been intense, which leads me to believe it's a lot worse than what she's telling us. From a safety standpoint alone, I need to talk to the principal.'

'I'm worried you're both homesick, and we're going to lose you to London again.' Her voice cracks with emotion. We loved living in London; who wouldn't? It's a vibrant, bustling city, but I always missed my parents and worried about the time they were missing out with Eloise, despite her regularly visiting them on school holidays. They weren't there for a lot of milestones and I've always felt guilty about that.

'It won't happen, Maman. I promise you. We're here to stay. I just need to make another plan for our future and work towards it.'

'A ten-year plan?'

I grin. 'Ha. All that forward planning, all that strategizing about the future, didn't exactly pan out. I'm beginning to wonder if putting undue pressure on myself was worth it.' My mind goes back to the epiphany I had about London Field Publishing never really being *my* dream. Sure, I got caught up in it, but my love is for the manuscripts themselves, and the authors who I work with. The collaborative process of bringing a book to life. Why can't my dreams be smaller, more manageable? More fun!

'All you have to do is follow your passion; the rest will come.'

'Step one is to take care of my daughter's happiness, then I can get serious about the rest of it.'

'And we'll be here to cheer you on every step of the way.'

'Now you're just trying to make me cry.'

'I'm so happy to have *mes belles filles* back. Life is better with you both here, and we'll do anything in our power to help.'

'*Maman.*' I'm not a crier by nature; I don't like the loss of control over my bodily functions, but my *maman* has the unique ability to make me ugly cry just by being *nice* to me. 'It's probably getting close to the time to search for a *pied-a-terre* of our own. That might help cement the fact this is permanent and also give Eloise her own space.'

'This apartment is too small, especially for Eloise, but I'll be sad to see you go when you do move. I hope you'll stay close.'

'Of course we will. I'll crunch some numbers and see where I'm at with what I've saved so far.' I'm fully aware of my savings down to the very last cent, but I'd like to run the figures and make sure I've got a small amount for emergencies that I can continue to build on.

'Dad and I have savings; we'd be more than happy to help.'

'*Non, merci,* Maman.' It's not just pride that stops me, it's the determination that I can sort out this mess myself. They're already doing so much for us. 'If you're happy having us then I'd rather do it myself.'

'We love having you both.'

* * *

The next morning, I call Valérie and let her know I'll be a little late to work. When Dad takes Eloise to school, I take the opportunity to call the school from the privacy of the apartment. The call goes to the switchboard and I ask to speak to the principal. When I'm put through, I say, 'Bonjour, I'm Coco Chevallier. My daughter Eloise started there recently.'

'Bonjour, Coco. It's lovely to hear from you. You'll be delighted to hear that Eloise's teachers have reported she's settling in well and her schoolwork has been of a good standard.'

'Well, that's not entirely true.' I go into detail about Léa and the taunts and how I promised Eloise I'd let her handle it herself but that she's not coping. 'If we could handle this sensitively that would be best.'

'I'm sorry to hear that. I spoke to Eloise myself just yesterday and she expressed to me that she was adjusting well and enjoying her classes. I'm aware though that students don't often report this sort of behaviour.'

'Yes, that's why I've been hesitant to get involved. She really doesn't want them to get in trouble in case it makes it worse. Eloise did mention that Léa is recently bereaved so perhaps her behaviour is connected to that? Acting out, in her grief? Maybe the school therapist—'

'Sorry, I'll stop you there, Coco. While I can't share personal details about any of our students, I do think you've been misinformed. I'm sure it's acceptable for me to say that as far as I know, Léa isn't recently bereaved.'

'Oh.' That stops me in my tracks. Eloise must have misunderstood, or perhaps the child who told her about it meant a different student? If Léa's not grieving, then what excuse does she have? 'There must have been a mix up, a...' I'd had this all figured out. Léa would get counselling and support and lay off Eloise. Now I'm not sure what the way forward is.

'It's OK, these things happen. I understand Eloise wishes to keep things private so as not to provoke them, but we do have a bullying policy in place as we discussed on the school tour. With your permission I'd like to call Léa and the other girls into the office and have a chat with them That way we can follow our policy and take actionable steps to help Eloise.'

'I understand you must follow protocol but I'm not sure that will help, especially if Lea's not... bereaved. I'd presumed that was a catalyst for it.'

'I hear your concerns. Even if I did pull Léa in without mentioning Eloise's name, they'd know it was her. They're rather shrewd at this age. It often helps to let them know we're apprised of the situation so they remember their manners and understand that we're keeping a close eye on the situation.'

I'm torn between keeping my promise to my daughter and making a good parenting decision. Eloise's safety is my number one concern so while she's not going to like it, it's probably for the best. Still, my gut roils at the thought.

'OK, if you're sure.'

'I'm sure we can sort this out. I'll keep you informed, and please call me if you have any other concerns. We want to make sure Eloise feels safe and happy at school.'

When I hang up, I flop against the bed. What have I done?

22

The next day, I'm at the bookshop early to make up for my lateness the previous day. I'm happy to be out of the tense apartment where I spent most of the evening waiting for Eloise to explode. Perhaps word didn't get back to her yet, *or* Léa and the girls realised they were being needlessly cruel and chose to stop. Did the principal decide against calling them in?

Every time I went to confide in her about the call, I lost my nerve. She is so fractious all the time, it's impossible to know how to handle her.

'Bonjour.' Valérie greets me, sliding a freshly squeezed orange juice along the bar for me. 'Did you have a nice evening?'

'Ah – *oui.*'

'Say no more. The angst of living with a teenager.'

'A teenager being bullied at her new school.'

'*Non!*'

I nod, slipping off my gossamer-thin scarf and taking my regular stool at the bar. 'It's OK, I'm hoping the problem will soon be solved.'

'It's hard being a *maman*, harder still being a solo *maman*.'

I lift a shoulder, playing it down. There are worse things, and while I often wish Eloise had a father figure, it's mostly when I'm tired or unsure how to deal with a certain situation. We're a strong little team of two most of the time. Or we were. 'I'm lucky to have my parents. But Valérie, please don't mention anything to Eloise if she comes in after school this week. She's been missing London a lot.' And then some. Lately I feel like my head is on backwards with all this trying to avoid land mines around her. 'Anyway, it's all fine. Everything is fine.' If I keep telling myself that, I'm hoping the universe will make it so.

'Ach, I am sorry, Coco. *Mamans* always bear the brunt of it. It will get better. So let me distract you with work. Today, things are going to be a bit different. I've got various book orders that need collecting all over Paris.'

'Oh, couldn't the orders be couriered?'

Valérie shakes her head, her curls catching in the rainbow-coloured lights behind the bar. '*Non*, it's too expensive. There are too many places to pick up from.'

'Wouldn't it be more expensive for me to go on my hourly rate?'

She scrunches up her nose. 'Such a head for numbers, our Coco. Your salary is just factored in, so it works for me. It means it's virtually free.'

That doesn't make economic sense whatsoever, but I let it go. 'Where am I going then? Should I take the bus or walk?'

'Here, there and everywhere, all over Paris. Quite the distance so the bus won't work, nor the Metro. I've asked Henri to help out to make the process more efficient for all parties.'

'Help out how?'

'By driving you, so you don't have to waste time waiting in bus queues, getting drenched in the rain.'

'It's spring, there's sunshine and no rain is forecast.' I narrow my eyes. 'And have you *been* in a car with Henri? I'm not convinced he holds a legitimate driver's licence. He did show me a card when I asked, but forgeries these days are so sophisticated. I really couldn't ascertain if it was the real deal or not.' When he gave me a lift home after book club, I was tempted to drop to the ground and kiss the pavement, so glad was I to be alive.

'I'm sure he's licenced! How bad can his driving be?'

I raise my brows heavenward. And then some more so she comprehends just how bad. 'The word *erratic* comes to mind. He can't talk and look at the road at the same time.'

She waves me away. 'You'll be fine. *Fine!* The streets of Paris aren't exactly Le Mans. How fast *can* he go in all that traffic? All those roundabouts, one-way streets. You're perfectly safe.'

'I'm not sure your reasoning is sound, but I need this job.'

'Then it's settled.'

'Gulp,' I say, gulping.

'Here is the man of the hour! *Merci*, Henri, I appreciate you doing me this favour, and I'll be sure to repay you in café crèmes and glasses of neat whisky.'

Neat whisky, seriously? 'You don't drive after shots of whisky, do you?' Actually, that would explain a lot.

'Bonjour, Coco. No, of course I don't. I'm not as irresponsible as you imagine. Are you ready to go then, Valérie?'

'Oh, you're going, Valérie?'

She gives a quick shake of the head. Is this because she's aware of his terrible driving skills and is worried for her own life? Is that why I'm going, like a lamb to slaughter? I'll have to keep him focused on the road and remind him of the many rules associated with driving, like it being vital to use the brake, not just the accelerator.

'Slight change of plans. I've, uh... sprained my ankle, so now Coco is going in my place.'

'Sprained your ankle?' I screech. The crafty minx. Is this all a setup? Well, two can play at that game. 'Why didn't you say? We should get you to a doctor.' She shoots me her best cease-and-desist glare, which I duly ignore.

'*Non, non*. There's no need, it's just one of those things. I'll strap it up and it'll be fine.'

'Ooh, I don't know, I wouldn't feel right leaving you here with an injury like that. How will you cope when it gets busy? Who will administer first aid if you require it?'

'I'll cope just fine,' she says between gritted teeth. 'I've got a first aid kit here somewhere.'

'See that?' I mimic the way she's grinding her teeth 'That's *pain* talking. Why doesn't Henri just pick up the books and I'll stay here and look after you?'

'*Oui*, I can do that, Valérie, it's no problem.'

She's getting huffy at me skewing her plans. 'It's much easier when one drives and the other jumps out. You know what parking is like, you'll be going in circles all day looking for a spot. It will be much quicker if Henri drives and you pick up the orders. Henri can loop around the block. You're making the pain worse, Coco, by fighting me on this.'

What a bluffer!

Henri's face pinches. 'Shall I get you some pain relief? Coco is right, you are grinding your teeth like the pain is too much.'

She gives him a fake smile. 'I've got a selection of pain relief right behind me if I need it.' She waves to the colourful bottles on display in the bar.

'I'm no doctor,' I say. 'but even I know that alcohol and a sprained ankle aren't a good mix.'

'She's right, Valérie. What if you have a fall? What then?'

'Would you two stop it! I'm perfectly fine. It's probably not even a sprain, it's probably a bruise.'

'If you're sure?'

How is he believing this?

'I'm sure.'

'Fine. We'll leave you to recuperate, Valérie. Be careful now, you don't want to bruise the other ankle.'

Her eyes shine with the victory of one-upping me. If I do meet my untimely death due to Henri's awful driving, she's going to feel bad and I'm going to haunt her for the rest of her life. 'I'll do my best to avoid that, Coco.'

23

Outside, Henri motions to his car parked half up a curb.

'Am I seeing things or is there more damage than just last week?' I ask, trying to hide the shock in my voice.

'Oh, that.' He waves away a body-sized dent on the rear quarter panel. 'People bounce when they're relaxed. There's a lot to be said for not seeing it coming, I guess.'

My pulse increases. It does look like the outline of someone's *derriere*!

'Entirely their fault, by the way. But I didn't swap numbers. Look at it, it's not exactly pristine.'

'It's not at *all* pristine.'

'Accidents happen.'

'How often do they happen, would you say?'

'Rarely.'

'I'm not sure I'm safe with you.'

'Stop, I can't handle all these compliments.'

I give him my patient mothering smile. The one that gives me a headache. 'It's just that a quick drive to my parents' apartment is one thing, driving around Paris for hours is almost *asking* for my life to be taken. I don't *want* to die in a fiery ball of junked metal.'

'Press the eject button on the dash if you need to.'

What! 'There's an—' His face dissolves into a grin. 'Not amusing.' His mirth is contagious though, and I find my own stupid turncoat lips smiling in return.

'It's only that when I'm driving, I'm easily distracted. There's something about the hum of the engine and the buzz of zooming up the boulevards. I find it thrilling.'

'Henri, this is a Peugeot, not a McLaren. You know what's also thrilling? Driving the speed limit.'

'I'll try my best.'

'Can I give you one piece of driving advice that has never steered me wrong?'

'If you must.'

'When you're talking, you don't need to give your full attention to the passenger. The general rule of thumb is to *always* keep your eyes on the road.'

'But the road is just one long trail of black bitumen.'

'*Merde.*' I make the sign of the cross, even though I'm not religious.

'Your chariot awaits. Where to first?' He opens the door for me, which I find rather sweet. Inside, I put on my seat belt, making sure to tighten it as far as it will go while still being able to breathe, before I finally bring up the email Valérie sent with directions.

'First stop, Librairie Galignani on the rue de Rivoli, opposite the Jardin des Tuileries.'

My soul briefly leaves my body when Henri spins the wheels and roars out, before bunny hopping. I'm nauseous already. He turns to me. 'What are we picking up there?'

'Remember the rule about keeping your eyes on the road?'

'*Oui, oui.*'

I use my invisible brakes, but they're useless. I take a deep breath and wish I'd been a regular church attendee. 'We're picking up an order of...' Wait, we've already got copies of this book, I've seen a heap of them around the shop. '*Lunch in Paris* by Elizabeth Bard.' I check the rest of the list – all books we already have! This whole mission is a farce.

'Oh, I've read that one. Great book.'

We get to our first destination, alive. Henri slows the car and we go sailing past the bookshop. 'What are you doing? You've just gone right past it.'

He huffs. 'You were supposed to jump out! Now I'll have to circle this huge block again.'

'What!' Is he insane? 'Jump out of a moving car?'

'A *slowly* moving car. It's not like you'd need to somersault onto the pavement or anything.'

'How do you know that for sure? How many moving vehicles have you dived from?'

He grumbles as we hit a red light. 'This is going to take all day if you expect me to find a place to stop and park at each and every bookshop.'

'Just find a spot. It can't be that hard. That way I have a chance of keeping all my appendages intact.'

He lets out a scoff, a rather maddening sound. 'Appendages intact! Exiting a vehicle going less than ten miles an hour isn't exactly dangerous!'

'This is probably a stupid question, going by the standard of your driving, but do you *know* any of the road rules for driving in France?'

'Coco, there are rules and there is common sense.'

'*Non*, there are rules and those rules should be followed.'

'You're quite the stickler.'

'Is that supposed to be offensive?'

'*Oui!*'

'Well, I relish being a stickler. It's kept me alive this long.'

I'm not sure what Valérie's end game with this faux mission is but I have an inkling it's backfiring. I expect she presumes being stuck in the car together all day will make us realise we're wildly in love. But instead we're probably going to return injured or dead, and if I *am* the one who gets the unfortunate job of jumping out of a moving vehicle, the odds of me being the deceased person are too high for my liking.

Henri screeches as the bookshop comes into view again. 'Are you ready? *Un, deux, trois...*' He counts as if I'm about to skydive.

'Henri, I'm not jumping! I'm not an adrenaline junkie!'

He lets out a string of expletives. 'We've missed it *again!*'

I can't help but laugh as he drags his fingers down his face like he wants to peel it off. 'Third time lucky?' I ask. 'When you come to a *stop*, when the car is *still*, I will alight.' How can I make it any clearer?

'*Argh!*'

Around we go again.

I text Valérie:

COCO

> This fool can't follow instructions. How desperate are you for these books considering we've got them all in stock in the shop?

We're at a red light when my phone pings with a reply:

VALÉRIE

There is a such a thing as being too clever you
know, Coco. Fine, abort the book-buying
mission but you're not to come back until
you've shared lunch at La Fontaine de Mars on
Rue St. Dominique. I'll make reservations for
12.30. You'll have to find something to do while
you wait. ;)

Do I tell Henri what's really going on? I don't want him to
think badly of Valérie, or like she wasted his time in some
ridiculous plotting with me, of all people.

My mind spins with excuses, but none seem very believable.
I'll blame the fictional customer! '*La vache!* Valérie has texted.
Bad news, the customer has cancelled their order.'

'They were all for one person?'

'Uh-huh.'

'Right, so back to base then?'

'*Non*, Valérie insists we have lunch at La Fontaine de Mars at
twelve-thirty.'

'Why?'

'To show her appreciation for your time.'

'That's hours from now. That's more of a waste of my time
than just going back to the bookshop.'

'Do you want to tell her?'

He shakes his head. 'What should we do in the meantime
then?'

'Take a wander through Jardin des Tuileries?'

'Sure.' Henri finds a parking space that's far too tight but
insists it's not. I hold my breath while he manoeuvres the
Peugeot, managing to tap the cars in front and behind. 'You're
going to get arrested.'

He guffaws. 'It's the way of things. There's no room so you
have to *make* room.'

'Your theory isn't sound.'

'Of course it is. Why do you think I drive such a beat-up car?'

'*Drive* is a stretch, wouldn't you say? Criminal negligence is more accurate.'

We exit the car and he takes a moment to lock the doors. 'You really think it's at risk of being stolen?'

'Something tells me you don't appreciate the battle scars my Peugeot proudly wears.'

I laugh. 'Your poor Peugeot.'

We enter the garden, which is fragrant with thousands of blooms. Henri tells me he's spent the last year visiting all the gardens across Paris. This surprises me because Henri doesn't seem the meandering, interested-in-nature type. 'Are you a big bird fan or...?'

'*Huge* bird fan.' He laughs. 'At first, it was for the fresh air, a way to clear my head. The sort of get-lost-among-people remedy that Parisians need. It helped get perspective on my life. The more I walked, the better I felt. I learned the history of each garden, felt an affinity for those who'd come before. As you probably know, so many literary greats walked these same paths, so I felt less alone, *and* if that's not the silliest thing I've ever said, I don't know what is.'

So he doesn't like sharing his vulnerabilities, I get that. 'It's not silly at all. Did you need perspective after your breakup?'

'You heard? Ah. From the book club members?'

I grimace at my mistake. 'They didn't say much. They're more concerned about your happiness than anything else.'

He gives me a soft smile. 'It's impossible to keep a secret in the book club.'

I laugh. 'I'm sure there are a few. Did your walks help?'

'Very much.' He slips his hands in his pockets as we walk through the garden.

'It must have been hard though, the ending of your marriage after so long.'

He considers it. 'I'm not sad my marriage is over, I'm angry. Angry at myself for letting it drag on so long. Angry at all that time wasted. Angry that she has no care or concern for our young child.'

Ah! It makes sense now. I didn't see Henri as the puppy dog type, waiting on the sidelines for her to return. 'You stayed in the marriage because of your child.'

He nods. '*Oui*. When she had the baby I thought she'd change, want to make a go of things, but she didn't and so nothing has been right since then.'

Is Henri one of those fathers who swoops in every second weekend to care for their baby? Most single dads I've met along the way expect praise for the sporadic weekends they do have their children, as if picking them up on a Saturday morning and returning them the following day is sharing the load with the mother. And forget sharing the mental load that comes with being a parent. I'm making assumptions, but it's hard not to when you're me and don't even have the luxury of sharing the care with a part-time dad.

'Is it worth holding on to that anger though?' I ask, surveying him. 'How does it serve you?'

He lets out a bitter laugh. 'It doesn't serve me at all, it just makes me miserable. My writing has suffered terribly. It all feels so pointless.'

'It sounds like you've had too many things happen all at once.'

He shakes his head as if shaking away his confession. When he looks back at me, his eyes are soft again, and he's lost the edge to his jaw. 'It's not all doom and gloom, is it? It's springtime in Paris.' There's something in the way he says it, an energy as if he is going to let the past go now that the dark winter is over and spring perfumes the air.

'Did you have a set time to mourn your marriage, Henri?' It's something I would do.

He smiles and this time it reaches his eyes. 'Maybe unconsciously? Suddenly I don't feel quite so despondent any more.'

'When Paris blooms in springtime, it's hard not to be swept away and enjoy every small moment.'

'And you, Coco, what is the real story behind your arrival?'

'You really don't want to hear all about that! We're happy to be back in Paris.' Well, *one* of us is but I keep that to myself. 'And I love working at the bookshop.'

'And your daughter, how is she handling being away from her dad?'

'Oh, her dad died. Sadly he was crushed and killed by a herd of bulls while he was running away from his responsibilities. Terrible stuff.'

His eyebrows shoot up.

'But we're fine.' We're clearly not fine. Eloise hates it here but I don't want to delve into that again, not today, because part of me worries my daughter really is never going to settle in Paris.

'I know all about you, Coco, single *maman*.'

'I prefer the term solo.'

'Solo *maman*, an editor, recently relocated from London. Lives with her parents in Montparnasse. Has a phobia about driving.'

'Only *your* driving. You are quite the proficient eavesdropper.'

He laughs. 'It's the reporter in me, always listening, ear out for a story.' *Mon Dieu*, he wouldn't tell *my* story, would he?

My new rule is don't trust men, but my rules haven't really worked, have they? I've held myself so tightly against hurt and it found me anyway. What's the harm in being honest? At least I'll know what kind of person he is if he shares my secrets and breaks my confidences.

'Do you want the truth?' I'm done holding on to that sense of shame since the thefts were exposed.

'*Non*, I only want lies.'

I shake my head. 'Lies, it is. I was co-owner of London Field Publishing...' I tell him the whole sorry story, leaving nothing out, including that Alexander has now hard launched his relationship with my editorial assistant and I am hiding out in Paris, humiliated.

Henri's lips quiver. 'Hard launched?' I love that he's skipped past all the criminalities and landed there.

He loses the fight against keeping his composure and soon we're both laughing. 'I'm still miffed he didn't soft launch first. Surely there's a method to these things?'

'Wow, Coco. Thank God that's all lies.' He bumps my hip and a thrill races through me. Is it his proximity or the fact that he didn't narrow his eyes suspiciously when I told him about the thefts and the way in which Alexander orchestrated it all to stay under the radar? 'Shall we have him killed? I have connections to the underworld, you know.'

'In the UK?'

'Especially in the UK.'

'I'll think about it. But I'd like a public apology first.'

'Broken legs it is.'

My own spontaneous laughter catches me unawares. It feels

good. 'Maybe broken hands, that would make it harder for him to steal from the next person.'

'Much more sensible. In all seriousness, I'm sorry you lost your publishing business. But I'm not sorry you're here.' He blushes. 'I mean… it's been good having a new face in the bookshop, even if you are argumentative.'

'*Moi?* I think you're getting us two mixed up.'

'I suppose that's a possibility.'

'You are a terrible liar.'

He grins. 'Will you start another publishing house?'

With a shake of my head, I say, 'I don't have the heart for it. And I doubt any authors would come near me.'

'People have short memories. You need to shout louder about your innocence.'

I throw my hands into the air. 'I'm not really a shouter.'

'You might have to be in this instance. If he's hard launching a distraction, you have to go bigger. Go bolder.'

Henri's probably right. Why do I still feel so frozen when it comes to Alexander? It's like I've allowed him to take my power away. 'Once we're settled here I will.'

We lapse into a comfortable silence, and I ponder everything I've learned about Henri. Maybe he's not such a bad person after all. Aside from his atrocious driving.

I check my watch; the hours have flown by. 'Almost time for lunch.'

* * *

We're shown to a table for two at La Fontaine de Mars. It's an authentic French bistro that's been in business since 1908 and serves traditional French fare like confit duck and gratin

dauphinoise. While it's always been a popular bistro, that popularity heightened after the Obamas dined here.

We sit across from each other, silent, as the waiter returns
with a bottle of wine and pours. We peruse the menu. 'What are
you thinking of?'

'The same as you, I'd expect.'

I freeze. Is this when he tells me he's going to order for us?
Alexander tried that carry on with me early on and didn't get
very far. I'm not sure what kind of power play that is, but I
stopped that before it became a thing.

When I twig, I say, 'The confit duck?'

'*Oui.* They do it better than any other bistro in Paris.'

We place our order, and soon a basket of sliced baguette is
placed on the table.

'I was thinking about your writing...' I take a sip of wine,
rolling it around my mouth.

'And?'

'You're in a rut.'

'I'm in a deep rut and my shovel is broken.'

I grin. 'What do you mostly write about?'

'Current events, literary Paris, lifestyle. It's fairly broad, but
it's also tedious. How many literary festivals can I write about
without rehashing the same old stuff?'

'Have you ever thought about personalising your articles,
putting a bit of your own life into them? Just an idea, but I used
to read a weekly lifestyle column in London and she'd write
quite honestly about the events, the pretensions and the
tedium. Without naming names, she'd highlight the preten-
tious sorts she encountered and all the behind-the-scenes
shenanigans. You're witty and acerbic, sometimes very much
so.' I lift a brow. 'I wonder if that would work? Make your articles fun so writing becomes fun? Just a thought.'

He surveys me over the rim of his wine glass. 'Your authors must really miss you, Coco. Do you always puzzle over a problem until you find a solution?'

'Have you seen *my* life?' I laugh. 'I've had a lot of experience with writers who faced similar issues. Like a prolific romance writer who felt she'd done every storyline already and wasn't finding any joy in her work any more.'

'What did you suggest?'

'A pivot to cosy crime with romantic elements. She took to writing murder a little *too* well.'

'You're lovely.' He blinks as if surprised the compliment slipped out. 'I mean, it's lovely the way you think of others, puzzling over a solution, including me. I appreciate it, Coco. And I'll give it some thought. Perhaps you're right. It's not just a block, it's also boredom.'

'It's about finding your passion for words once more.' And really, I should take my own advice, figuring out how I'm going to follow my passion for editing and earn a decent wage for us to be able to find our own place in Paris.

'*Merci,* Coco.'

24

My work week comes to an end. I'm on a high after a happy day spent at the bookshop. I'm still secretly buzzing from the lunch date with Henri the day before, which I take great pains to disguise. In the lulls, I spent some time thinking about the weekend and where I could take Eloise that she'd enjoy. The Palace of Versailles, perhaps? She's never been and it's one of the must-sees despite how hectic the queues are.

I arrive home and hang my scarf on the hook behind the door.

'*Bonsoir?*' I call out. 'I've got one spicy saucisson pizza!' Friday night has become the official evening that I grab a take-out on my way home.

Maman appears, face lined with worry.

'What is it?'

'You better go chat to Eloise. Today wasn't good.'

I take a deep breath. '*Merci,* Maman.' I find Eloise in our room, legs bunched up beneath her, head resting on her knees.

'Eloise, are you OK?' She lifts her tear-stained face and

there's a look of rage in her eyes. Ah. She knows I called the principal then.

'You promised!'

I sit beside her on the bed. 'I know, but one of my roles as a parent is to do what's best for you.'

'You could have warned me! But you didn't! They called Léa and the two girls in and they got in so much trouble. Now they're going to make my life hell.'

'Don't say hell.' It's a just reflex but I want to slap my own face.

She shoots me a glare. 'Well? Is that all you have to say?'

'Darling, I intervened because I was worried about you. If Léa is holding you hostage and encouraging the other two girls to do the same, then steps have to be taken. There's ignoring bad behaviour and then there's ignoring clear warning signs. I want you to enjoy school. To make new friendships, like you had in London.'

She scoffs, a gargling sound through her tears. 'Well that's not likely to happen now! If anything they're going to ramp things up, aren't they? Léa got suspended!'

'Why?' The principal didn't mention a suspension, and if they were following protocol lined out in their bullying policy, a student would get a warning first and then a suspension if behaviour continued. Unless... 'What did she do to deserve a suspension, Eloise?' Fear grips my heart, but my daughter only ignores me. '*Tell me*. What did she do?' My voice is icy calm as my heart continues to beat too fast.

A fresh batch of sobs breaks out as Eloise lifts her ponytail in my direction, and I let out a gasp when I see the damage. 'She *cut* your hair?' Her glorious mane of curls has been hacked away, leaving a zigzagged mess. The Rapunzel taunts.

Eloise nods.

'Why didn't the school call me?' White-hot rage pierces my temples.

'They called here and spoke to Grandad. He picked me up early.'

'They should have called me.'

'Really?' She gives me a weary smile. 'And what would you do, Mum? Storm down there and scream at them? *You* did this. *You* made it worse. The principal told me about your call and how she took Léa and the girls aside. Next minute Léa's chopping my hair off in art class, thanks to *you*!' All her emphasis feels like bullets hitting me square in the chest. Bang, bang, *bang.*

'My job is to do what's right for you whether you can see it or not. I wanted to tell you I was calling the principal but I knew you'd explode. I'm walking on *eggshells* around you, Eloise, and it doesn't feel good. How is *their* destructive behaviour my fault? That child is escalating, and no matter what you think, the school needs to be informed. Léa deserves to be suspended. In fact, she should be expelled, and I'll be pushing for that on Monday morning.' My own temper flares at my daughter, and I burrow it down. I should have been upfront with her, but it's like fronting up to a wild tiger.

'NO! Just leave it! You're making it a thousand times worse!'

I lean my head against the bedhead. Have I made it a thousand times worse? Is this fixable or will Léa come back from her suspension worse than ever? 'Do you want to change schools?'

'Again? God. No. Just leave me alone.'

'Fine, but you might want to know that I reached out to the principal concerned that with Léa having lost her *maman*, maybe she needed some support, but I was told she isn't bereaved, so she has no excuse for this behaviour. We'll go to school together on Monday and sort this out.'

Eloise gives me the dead-eyed teenager look and points to the door.

25
———

'Bonjour, we're here to meet with the principal.'

'Go through, she's waiting for you.'

Eloise trails behind me, holding herself tight. It's hard to get used to her new blunt bobbed hairstyle. I'm still doing a double take when I see it. It's only hair, it will grow back, but it's the violence of such a thing that gets to me.

'Welcome, Coco and Eloise.' The principal ushers us into her office, big smile in place, as if that will placate me. 'Take a seat.'

I don't bother with small talk. 'I'd like to know why Léa wasn't expelled. Surely committing an act so heinous as taking scissors to another student warrants that?'

She gives me a patient smile, as if expecting this sort of upset from me. 'As per our bullying policy, Léa was suspended due to the nature of the incident. Expulsion is only used in serious cases.'

Eloise frowns.

This is unjust!

'We have cameras, so we were able to thoroughly investigate.'

'Cameras clearly don't bother them.' I find it hard to catch my breath. The more I sit here the angrier I get while the principal wears that same smile as if we're simply talking about the weather and not a child attacking another with a pair of scissors!

'As Eloise has probably told you, they have art class together on a Friday. We've studied the footage closely and we can't be sure Léa purposely meant to cut Eloise's hair – it really *does* look like an unfortunate accident.'

I gasp. 'Oh, *come on*! How do you *accidentally* chop off someone's hair! You must be joking. This coming from the girl who has been teasing her about her "Rapunzel" locks. It doesn't take a genius to connect those dots.' Eloise presses a hand to my leg as if to quieten me, but I will not be silenced.

'I do understand your anger, Coco, but really we can't be certain it was done maliciously. Even Eloise isn't sure, are you?'

Eloise drops her gaze.

'*Eloise!*' Seriously? 'Tell her the truth. You know she did it on purpose.'

Eloise gives a tiny shake of the head, implying she's not going to speak up. She must be so afraid of Léa to act like this.

'In light of that,' the principal says, 'we did suspend Léa, because an accident like that is dangerous, and at age thirteen she should be responsible with a pair of scissors. We've given her some time to reflect and she'll back at school tomorrow. I'll be monitoring them myself.'

Time to reflect! '*Tomorrow?* She got suspended for one day?'

'She left a few hours earlier on Friday. While suspension is a reset, we're also mindful of our students missing too much school. It would be counterproductive, *non*?'

My head is going to explode. 'This is unbelievable. How will you protect my daughter? How do you envisage she'll make friends when the rest of the cohort follow Léa's lead?'

'As I said, I'll be monitoring the situation myself, by cameras and in person. We're going to hold an assembly for their cohort and remind students about the effects of bullying and the consequences they'll face.'

'Do students really listen in an assembly like that?'

'I appreciate that you're upset, Coco, but Eloise isn't entirely innocent here either.'

My jaw drops to the floor. '*Excusez moi?* You're blaming Eloise now?'

'No, I'm not blaming anyone. I'm saying there have been less than perfect behaviours by many students and we're doing our best to navigate this situation and reach a harmonious conclusion.'

The nerve! The gross unfairness. 'I'll be expecting a phone call from you each day, assuring me my daughter is safe and being kept well away from Léa and her two friends. I'm sure it goes without saying but I expect they won't be together in art class around scissors any more?'

'We think it's best they learn to—'

'*Non*, I think it's best Léa is moved to another class. What if she slipped with those scissors? What if she sliced into my daughter's neck? No, I want her moved.'

26

By the time Thursday comes around I'm excited about the next session of book club – the informal, reading meet-up – this time I'm ready for it. Nothing can get under my skin, not after the meeting with the principal and the subsequent silent treatment from Eloise.

I'm happy to get out of my own head and forget for a while. I'm considering moving her to a new school, but my *maman* keeps talking me out of it, telling me it's not right to teach her to run away from her problems. I'm going to see how the next couple of weeks go, and if there are any more incidents then I'll pull her out. It's not running away if it's not safe there, and the school *can't* assure me she's safe. Kids are wily, and now Léa and the two girls know they're being watched on CCTV I'm guessing they'll make an effort to misbehave out of sight.

I've just finished setting up the book club area when Henri arrives downstairs. I give him a wave from my perch in the book loft. I haven't seen him all week, and honestly, the bookshop was a little less fun without him here. Probably no one to tell me I'm doing everything wrong made the days go much slower.

The week has been quiet, actually, so it gave me time to pitch some ideas to Valérie about how to get more bodies inside, not just for the bar area. She's agreed I can start up a writing club and I'm also going to offer the space for book launches. I'll have to grovel to a few publishing pals, but I'm ready for that now. I take one last look around the book loft, and feeling satisfied, I go downstairs to welcome Henri.

'Bonjour, Henri. Where have you been all week?'

He takes his usual seat and waves to Valérie. 'Vacuuming. Cleaning my apartment from top to bottom, like you suggested.'

'Ah, the cure to writer's block! Did it work?'

'*Non.*'

'Time for third on the list then?' I blush as soon as the words leave my mouth.

He grins and it lights up his whole face. 'Remind me what was third on the list again...?'

I bite down on my lip. The damn man, is he flirting with me? 'Was it... a long soak in the bath?'

'No, that wasn't it.' His eyes twinkle.

'Was it...?'

'Ah!' He holds up a finger. 'You suggested sex would cure it? Didn't you?'

My legs go like jelly, as this feels almost like a proposition, and right now that sounds like an enjoyable way to spend a lazy day. What! It's looking at the sparkle in his eyes, the challenge he presents that's doing this to me. Normally, I'd blush and fumble and sidestep this interaction; hell, I'd probably run a mile, but the new me is throwing off those shackles. Because why not. I'm sick of being the staid one. 'I believe I did offer up sex...' He startles. I leave the sentence hanging for a moment and enjoy watching the apples of his cheeks pink with warmth. '...As a potential cure.'

He shakes his shirt as if he's suddenly hot and he goes to speak and stops himself. 'Perhaps... sex *is* the answer to my troubles?'

I want the ground to swallow me whole. Is he implying...

'Why don't I write about sex! You're a genius, Coco.'

'Er... write about it how?'

'After our walk the other day I felt like you shook something loose. Something that has been holding me back for so long. Why do we mire ourselves in all the bad things after heartbreak or divorce? Why do we allow ourselves to wallow for so long, as if the pain becomes a new appendage, dragging along like a lame leg? I'm going to write about what comes after. Finding joy in the small things. Like sex. Like walking. Reading. Joining a book club, even.'

'Maybe not this book club.' I'm still hyper focused on the sex thing while he laughs as if I'm really funny, but again I'm a couple of steps behind.

'I've been writing from the point of view of a man who lost his way, which is fine, but dull, so dull even I couldn't stand to read my writing. I need to inject energy back into my work and my life.'

'I'll help however I can.'

'Dinner?'

'Excuse me?'

'Would you like to go out for dinner one evening?'

'Is this for research for your article?' I'm slightly dubious as to his motivations.

He cocks his head as if amused. 'Purely for fun.'

'OK, just so long as it's not for sex.' What! My brain is scrambling. Someone hit the reset button! 'Ah – not that I'm opposed to sex, it's more that I don't want my performance to be judged for an article.' There, that should clear it up.

He gives me a look I can't quite decipher and his mouth opens and closes like a fish. The man is struggling, probably with the worry about his word count now that he has a solution in mind.

'I'll bring your coffee. Are you staying for book club?'

'*Oui*. I'll head up there now.'

Ziggy and Lucy arrive and I follow them upstairs with a tray of drinks.

Ziggy throws herself on a daybed while Lucy swishes her floral dress as if waiting for a compliment. 'Lovely dress,' I say.

'*Merci*,' she says.

Both women chat to Henri.

Soon the book doctor Isidore arrives followed by American Agnes and Nikolina. No sign of the double denim-wearing Allegra. She might be a victim of the pop-in syndrome they mentioned. Agnes chats to Ziggy as if they're the best of friends. Isidore surveys the tiny nails on her tiny hands while Lucy shares photos of her new foster cat with Nikolina. Henri sits close to me, arms folded, as he gazes outside to the Eiffel Tower in the distance.

There's no sign of the former resentments, not a raised voice, or a glare, or a muttering under a breath from any of the book club members. They are the same people yet are acting completely different. They're calm, too calm.

'What's going on here?' I eventually ask.

All eyes turn to me. Am I misreading this or are they suddenly wearing guilty expressions? When they throw fleeting looks towards Henri, the jig is up. Henri's given them all instructions to play nice. It's sweet of him and I'm really not used to a man having my best interests at heart.

'Henri has warned you all to be nice to me so I don't run away screaming, hasn't he?'

Agnes lets out a long breath as if relieved the secret is out. 'Yes! We're to be docile and not argumentative. But honestly, I don't know if I can be that person, Coco. I'll try but the arguing is what keeps me young.'

Ziggy nods her head as if she agrees with Agnes. 'Me too. Arguing with Agnes keeps me sharp. Without that, I might turn soft.'

What?

'We might get loud,' Nikolina says. 'But that's just so we're heard. There's a lot of love and respect here.'

'Speaking of love,' Lucy waggles her brow, 'Ziggy may have found the cure to her broken heart.'

'Oh?' I say. 'Did Valérie help?'

'Of course,' Ziggy says as if I'm dense. 'She gave me a passage by Rumi: "Your heart knows the way; run in that direction." At first I took it to mean literally running away, from the embarrassment after my online relationship fizzled out in such a humiliating way. Like, people didn't believe I could be so heartbroken about a guy I never met in person.'

'And they're stupid,' Lucy says, siding with her friend. 'These days with video calls and the way technology is, it's almost like meeting in real life.'

'*Oui.*' Ziggy shoots her a grateful smile. 'Anyway, so I felt like Valérie's passage was inspiring me to run in the opposite direction of my mistakes, in order to protect the heart at all costs. I'd put the idea of love on the backburner and got on with life. When out of the blue the other day, this guy approaches me at a café and asks me to help him translate one of the poems from *Un Baiser D'adieu.*'

Could it be, the Australian customer who wanted to woo the woman who sat beside him at the same café every day? The 'Tolstoy but make it fun' guy? It couldn't be. That would be a strange coincidence. Especially since I sold him that very book!

'And...?' Agnes probes. 'What's so earth shattering about that?'

'Well, I've been sitting at the same café for weeks at the same time of day and he's always there. I've been trying to work up the courage to talk to him but I just couldn't.'

'That's not like you,' Agnes says, her voice gentle.

'I know, I just felt like I couldn't handle another rejection, you know? Anyway, this guy attempts to speak French but he's hopeless, and he asks me to help him translate one of the poems. He's heard me chatting on my phone, he says, so he knows I speak English as well as French.'

Is this bookshop really magical? How can this be? I helped him. I just didn't know he was smitten with Ziggy!

'And then we picked the same book for book club, it felt like a great big neon sign, like Cupid pointing the way.'

'Where's he from?' I ask, needing confirmation.

'Australia.' Her face falls. 'He's going back home soon.'

It is him!

'"*Your heart knows the way...*"' Lucy says.

'"*...Run in that direction.*"' Nikolina gives her the nod of approval. 'Valérie's passage was pointing to the future, not the past!'

Ziggy lets out a nervous laugh. 'I mean, I *could* go for a holiday to Australia.'

'Valérie's passages are always inspiring,' Isidore says. 'You should go.'

A gentle breeze blows in from the window, fluttering the pages of the books in the Madeline library, almost like even the air around us is in agreeance.

'I'll think about it,' Ziggy says. 'Now, are we reading?

Because I'll have to translate these poems for my Australian boy and I'd like to get your take on their meanings first.'

'Why don't you just buy him the English translation?' ever-practical Agnes says.

Ziggy pulls a face that reminds me of my daughter, with the 'duh' implied. 'Where's the romance in that?'

'Oh,' Agnes says. 'I'm so out of practice.'

'You're married aren't you?' Lucy asks.

Agnes nods. 'Fifty years next month, so we're not exactly in the honeymoon period any more.'

Ziggy gets a mischievous twinkle in her eyes. 'If you read a bit of spice it might give you ideas...'

'Are you talking about sex, Ziggy?'

Ziggy falters. 'Ah... I'm talking about intimacy. Romance. Finding inspiration in the books you read.'

'My husband would die.'

'From sex?' Ziggy's eyebrows pull together as if she's actually concerned about such an outcome.

Agnes shakes her head, exasperated. 'From me being too forward.'

'How is that—'

I sense the start of trouble, so I quickly redirect the chat.

I take my trusty clipboard and read from a cue card.

'Welcome, all. I'm mindful of the time and giving ourselves enough after to chat about what we've read as long as we don't share any spoilers for those who haven't finished the poetry book... Who has finished it?'

Everyone's hands shoot up except Ziggy. 'Sorry but I've been busy with my handsome Australian. I'll finish it today though so we can chat about it early if everyone wants to?'

'Sure.'

'Let's read!' Everyone finds a spot on either a daybed,

hammock or bean bag. I'm dithering where to sit when Henri pats the space next to him on a chaise longue. I get a small thrill at the offer and join him. The seat cushion isn't as buoyant as I thought and we roll into each other, our bodies touching. It should be no surprise he smells delectable. He's really the whole package, and usually that would be a red flag. An avoid-at-all-costs situation, because just who is he trying to attract being gorgeous, and caring about his appearance and his cologne? But perhaps not all hot men are bad boys? The jury is still out.

'Sorry,' I say, trying to disentangle myself, but I only make it worse as we sink deeper into the cushions.

'Perhaps it's easier to stay like this?' he asks.

'But we're a tangle of limbs.'

'Is that so bad?'

'No, you're not offensive to look at, I guess.'

'Lucky me.'

'Welcome.'

'You're not offensive to look at either, in case you were wondering.'

'*Merci.*'

'We should read.' He motions with his free hand, the one not stuck around me, that we're being watched. I'll never live this down when it's obviously a chaise longue malfunction.

'We better.' I can't help stealing glances at him as we read. What is this? There's something about the man that makes me lose all reason. Either he's driving me to distraction when we argue or making me woozy with desire at times like this. It seems like everyone is falling in love in Paris, and it's making me yearn for the same.

Bad idea, Coco.

Too soon, my alarm beeps, signalling the end of the reading

session. It takes some effort to remove myself from Henri. When I do, I fix my hair and smile as I try to get my thoughts in order. For some reason I can only think of Henri and how I felt with his body pressed against me. Am I that lonely that the simple touch of a man sends me spiralling? Or is it because it's *that* man?

I call the group to order, ignoring Henri's gaze. Well, trying to.

'I'll start us off. I found *Un Baiser D'adieu,* a revelation. Heart searing, heart-soaring. Relatable, on so many levels, the human condition so clearly flawed, but so special nonetheless. I don't think I've openly wept reading poetry before like I did with this – maybe it's because I related to the mother-daughter relationship and the struggles that ensued with the last poem in the book...' What I can't say is that when I read that one at home I cried buckets, with my daughter beside me, the only time last week she wasn't glaring at me, and that's only because she was fast asleep.

Henri cocks his head and surveys me. '*Oui,* I related to the ups and downs of their relationship too in the last poem. Families are often full of dramatics, but theirs didn't feel dysfunctional. It felt more like they were preparing for battle, as if readying themselves to fight this unnamed thing, the intruder into their lives, but it's left vague for the reader to figure out. What do you suppose they were waiting for?'

'They're expecting the father to come back,' Agnes says, her tone brooking no argument. 'It's obvious. There's many a reference his departure is causing stress, financial worries, and they lose their house. It makes sense they *need* him back but they're nervous about it because he's got a drinking problem.'

Ziggy vehemently shakes her head. '*Non,* I got the sense they were relieved he'd left and even amid their struggle, anything was better than having him in the house, his volatile nature, his cruel words.'

The book doctor pulls a cushion onto her lap. 'They were afraid of death. They hint at this ever-present malignant blackness.'

'That's just a poet trying to be fancy, trying to confuse,' Nikolina says. 'They can't just say *Mon Dieu* I hate my mother. My boring life. My horrible dad. Look, it was readable, but would I dive into another poetry book? Probably not. I prefer sinking into a thriller, a whodunnit. I did find the poem about the dog and the puppies moving. There was a childlike innocence to it.'

'The title says it all, doesn't it? *A Kiss Goodbye*. I loved it,' Henri says, awe in his voice. 'I would never have picked that up, so I'm thankful to whoever suggested it.'

'It was me.' Ziggy puts up a hand.

Did Ziggy suggest it too? I never actually checked the other suggestions, just threw the tote bag back behind the bar and left for the night.

'I suggested it too,' says Isidore.

'Likewise,' I say, miffed. 'Isn't that odd? I've never encountered that at any book club I've been to before.'

They shrug as if it's nothing. Maybe, like me, they've seen the many stacks of it around the bookshop and were intrigued. But they're not making eye contact and are acting rather sketchy. Come to think of it, there's much talk on TikTok about the author. No one knows who they are, which is strange since Gen Z on TikTok are responsible for its meteoric rise. This group is nosy, that's one thing I've learned, so why don't they care?

'Ziggy.' If her name is Obsessive Fan Girl, surely she'll have the inside scoop. 'What's the story with the author? Do you know? From what I've seen there's no social media for them. I don't even know if the author is male, female or nonbinary.'

Ziggy opens her palms. 'Haven't heard. Why?'

'Well, aren't you interested?'

'Not really. I'm sure the author has their reasons.'

'Probably a recluse,' Nikolina says.

I'm not convinced. I'm not sure why. Is it that this slim volume of poetry is everywhere? Not only here in the bookshop but all over social media. And that's not unusual when a great book takes off, but what *is* unusual is the author is a mystery. A mononymous name, no author photo, no author biography. *Nothing.*

'Poets are a different breed,' Agnes says. 'They probably didn't expect worldwide fame.'

Another thought hits. What if the poems are based on real life? And the person they were running from (if they were running from a person, that is) is an actual danger to them? Or it's the very opposite!

'Actually,' I say, 'we're reading these like they're based on real life but there's a very real possibility that they're fictional.' And here I am getting carried away with it all.

Agnes grunts. 'You're right. That's the power of them; they felt so *real*.'

Lucy holds the poetry book, her eyes still glassy with tears. 'Lucy? Your thoughts?'

'I found it heartbreaking. Even after I read the more uplifting poems I couldn't shake off my despair from the sad ones. It's a beautiful book but has to be read in the right mood. As for what they were waiting for, I don't know. I don't want to know.' She clutches her heart. 'They'd run away and whatever they ran from, caught them in end. They tried to hide but it was of no use.'

'I wish I liked it as much as the rest of you,' Nikolina says.

'That's the beauty of reading,' Isidore says. 'Even if you didn't love it, Nikolina, you must admit it provoked a reaction. It touched you, therefore, it's done the job intended.'

'That's a great explanation. On that note, what makes a good book? Is it that you were moved or does it have to be more than that? Do you have to love every single page or is it enough to enjoy moments that made you think, reflect, cry, rage?'

The group gets into a heated discussion and this time I just let them go, listening in and enjoying the banter, the arguments, the occasional literary put down. Even Agnes reluctantly agrees the small book of poetry is one of those books she will read again when the time calls for it, it having made her homesick for her own adult daughters who live in Wisconsin, so very far away.

'Why did you move to Paris?' I ask, imagining a world where oceans separate me and Eloise and shuddering at the thought.

'My husband wanted to,' she says. 'He's a historian and was offered a position here many moons ago sorting the archives at the Musee D'Orsay. His dream job.'

'And you? Did you relish the idea of living in Paris?'

'Not at first. But one must do the right thing in a marriage. We made a vow, after all.'

'Ah, I see.'

'He's retired now, but he still goes off every day, as if he's still working.'

'Where does he go?'

'That, my dear, is the greatest mystery of all. I enjoy my solitude and we live very separate lives.' While she sounds upbeat, it doesn't ring true. Does Agnes need the book club, the bookshop, a lot more than she lets on? Her married life sounds rather lonely.

27

Another week slips by as I'm tidying up the bookshop when my phone rings. I dig in my jeans pocket to find it.

'Bonjour?'

'Hello, Anais.'

'Sally?' My first ever acquisition at London Field Publishing and one of my favourites.

'Yes, it's me, love. How's Paris treating you?'

I take a moment to decide if I'm upset with Sally calling out of the blue like this, and decide to hear her out. 'Well, I'm not getting the double takes and the whispering behind the hands like I did in London.' I try to infuse my voice with a lightness I don't feel. My Paris life isn't exactly all rainbows and butterflies yet. Not with my daughter, at any rate.

'I'm sorry, I really am. That man did a number on you, that's for sure. I'm sorry for my radio silence too. Not just mine, all of ours, but we were advised to have no contact until it was all sorted.' The liquidators were waiting on further funds to come in from various eBook platforms and bookshops, who often pay months down the track, so there's hope that we're nearly there in terms of everyone being paid fully now, as I couldn't get those funds any faster and they weren't due until now anyway. I'd received an email this morning saying all the loose ends would be tied up by the end of the month and that would be that.

Then I could go after Alexander, having the full financials.

'So it's all sorted? Finished?'

'For me. A few others are still waiting but they've been told they're working through them all.'

'It's a relief.'

'For everyone I expect.'

There's an awkwardness between us that wasn't there before. It can't be helped I suppose. 'Coco, none of us were happy that you were given the short shrift. Your cantankerous pal, the retired DS Phillip got his mates to personally look into it. Ooh, I'm probably not supposed to mention that, and over the phone no less. Next minute I'll have Scotland Yard around here.' We laugh. Phillip is a stickler for the rules, and I can relate, so for him to have asked his police mates is unusual.

'And?'

'And they say you've got a strong case and you shouldn't let it go.'

'They were suspicious of me though.'

'Well, you've got oodles of proof now, haven't you?'

'I do, but I'd have to file a civil suit and bleed myself dry with legal fees.'

'Maybe. Maybe not?'

'Did Phillip put you up to this call?' I miss Phillip complaining about the state of the publishing industry and his writing colleagues who get their policing facts wrong.

'He did. He might have a little rabbit up his sleeve.'

'Do tell.'

'This isn't the first time Alexander's pulled a stunt like this.

He's done it before and settled out of court. DS Phillip wants you to call him. He might be retired but he's got an idea.'

'Well, that changes things.' He's settled out of court! 'Who was it?'

'I'm sworn to secrecy. Blame DS Phillip. But if you needed a little spurring on, Alexander has announced his engagement to Molly-Mae. They purchased a lovely little cottage in St Ives, in Cornwall. I'm sorry, Coco.'

I assess how I feel about the impending nuptials... Oddly at ease. They deserve each other, but as for the cottage, a quiet rage boils inside of me. 'He's not even trying to hide it? How is he so brazen with stolen funds?'

'There are whispers he and Molly-Mae are going to launch their own digital publishing firm – but we're not sure if that's Alexander putting feelers out to see what reaction he'll get.'

I rub my face, probably smearing my lipstick. 'I see.' I seem to be the only one who is suffering after the fall out. That hardly seems fair.

'DS Phillip said his door, or phone in this case, is always open.'

'Thank you, I might take him up on that. So where did you land after all this?'

Sally names another boutique publishing firm. 'Only signed for two books, though, Coco. In case you return to the industry. I don't mind admitting I'm struggling without you. I miss your editorial magic touch, the way you don't stop until you get the best story out of me. I always knew you were a wonderful editor, I just didn't realise how much you shaped the manuscripts and made them better until you weren't there.'

'Thank you, Sally. That is really lovely of you.' I do miss that part of my life. Reading Sally's messy drafts and then going for a walk around London to ruminate about it. Letting the story sink in while I ponder about what can make it stronger.

'Keep me posted, won't you? If you start up again, or join another publisher, I'd love to go back to where we were.'

'I will, Sally. I miss working with you too.'

After we say our goodbyes and I hang up, Valérie calls me over to the bar. 'What was all that about then?'

I'm numb. Not much can shock me when it comes to Alexander any more, so even the cottage and the engagement doesn't hurt me like it should, but what does blow my mind is that he's done this before and gotten away with it. I'd never heard any rumours about him and if he settled out of court, that would be why. And now he's planning on starting another company, while I've lost my investment and my dignity. He doesn't get to do that twice and get away with it.

'Sit,' Valérie says. 'And tell me what's going on. Your complexion is grey so you must've had some sort of shock. Now, before you launch into it, I know all about London Field and what happened.'

'You do? How?'

'Google.'

Oh God. 'That's why you gave me the job?'

'No, that's not why. Do you see any other weekday staff here? No, the job is legitimate. You recall you dropped your business card here the first day we met?'

'Yes.'

She shrugs. 'I was curious. It's not magic that fixes a broken heart. It's details. And I wanted to know what made you hold your sadness in such a physical way. And so down the rabbit hole I went.'

I cup my face. 'And you didn't think to tell me?'

'Why? What would it matter? I'm only telling you now so we

can skip to the next part of the story, the phone call and what's happened today.'

Am I upset about the intrusion? I suppose not, because this is Valérie, who has trusted me even knowing that I'd run from a scandal in London. Who sensed I needed a life raft and sailed on by with her hand outstretched.

With a deep breath, I tell her what I've learned from Sally.

'You need to take action now, Coco.'

'I know. I'll call DS Phillip, see what his idea is.'

'Good plan. Now, why don't you head off for the day?'

'*Merci*, Valérie, but I'll be OK. I've got to tidy Library Madeline. There have been a lot of customers up there today and it's a mess.'

'It's always a mess up there, that's why I don't tell anyone about the book loft. If they find it, then that's all well and good, but otherwise, all those stairs, it's too much.'

'But it's such a beautiful area with the view of the Eiffel Tower and sunlight streaming in.'

'It really is, so why don't you take a break then? You haven't stopped today, you haven't even had lunch. Why don't you go upstairs while it's quiet and I'll ask Henri to ferry some lunch up to you, because those stairs will be the end of me.'

'No, it's—'

'I'm not asking, I'm telling. Off you go.'

'OK.' I head upstairs, glad for a moment to clear my head.

Not long after, a sheepish Henri appears, carrying a bottle of white wine and two glasses. 'I've been sent to cheer you up. Liquid lunch OK?'

I laugh. That Valérie is always scheming when it comes to me and Henri.

'Sure.'

He sits beside me on the daybed. It feels rather intimate but also comforting, like I've made real friends here already at the bookshop and those friendships will continue to deepen as time goes on. It makes me think of Eloise, not having the same good fortune.

'Valérie mentioned a phone call...?'

'Alexander is engaged. They've bought a cottage in Cornwall, in one of the most picturesque villages in the UK. They're putting feelers out about starting their own digital publishing company. Meanwhile, I'm living with my parents and sharing a bedroom with my daughter who, by the way, isn't speaking to me. I'm no mathematical genius, but I'd say the only person suffering in this equation is me.'

Henri's sympathetic smile almost pushes me over the edge. I'm not upset, so why do I feel like crying? I'm angry, dammit. I'm tired of always feeling like less.

'I'm so sorry, Coco.'

'I should have asked your underworld pals to kill him.'

He laughs. 'There's still time.'

I bring my knees up to my chest. 'He's now living the kind of life I wanted. Am I'm too pedestrian for the fairytale? Maybe not all of us get the veil, the husband, the white picket fence.' I cup my face, wondering why I'm blurting all this out to Henri when I've just told myself that none of that matters, all that I'm concerned about is the destruction of London Field Publishing, but I guess I can only bury my pain for so long before it rises back to the surface. It's not that I miss Alexander, it's that I want to find someone who loves me enough to propose. To plan a dream life with. I haven't even got close to that happening, so what does that say about me? Am I so unlovable?

'It shocks me, that it's all working out for Alexander, the villain of the piece.'

'Well, even if it is working out now, he's still the bad guy, and everyone in the industry knows that. Whereas you're known for stepping up and doing what was right, even at great personal cost to you.'

I manage a wobbly smile. 'Do you ever see yourself getting married again?' Right now, I'd much rather imagine Henri in a suit waiting at the end of the aisle than Alexander, which is the picture that's front and centre right this minute.

Henri considers it. 'Marriage isn't all it's cracked up to be. But I'd like to fall in love again. It's hard, being a single dad, but you understand.'

'*Oui*, I do. It's why I didn't date for the longest time, wanting to preserve our homelife just for us. But now I wonder, have I left it too late?'

'Why would it be too late? You're young.'

'I feel older than thirty-three, somehow. Even my daughter worries I'll end up alone, living with a virtual assistant called Alexa for company.'

He grins. 'It's scary, isn't it, to think of our children one day being independent and gone from home. We'll have all that freedom and not know what to do with it.'

There's something so authentic about Henri. He could be throwing all sorts of platitudes my way to cheer me up and get back to his work, but he's just sitting here instead being real. 'We could get married,' I say, arching a brow.

'I'm all for spontaneity...'

'Stop! I don't want to hear the "but".' I laugh. 'I mean, if all else fails. Say, when I'm forty or so, when my daughter has truly left me for her own exciting life at university or whatever, we can get married so we're not alone.'

'A marriage pact for lonely, sad people?'

'*Oui,* exactly like that.'

'I'm in.'

I give him a wide smile. 'Deal.' I hold out a hand so we can shake on it. 'If we find ourselves single at forty, we'll get married and live happily ever after.'

Henri rubs his chin. 'This is probably when I should mention I'm forty next year.'

'What!'

'You already made the deal. No reneging.'

I'm not sure why the silliness of the conversation amuses me so much, but soon we're in fits of laughter.

When the laughter subsides, I find myself close to Henri; our knees brush, our heads are dipped forward. As we gaze at each other, time slows then stops, a caesura. The moment feels weighted, as if this elongated pause is for my benefit – a sign pointing *this way,* in case I miss or misread the signals, which I so often do.

I'm almost floating with the sensation pulsing through me, and so I trust in that. I lean closer, our faces a breath apart, waiting a beat for consent, some tacit approval. He traces a fingertip along my cheek, the softest touch, but it sends my nerve endings into a frenzy. There's no sound except the thrumming of my heart, the siren wail of my pulse, as I press my lips against his, slowly, then all at once, I give in to the kiss.

The world fades to black but inside my mind is a riot of colour as he cups my face and the kiss deepens. I'm electrified, startled back to life. I'm Snow White, awoken with a kiss from the prince. It *feels* like coming home, and how can that be? Like the touch and taste of him is familiar.

I'm woozy with it all when a voice breaks through the love-struck bubble.

'Mum! What are you *doing*?'

I jump back from Henri as if zapped, stung, to find Eloise standing there, glowering, backpack slung over her shoulder.

I will myself to snap back into maternal mode. My brain scurries to reboot, but too many wires are crossed, as if I can't find the path, the way back. 'I... we... there...' It's a muddle. I suck in a breath as dizziness comes. The tingle of Henri's fingertip along my cheek still pulses, yet his hand is now by his side. There's the thought of panicking, but I'm done with that. I don't want to fall prey to it ever again. I have done nothing wrong, then or now. I steel my shoulders. Focus on the matter at hand. 'Why aren't you at school?'

She harrumphs. 'They've been trying to call you for hours! In the end, Mémère had to leave work to get me! And you're just here... kissing this guy? My life is legit falling apart right now and you don't even care!'

I take my phone from my pocket. No missed calls.

Henri's touch glances over my arm. There's a message in that briefest of connection. It's reassurance, it's support. 'I'll be downstairs.' He leaves us, giving Eloise a quick wave as he goes. Politeness stops her from being rude and she gives him a tiny wave in return and then turns her fire on me.

28

I don't apologise because I'm not sorry. In fact, I'm not going to apologise for being me ever again.

'What happened at school?'

Emotions flick across her features. Hostility, pain, panic. 'I got *bloody* suspended.'

'Don't say bloody!'

'*Mum!*' She stamps her foot, and the gesture is so very childlike.

I scoop my hair back and redo my ponytail, trying to compartmentalise the before and the after so I can listen to my daughter. 'I don't like it when you swear. Why did you get suspended?'

'Because of Léa, why do you think?'

I stand and make my way to her, giving her shoulders a reassuring squeeze. 'There must be more to it than that?'

'I don't *know*! All I know is I'm not going back to that school, like, ever! I want to go back to London.'

I sigh. 'We've talked about this. I'll have to call the principal.' I find my phone next to the daybed and check the time. It's probably too late to call the school now, it's just past four, when the office closes.

'*Wait.*' She grabs my wrist. 'What was going on with that old Jude Law guy?'

'I stopped overthinking, and it was' – *glorious* – 'nice.'

'Great, now we'll *never* get back to London.'

29

The next day, I'm serving a rather testy customer, who is adamant that she should be able to swap the books she paid for last week for different ones. 'I understand what you're saying,' I enunciate slowly once more. 'But this isn't a library, or a book swap. We don't allow customers to pay for books and then exchange them for different books. If we did it would be very hard to keep the bookshop afloat.'

The woman, who is wearing athleisure, gesticulates wildly as she makes scoffing sounds and tries to get the attention of other customers milling close by. 'That is just ridiculous. I paid good money for these.'

My gaze drops to her selection. She chose books from the second-hand sale bins, so in total she paid three euros for three books. 'You chose really well,' I say, trying to placate her. 'I'm sure you got three euros worth of value reading them.'

'One of them wasn't very good. Can't I just swap them for three more?' Part of me wants to give in, anything to move her along, but what if she comes back again and wants to swap for full priced books, and I've set a precedent, because I ran out of energy dealing with her?

'Sorry, *non*.'

Valérie swishes in, back from wherever she goes for a few hours during the day. As usual, her sunny smile is gone after these mysterious outings. 'Ophelia,' she greets the woman. 'You're not trying to swap books again, are you?'

Ophelia blushes. 'One of them wasn't very good.'

'Come on, let me make you a coffee and you can tell me all about it.'

'Fine, if you insist.' Ah, does Ophelia like sharing a coffee with Valérie, more than the idea of swapping books? The longer I'm here, the more I recognise all the small ways Valérie helps people, especially those suffering from loneliness. It's easy to feel lonely in a big city like Paris, where you can feel faceless and nameless in the crowds.

I send Valérie a grateful look and move to the next customer. The day slips away as I serve customers and restock shelves. When there's finally a lull, I find Henri in his usual chair. We didn't get a chance to speak after our kiss, and so my plan is to dust the shelves around him to get his attention.

I hum an upbeat tune as if I'm just peachy, as if this is any other day and not The Day After The Kiss.

'You're in a good mood,' he says with an eyebrow raise and a rather smug smile. 'Haven't you already dusted here?'

'*Excusez moi*, how would you know where I've dusted?' He wasn't here, he can't prove it.

'You dust and vacuum every morning at precisely 10 a.m.'

I'm a creature of habit. 'Yes, well, I've decided to dust twice a day, for the benefit of our customers.'

'Can we talk for a minute?'

Valérie wanders down the bar, closer to where we are. She

doesn't know about the kiss, but I'm sure she senses the tension between us. 'That sounds ominous.'

I sit opposite him, fidgeting with the duster.

'Not at all. I hope everything was OK with your daughter yesterday?'

I sigh. Real life. 'Can we talk about *anything* other than that? I'm... at my wits' end with it all at the moment.' I don't want to scare him by explaining thirteen is HELL. And moving to a new school with a mean girl bully is worse. I also keep quiet that my wilful child went straight home and told my parents that she caught me kissing 'some rando' at work and made it sound a lot bawdier than it was in reality.

'In that case, I was wondering if you're free for dinner tonight? My parents are in town, you see. And there's a little bistro around the corner that is always good.'

Mon Dieu. Pressure gathers in my brain. Doesn't he know we were *joking* about the marriage at forty thing? This is moving too fast. It's too soon. Concern dashes over his features. 'Or, if you'd rather not, I understand. No hard feelings.'

This is one of those situations where it's better if I'm honest. 'It's just... isn't it a bit too *soon*, a bit *premature* for me to meet your parents? I mean, the kiss *was* spectacular as far as kisses go. And I'm all for commitment. But there are important stages... I... uh... believe you're skipping, by moving ahead at such a rapid pace.' There. It's best to be upfront and honest. Otherwise next week we'll be sampling wedding cakes and researching honeymoon destinations and really, how well do I know this guy? I can't base my future on one kiss. No, I must stand firm on this, even if he got his parents to rush to town so quickly. I only hope they're not upset at the slight.

He almost swallows his lips as he tries to stem... laughter?

'What?' I cry. 'What's so funny?'

With a hand up, he manages to control the urge and eventually sputters. 'What I meant was, my parents are in town to visit for the weekend, therefore, they can babysit so I can go out with you. Alone.'

I want to slap my own forehead. 'Ooh! Ha! What a relief!'

'A relief?'

'Yes!'

We lapse into silence before giggles get the best of us.

'Around seven this evening? I want to take you to Les Éditeurs.'

I smile. 'Because I was an editor?'

'And you will be again.'

'I'm not sure about that but I have heard good things about the bookish bistro, so I'd love to try it.'

'I'll pick you up?' he asks.

'*Non, non*, I can meet you there.' Not only am I terrified of his driving, but I'd also rather keep this dinner date private for now. Eloise doesn't need to see me flaunting Henri around when she's on such an uneven keel. She's spending today at home, having been suspended the same length of time as Léa, but is due back at school on Monday. I don't have the details about her suspension as I've been playing phone ping pong with the principal, so I'm hoping I catch her return call this time.

'Great. I'm looking forward to it.'

'Likewise.'

* * *

When my phone flashes with the school number, I shake it at Valérie to let her know I'm slipping out the back for a bit.

'Bonjour.'

'Bonjour, Coco.' The principal's tone isn't as conciliatory this time. I'm frustrated with Eloise, who refused to talk about it with me. Punishing me for the kiss, I suppose. I'd have been mortified too at that age if I'd caught my parents smooching, so I don't take offence. It does make this phone call much harder though, having no facts at hand to fight her case. 'I'm sorry we've kept missing each other's calls.'

'*Oui*, Eloise said you tried to call me numerous times yesterday but I didn't have any missed calls from the school.'

'Eloise told us not to call you yesterday. She insisted that your phone would remain off at work.' What? Why would she lie like that?

'Oh, it's a new job,' I finally manage.

'Look, I think the best way forward is if we have a mediation with both families. The situation hasn't been resolved and it's only getting worse.'

'Mediation? Isn't that a bit drastic?' I hate things like this where I have to face off with a family unit, and there's only me. I always feel so scrutinised, so under the spotlight, so *alone* as a solo mum.

'In light of the incident, I don't think so.'

'What incident? Why did Eloise get suspended?'

'She didn't tell you?'

'No, she's been rather upset of late.'

'Eloise slapped another student.'

'*What?*'

'It was witnessed by others.'

My daughter would never raise a hand to anyone. I know this to be true. 'Was this alleged slap caught on camera?'

'Well, *non*, but I investiga —'

I cut her off. 'Let me guess, the girl who made the complaint was Léa?'

'*Oui*, Léa made the complaint and I believe her.'

'This is unbelievable. What did Eloise have to say about it?' Surely she wouldn't have sat there and taken the blame for an act she didn't commit? Eloise might be moody at times but she's not aggressive.

'Eloise refused to talk about it.'

'Because she's *intimidated* by Léa! She's probably scared to speak up, especially as you're supporting the bully herself. Why is that?'

Her voice remains maddingly calm, as if she's trying to lull me into believing my child would purposely hurt another. 'Will you agree to a meeting with the family? I think it's the best way forward.'

'What other choice do I have?'

'I promise, we'll sort this out. These types of meetings are largely successful.'

'Fine. Let me know when and where.'

'I'll confirm with Léa's family and send you an email with possible dates and times for the meeting, which will most likely be later next week.'

30

After work I rush home raring to have a proper sit down with Eloise and grill her on the so-called incident, as so far she has refused to tell me anything. I need every minuscule detail so I'm ready for the upcoming meeting. I'm still processing it all and need to work out what our rights are in this situation. I don't believe for one minute that Eloise slapped Léa. For a couple of reasons: firstly, my daughter is not violent and has never displayed aggressive characteristics that make me believe she's capable of that. Secondly, this alleged slap wasn't caught on camera, which is convenient. Who were the witnesses? If Léa does intimidate the cohort as much as Eloise says, then surely those children would say anything to remain in Léa's good graces?

Back at the apartment, I'm frustrated to find a note.

I've taken Eloise to dinner and a movie. Maman x

Well, I suppose that gives me time to get ready for my dinner date with Henri. I shower and change into a summery dress and a pair of strappy sandals. I've been so caught up in Eloise all afternoon, I haven't given much thought to tonight. What if the conversation is stilted? Or what if he's one of those odious types who drinks too much and we end up in a slanging match?

I write a note for Maman telling her I'm out to dinner with a friend and head outside to order an Uber. The driver and I chat about the state of the economy before he deposits me in front of the Les Éditeurs, coming to a full stop, I might add; none of this jumping out of a vehicle at speed.

Henri, ever the gentleman, is standing out the front. It's touching that instead of waiting inside at a table, he's waited for me so we can walk in together. Little details like this show me what sort of man he is.

'*Bonsoir*, Coco. You look beautiful.'

'*Merci*. You look…' What? Handsome, too formal? Hot, too suggestive? Shockingly good looking, too desperate? '…Well.' There. Sufficient.

'Ah – *merci*.'

He seems tongue-tied so perhaps I better limit the compliments. Maybe he's got a hidden nervous disposition that lies just beneath the surface?

'Shall we?' He offers his arm, which I take. It's all rather wholesome and sweet. When I feel the outline of his muscles through his light jacket, a swoony thrill runs through me.

We're seated at a table and talk soon turns to the book club. 'Agnes isn't well,' Henri says.

'Oh?' Agnes is one of those formidable women who appear indestructible. 'I hope it's nothing serious?'

'Well, it is rather. She's been admitted to hospital. Valérie called me and asked for a lift so she could check in on her.'

The waiter takes our order. I'm relieved when Henri doesn't

suggest I order a salad like Alexander so often did. 'I'm glad Valérie is with her. Do you need to get back to pick her up?'

'*Non*, she's going to catch a taxi. But here's the thing. The reason Valérie didn't take a taxi in the first place is because Agnes asked her to stop past her apartment and get her some clothes and toiletries, so it was easier for me to drive her there and then back to the hospital.'

I narrow my eyes. 'Why couldn't Agnes's husband take her things?'

'Exactly.'

'What did Valérie think about that?'

The waiter returns with our wine and pours. 'She didn't think much at first. She was more worried about getting whatever Agnes needed and getting to the hospital to make sure she was OK. We both sort of presumed maybe Agnes's husband was away, or caught up at work, or already at the hospital.'

I take a sip of the wine, rolling the passionfruit taste on my tongue. 'And he wasn't?'

Henri grimaces. 'Agnes told Valérie where the spare key was hidden, so she let herself in only to find him sitting on the sofa watching television.'

'Did he know about his wife?'

'Valérie queried this and he said he knew and that he'd see Agnes whenever she was discharged.'

My heart hurts for Agnes. 'That's so callous. Or is it that whatever she's in for is minor, and maybe her husband hates hospitals?'

'They suspect it was a heart attack.'

My hand flies to my throat. 'And he's at home on the *sofa!*' Poor Agnes. 'What a beast of a man.'

'You know, it explains a lot about Agnes and all her bluster. She's in a loveless marriage.'

'We don't know that for sure.'

He makes a face. 'We sort of do. Valérie told me. She was incensed after seeing him sitting there so relaxed, as if Agnes didn't need any care or comfort.'

'Oh no, what did Valérie do?'

'I'm not entirely sure, but I could hear her yelling at him from all the way down the road where I was double parked.'

'I can't imagine Valérie yelling, somehow.' I try and picture her enraged and fail. Aside from the times she disappears during the day and comes back glum, she's cheerful, happy.

'We should visit Agnes, let the book club know too.'

'Yes. You really are soft under all that muscle, aren't you?'

He laughs, feigning shyness. '*Moi?*'

'*Toi.*'

After dinner, we stroll along the Seine as the Eiffel Tower sparkles in the inky night. Dinner cruises chug along the river and the air is fresh with promise.

Under the leafy canopy of a horse chestnut tree, Henri stops.

I hold my breath, my body feeling like liquid beneath me. I take his collar and pull him against me, making my intent clear. We fall against the trunk of the tree as he holds my hips and drops his head to kiss me. Stars explode inside me. I'm sure I've never felt so woozy as this before. Blame the wine, the night, the man, the chemicals in my brain that scream at me that I haven't *felt* like this before. Were they all frogs and this is the prince?

There's a sensation of falling, a heady dizziness as our hands explore the outline of each other's bodies. I so badly want to give in to this wildness, abandon all sense and let my desire take over, but common sense prevails when he pulls away for a moment, leaving a space between us, the space where his body was a mere moment ago, pushing against mine.

The street comes alive again. There are people milling about, staring.

I can't help but laugh. *Sensible* me doesn't subscribe to public displays of affection. Doesn't behave in a tacky uncouth manner, but this *new* me wants to ravish this man, consequences be damned.

Is it so base as only a physical attraction? I trace his bottom lip with a finger, wanting to leave an imprint and to take the memory home. If I'm honest with myself, this is more than just a spark. More than desire. The very first moment I laid eyes on him, I felt that recognition. That weighted pause, the caesura moment, but I allowed the knowledge to slip past because my confidence was shattered, my heart already bruised and sore.

But how to say all of this? Does it even need to be whispered out loud? If it is what I hope for, I won't have to do any encouraging.

'I'm fighting an internal battle so hard right now,' he says, tucking a lock of my hair back from my face.

'Oh?'

'I want to take you home, but I can't, and we should go slow...'

I let out my own frustrated laugh. '*Oui*, such delicious torment.'

'Argh.' We kiss again and I let myself melt into his arms, realising that my own happy ever after may come much sooner than expected. Did The Bookshop for the Broken Hearted have a hand in this...?

31

'What's got you so rosy-cheeked?' Valérie says on Tuesday when I practically slide into work on a cloud after another flirty text exchange with Henri early this morning.

'A full eight hours' sleep and the required amount of water to stay hydrated is my best guess.' I give her a dazzling smile that I just can't seem to swallow down. I'm beaming and cannot contain it. Even the email from Eloise's principal confirming the upcoming mediation with Léa's family hasn't dulled my shine.

'You are a very bad liar.'

I laugh. 'Yes!'

'Love has found you, just like I predicted, *non*?' She gives me a maternal smile like she's proud of me, which is rather sweet.

'I *love* Paris.' Henri and I agreed to keep our dating on the downlow while we get to know each other better. That way, if it doesn't work out, we won't have to explain ourselves and we can just pretend it never happened. Everything is sweet though, and the world is in full technicolour, until my phone alerts with a reminder. I hate having to ask for time off, especially as I'm the only help Valérie has during the week but it can't be avoided.

'Is it possible to leave early tomorrow? I've got a meeting at Eloise's school. I can make up the hours by coming in at the weekend, or skipping lunch?'

'You shouldn't keep skipping lunch. No need to make it up, you stay later when it's busy so I actually owe you. And it's family first here, you know that. Is everything OK?'

'She's being bullied and now they're trying to turn it around on her. It's upsetting to say the least.'

'I'm sorry to hear that. I'm surprised we haven't seen Eloise in here. I thought she wanted to study in the bookshop after school.'

'That's my fault too. She's avoiding me after I called the school and intervened. I'm currently going through a long spell of the silent treatment.'

Valérie pats my hand. 'It does get better. This monstrous age soon passes.'

I inhale the hope of such a thing. 'Soon?'

She laughs. 'Soon enough. Next she'll be at university, working or travelling abroad and you'll remember this time fondly.'

Eloise on a beach in some tropical country flashes in my mind's eye and a week ago that would have given me heart palpitations, but now I sort of understand a little better. Maybe it's me having something joyful in my own life, or at least the beginning of it with Henri, but my entire focus for once is not on my daughter, who doesn't want that attention from me, or maybe it's just a realisation that she's not a small child any more and one day soon she'll be an adult and I'll have to let her go. Have to let her make bad choices and learn from her mistakes. Have to let her have fun, even if she chooses to holiday on a beach in a country far away. Is it a signal that it's OK for me to want more for myself too?

Not just work. Not just Eloise. Chasing my own happiness even with all my past mistakes so close they're still sitting in my shadow. We're all learning as we go, we're all imperfect.

It's not a crime to want to find love. To hope a man loves me so much he proposes. Why can't I wish for the fairytale happy-ever-after in my own life?

All this musing about life and love and letting go reminds me. 'How is Agnes? Henri said they suspected she had a heart attack?'

Valérie's smile turns into a frown. '*Oui*, they confirmed she did suffer a minor heart attack. She's blaming the rich French food, of course.'

'Oh, *Agnes*! Will she be all right?'

Valérie lifts a tray of glasses from the dishwasher. 'She will be. They've put her on medication and suggested she lose some weight and cut back her red wine consumption.'

'How did she take that news?'

'Not too well.'

'Henri suggested that we get the book club together to visit her. Do you think she'd like that or would she actively despise the intrusion?'

Valérie takes a tea towel from the rack and lifts up a cocktail glass to polish. 'She will pretend to hate it, but secretly she'll love every minute. It's a great idea and she could really use her friends at the moment.'

'What's the story with the cold, callous husband?'

Valérie frowns. 'He *is* a cold fish. I've always suspected Agnes's marriage wasn't a happy one, but I still got the surprise of my life, finding him at home like that. Not a care in the world, watching... well, you don't need all the details. The man is a dictator, ruling her every move, did you know that?'

I can't imagine anyone dictating to Agnes. 'Really?'

'Really. Right down to the type of books she reads. All that protesting she does about modern books – that's his influence, but I didn't ever want to mention it, so keep that quiet. I've probably made things much worse for her when she gets home, but I told him what I thought about men like him, and none of it was positive.'

My chest tightens with the thought of Agnes living with a man like that. 'Why does she stay?'

'Why does anyone? Loyalty, probably. Agnes is a steadfast sort. Maybe also fear of the unknown. Her age might be a factor. Anyway, it's not for me to guess, but I will be giving her some advice when she feels better. No one deserves to be dictated to.'

The scenario reminds me of some of the poems in *Un Baiser D'adieu*. Did Agnes recognise her own situation in them? There's fire in Valérie's eyes. It's almost as if she's reliving her own past. Did she once have a controlling husband too? 'Will she listen to you, do you think?'

Valérie guffaws. 'I'm not sure. His control is so ingrained, but I have an idea that might appeal and I'm going to ask her because sometimes the greatest thing you can do for a person is offer the hand of genuine friendship and let them know they have a soft spot to land when all else fails.'

32

By the next afternoon, I've managed to get hold of the usual suspects from the book club and I apprise them of Agnes's situation. I don't mention her husband or any of that, only that she's had a minor heart attack, and that, if they're up for it, we're planning a group visit.

I'm just hoping all of us turning up at once doesn't trigger a second heart attack. I send the group another blanket message.

COCO

> It's best if we keep stress at a minimum for Agnes so let's refrain from any literary debate. Coco x

I'm tallying up the takings earlier than usual, getting ready to leave Valérie in charge so I can head to the mediation at school, when my phone chirps with a text.

ZIGGY

> Can I please take her one spicy book as a joke? It will make her smile, I'm sure of it. Zigs ;)

I shake my head.

Only if you want to be banned from book club.

I find Valérie in an intense discussion with a thin woman who looks slightly familiar. She's wearing a band tee and denim shorts and I struggle to place her. Her hair is neatly tied in a long plait.

'Sorry to disturb you, Valérie, but I'm off to the school meeting now.'

'Is it that time already? Quickly before you go, meet a new friend of mine, Rachelle.'

When Rachelle spins to face me, I realise it's the young girl who Eloise watched stealing a book. The one who'd looked down on her luck. 'Bonjour, Rachelle.'

'Rachelle is going to help in the bookshop at the weekend and might even cover a shift or two in the bar Thursday and Friday evenings.'

I give her a warm smile. I bet Valérie approached Rachelle and not the other way around, by giving her a solution that helped her retain her dignity. 'You're going to love it here,' I say, meaning it.

Rachelle wrings her hands as if she's nervous. '*Merci*, I'm grateful for the opportunity.'

The Bookshop for the Broken Hearted is magical. The lost and sad, and lonely and broken who find their way here *are* eventually cured, but not by a potion, not by a passage, but by Valérie herself. A woman who doles out an abundance of love and support, friendship and advice, food and drinks, books, to whoever needs it.

She gives a literal helping hand up.

What made her this way? Or *who*, might be the question.

There's no time to ponder it as I give them both a wave and head out in the direction of Eloise's school.

I arrive at the office earlier than the scheduled time, which gives me a shot of confidence. The secretary shows me through, and I greet the principal cooly. I'm still not convinced that she has Eloise's best interests at heart.

'I'm sure they'll be along soon.'

I nod, holding my purse on my lap like a safety blanket.

The principal calls to her secretary, 'Can you check that Eloise and Léa are on their way please?'

A girl appears at the door, a timid expression on her face. This must be Léa. Her acting skills are on point. She's playing the part of fragile teen very well.

'Come in, Léa, and take a seat. This is Coco, Eloise's *maman*.'

'Bonjour.' She speaks so softly I can barely hear her. I give her a small nod. It's easy to hold on to my iciness when I remember my daughter's hair being cruelly chopped off and all the teasing and taunts.

My daughter appears at the door. 'Eloise,' the principal says, 'join your *maman* there and say hello to Léa.' Eloise's face is like thunder, her whole demeanour hard, sharp, a stark contrast to Léa, who is continuing with her cowed act.

'I'm sure it won't be long now…' the principal says, checking her watch again. 'And then we can begin.'

'I hope not,' I say. 'You said four and I managed to get here by four.' Being kept waiting like this is probably a power play by the happy parents. It ratchets up my nerves and my anger. I'm coiled, ready to fight for my daughter and for fairness to prevail.

Another ten minutes goes by and I'm about ready to explode. 'Can you call them? This is the height of rudeness. We do have other places to be, you know.' The tiger mum part of my personality is not pretty, I'm aware of it, but it's a part of me that will always speak up and be in Eloise's corner, more than I do for myself at any rate.

The principal picks up the phone then drops it again. 'Ah, here he is. Monsieur Beaufort.' *Merde.* I suppose we have to continue waiting for Madame Beaufort.

When I turn to eviscerate Monsieur Beaufort with a glare, confusion reigns. My first thought is Agnes – did she have another heart attack? Then my next worry is Valérie. It takes me a full minute for my brain to catch up and when I do, all colour drains from my face. 'Do not tell me Léa is *your* daughter?' My voice is high, like a shriek. Of all the ways my life could be flipped upside down, I wouldn't have guessed this would happen.

His eyes flash with hurt, then... anger? '*Oui*, and that would mean *your* daughter is the one who *hit* Léa. How could you not tell me? Did you think I wouldn't find out?'

'What do you mean? I didn't know!'

'Take a seat,' the principal says with a sigh. 'Let's discuss this like adults, shall we?'

There's a pain in my chest, as if my heart is breaking all over again. 'I'd like it known that I do not for one minute believe that Eloise hit Léa. It's rather coincidental, is it not, that it wasn't caught on camera?'

Léa gasps. The audacity of the child. Acting in such a way to fool everyone around her. Maybe she's conniving like her mother; who would know?

'That's exactly why she did it there,' Léa rails. 'So she wouldn't get caught. Luckily my friends were there and saw it happen.'

'How can you imply Léa's lying?' Henri asks, gruff. 'They took pictures of her reddening cheek just after it happened. You could still *see* the imprint of your daughter's hand on her face, that's how hard she hit her.'

'Eloise?' I say, beseeching her with my eyes to speak the truth.

'I hate it here.'

I bite down on a scream. This is not the time for teenagerly mutterings.

'Did you slap her, Eloise? That's the crux of it. Now, I *know* you'd never do something like that, but you have to speak up for yourself.'

Henri grunts. 'She's never going to admit to it when you put it like that, is she? This is a waste of time. We're leaving. Come on, Léa.'

Léa wipes away a crocodile tear and hastens after Henri.

I cross my arms. 'Now what?'

The principal rocks back in her chair. 'I have no idea.'

33

We make the trek back to the apartment, my footsteps heavy. 'Eloise, why won't you speak up? If you don't, you're going to get the blame. Her timid act is very believable, and you sat there acting petulant and moody, which did you no favours.'

'You're just mad because Léa's dad is the Jude Law guy, right? And that's going to make things super awkward now.'

'Well, yes it is, but that's not why I'm mad. I'm mad because we barely heard a word from you, and it doesn't help your defence. I can't help you if you don't confide in me.'

She lets out a frustrated shriek. 'Because I don't *care*. I don't care about any of it. I just want to go home.'

'This is home. I have told you so many times. What if this continues, and you both get expelled because you didn't tell them the truth? That will affect your entire future!'

'I have no future.'

I shake my head. 'I can't talk to you when you're like this.'

'Good.'

I get her home, leaving her with Maman. 'I'll tell you later,' I say, not able to hide my annoyance. 'I've got to visit a friend at the hospital. I'll be a few hours.'

'Take your time.'

* * *

I wait outside the entrance of the hospital, checking my phone for a message from Henri. Part of me hopes he'll see reason, or that Léa will crumble and tell the truth and he'll apologise. I'm not even sure if he'll come to the hospital now, and if he does, it's going to be awkward.

When he mentioned his child, I'd presumed she was a toddler by the way he spoke about having a babysitter for her, as if she was very young. What are the chances these two girls found each other and actively hate one another? It's a disaster. Now it makes sense why he always leaves the bookshop around 4 p.m. every day. All those signs I didn't see.

'*Bonsoir.*' Ziggy and Lucy arrive, each carrying a huge posy of flowers. Trailing behind them is Nikolina holding a bunch of magazines to her chest.

'Isidore is in Lyon, so she won't make it but has sent a gift basket,' I say. 'If we're not waiting on anyone else, we may as well go in?'

'Wait,' Lucy says. 'What about Henri?'

Just as I'm about to make an excuse for his absence, he arrives, ignoring me as he kisses everyone else hello. How rude.

'What about a kiss for Coco?' Ziggy asks, grinning. 'Don't tell me you two have had a lovers' tiff already!'

'What do you mean, lovers' tiff?' Henri asks.

'Sparks were flying at the last book club, we've all been talking about it. Valérie is planning a literary-themed wedding, did you know?'

Mon Dieu. 'Well, we better get in there. I can't stay too long as I have to get back to my daughter.' I give Henri a long look. 'She's not doing too well after being bullied relentlessly at her new school.'

'Or perhaps your daughter is the bully?' Henri fires back.

'That is laughable.'

'Yet no one is laughing.' He catches my elbow. 'Please, Coco. Ask her to tell you the truth.'

'Are you aware your daughter chopped off Eloise's hair, after calling her Rapunzel and repeatedly telling her she should cut her hair short to meet the current style?'

'It was an accident.'

'How? Make that make sense.'

'We're not going to agree, so it's best we keep our distance.'

'Well, I agree on that at least. Eloise is everything to me and her happiness comes before everything else.'

'But she's not happy, is she?'

'That's none of your business.'

He puts his hands up in surrender and I now see where Léa gets her acting skills from.

* * *

Agnes's skin is grey under the harsh hospital lighting but her eyes light up when she sees us at the door.

I'm a little taken aback when Ziggy rushes forward and throws herself on Agnes, crushing the bouquet of flowers between them. 'I've been so worried about you.'

Agnes pats the top of her prone head. 'I'm fine, Ziggy, nothing a few days' rest can't fix.'

'We have gifts!' She produces the squashed posy. 'They'll bounce back in some water.'

'Thank you. You didn't have to...'

'I'll find a couple of vases,' Lucy says, holding her bouquet up.

'They're beautiful, thank you.'

Henri hands Agnes a box of chocolates. A clearly terrible choice, considering what her doctors have said. I bite my tongue against mentioning it, knowing I'm still feeling rather sensitive around him and am probably being harsh.

Nikolina places a stack of gossip magazines on the table. 'Now, don't even start with me, Agnes. These were all I could find on short notice, and who doesn't like a bit of celebrity nonsense from time to time?'

Agnes lets out a chortle. 'I don't mind a bit of celebrity nonsense.'

'What?' Nikolina reels. 'But you always say...?'

'Forget what I always say. That Agnes died in the ambulance on the way here. She clutched her pearls and went towards the light. The reincarnated Agnes likes gossip mags and trashy TV and—'

'Spicy books?' says Ziggy hopefully.

'The spicier the better.'

'Ah, Agnes,' I say, feeling like someone has to be the voice of reason. 'Are you sure with your heart that you should be reading a racy book?' Although if my theory proves correct... 'You've been reading them all along, haven't you?'

A blush creeps up her cheeks. 'They're scintillating. I love them all. Hockey romance, reverse harem, billionaires, rock-stars, shifters, you name it, I'll devour it, only now I won't need to hide it any more.'

'But why did you feel you needed to hide it?' Lucy frowns.

'My husband has always been very prim and proper. He once caught me reading a Regency romance and asked me if I was losing my marbles; did I need to read something so base as that for cheap thrills. I know, I know, it's offensive, but his opinion always mattered so much to me. So I read in secret and took every opportunity to denigrate romances so I'd never be suspected of adoring them like I do. How did you know, Coco?'

I arch a brow. 'You knew the plot of so many of the latest bestsellers.'

I take a moment to hand her my gift. As she opens the card and reads, one lonely tear rolls down her cheek. 'How did you know?'

'I can spot a writer a mile away.'

She blusters, as if she's embarrassed. 'I'm not a writer. I've just been scribbling for a long time.'

'What is it?' Nikolina asks, pointing to the card.

'Coco has offered to read my manuscript and give it an edit whenever I'm ready. And how did you know about my novel being finished? Did I give it away, somehow?'

I laugh. 'I've been sworn to secrecy.'

'Ah, Valérie told you I'd finally written "The End" on my little project. Well, I won't hold it against her as I'd love your editorial input, Coco. I really would, but be warned it's probably a disaster.'

'What kind of story is it?' Lucy asks, perching on the foot of the bed.

'Cowboy romance. What else would it be?'

We all giggle along with the newly reincarnated Agnes and I can't help but feel these people came into my life for a very good reason. Even Henri, although he still won't meet my eye.

'I've got you to thank for this, Coco,' Agnes says.

'Me? Why?'

'When I first met you, you said something like, by embracing all kinds of stories you learn so much about others, and about yourself along the way. It's time I did that. Embrace every story, even my own.'

We spend an hour with Agnes before we're asked to leave as visiting hours come to a close. 'At the risk of being banned from book club, I snuck these in for you and now I'm glad I did.' Ziggy pulls a couple of books from her handbag and hands them to Agnes. 'Spicy books for our spice queen!'

I can only shake my head. Outside, the sky has darkened and the air cooled. We say our goodbyes and Henri leaves before I can ask for a quiet word.

34

A week later, the bookshop is busier than ever as the spring days grow warmer and the promise of summer creeps closer. I'm preparing for an impromptu book club catch up, as I've got some questions for the group. As I arrange the space, I find myself unable to look in the direction of Henri's empty chair, which has been vacant since our falling out over our daughters.

'Why don't you call him?' Valérie says. 'Talk it out.'

'I can't.'

Soon, the book club members arrive and I'm quickly swept away by the chatter. It's a more subdued group without Agnes and I miss her dominating presence, but she's still recuperating at home. Henri's absence is also remarked on. I brush it off, not wanting to get into it.

I direct the conversation back to *Un Baiser D'adieu.* 'Thanks for coming today. I had something to discuss.'

Ziggy sends me a questioning glance. 'But it's not Henri?'

The group waits in anticipation.

'No, it's not Henri, it's about the poetry book by Larivière.'

Ziggy runs a hand through her short tufts, now bright blue, and says, 'OK?'

'I read it again, sort of forensically this time. Looking for clues, locations, themes, things like that.'

'And?' Lucy asks.

'Do you remember the poem, "The River, oh the River"?'

There are murmurs of assent. 'If you go upstairs, everything you can see outside that window is mentioned in that poem and there are a lot of references to this exact area.'

'Well, the river is long, Coco. You can see it from many vantage points.'

I swallow a frustrated sigh. 'It's more obvious than that. There's a line about *Le Petit Prince*, which I always thought jarred a bit, but if you go upstairs and look out the window and straight down, on the side of a building are the words faded but still visible: *Le Petit Prince*. Now, that can't be a coincidence?'

'I don't know,' Lucy says. 'Isn't it best left a secret?'

Isidore shakes her head. 'Secrets only stay buried so long. That's the way it is.'

'Has anyone heard from Agnes?' Ziggy asks.

Why are they so disinterested? I let it drop for now. The bigger question is why am I on a witch hunt for this author? It just feels close, like there's a mystery to be solved, but not even the so-called obsessive fan girl Ziggy is interested. I've never been so moved by a book of poetry before, and I can't seem to let it go. There are a lot of mother and daughter references so perhaps that's why I'm so stuck on it, because it feels like Eloise and I are so fractured right now.

'I saw Agnes yesterday,' I say. 'I took her a bunch of books. She's looking much better.'

'Is she staying with her husband then?' Lucy asks.

'Looks that way.'

We all fall quiet.

35

Maman calls me into her bedroom when I get home and shuts the door quietly. 'What's up?'

'There's something you should know.'

I pinch the bridge of my nose. I cannot take any more bad news. 'Are you OK? Dad?'

She waves me away. 'It's Eloise. I got to school late to pick her up because I got held up at the *fromagerie*, you know how Oliver chats, but anyway, when I did finally get there, Eloise was by the gates with a group of kids who were all hurling insults at Léa.'

'Oh? Eloise has found some new friends?'

Maman's top lip vanishes as she bites down. 'Time to take your blinkers off, Coco. All of those children, including Eloise, were being horrible to that poor girl. I hate to say this, Coco, but from what I could hear, Eloise was the instigator.'

'Probably because—'

'Stop.' Maman takes my shoulder and says in a firm voice, 'The time for excuses is over. None of us believe Eloise is capable of the acts she's been accused of, but I saw with my very eyes and heard such awful taunts coming from her. We need to have a chat with her right now.'

My breath leaves me in a whoosh. Could I have got this so wrong? Is my daughter the bully? Has she been the bully all along? I think back to the meeting, the cowed, timid posture of Léa, compared to Eloise's gritty, petulant mood.

I cup my face. And Henri. I've accused his child and shrugged off the fact that Eloise slapped her. Did she slap her? Eloise hasn't admitted it, but what if she did?

My shoulders slump as I go to the bedroom. 'Eloise. Kitchen. Now.'

She takes her merry time and slides onto the chair, a look of abject boredom on her face. 'What?'

'I'll sit here all night if we have to, but I'd like you to tell me the truth about Léa. Starting from our conversation where you told me they called you cheugy, and bullied you about your hair and your clothes and the apartment you live in.'

Her gaze slides to Maman, as if knowing she ratted her out.

'Tell me now, and I want the truth this time.' I'm fizzing with anger but I keep it in check. This is my daughter, and if she did do these things there must be a valid reason. I hope there is.

Eloise heaves a sigh as if this is beneath her. 'Léa did say all those things about my hair. She'd call me Rapunzel but it in a sweet way. Her two best friends are the ones who told me I should cut it into a more modern style and made jokes about me.'

I'm blindsided. She *lied* to me about all of it; even that day when I thought she'd taken me into her confidence, that was all a lie? 'So why go to this extreme?'

She drops her head. 'I don't know. I was mad. Léa is always so happy, so friendly. The other two girls talk about how she lives in this big apartment by the Eiffel Tower. Like she's got literally *everything*. And every day she'd come to school with, like, new shoes, a bag, the latest iPhone.'

'This is all done over jealousy?' I'm so disappointed in her I can barely breathe.

Eloise glares. 'Her life is *so* easy. And mine isn't.'

I scrub my face. 'Did you slap her?'

At this, her resolve crumbles and when she regains some control she says, 'I did. And I did it outside where I knew there were no cameras.'

My heart plummets. 'Eloise. *My God.*' My stomach roils at the knowledge that she's made this child's life hell for absolutely no reason. And I was none the wiser. Henri's child. If I were him, this would be unforgiveable.

'Léa cut my hair on purpose. She did! I *think*.'

'You *think?*'

'I spun around and my ponytail flicked out as she went to cut a piece of cardboard for our art project but I'm sure it was done on purpose! The timing of it...'

Now the trust is gone, I don't know what to believe. 'Why would she do that? You even said she's been sweet as pie the whole time, and it wasn't her teasing you or doing anything of the things you accused her of?'

'Because I told her you were dating her dad,' she stammers, flustered.

'You *knew* he was her dad?'

She pulls her *duh* face. 'He's all over her Insta.'

'But I wasn't dating him when she cut your hair. I'm *not* dating him.' What I don't say is there's no chance now. Not after this.

'Yeah, I know that, but I wanted to make her mad and I thought telling her he was dating you would upset her. It didn't!

But it also came out that she'd lied about her *maman* being dead. Who *does* that?'

'What do you mean?'

'She told everyone her *maman died* when really she ran off. Everyone found out recently when there were paparazzi shots of her *maman* online with her new reality TV boyfriend. Don't you think that's *awful* of Léa to lie like that?'

I close my eyes against the nightmare of this situation. I feel like I don't even know my own daughter, and how can that be? 'Eloise, have you no compassion? So what if she lied about her *maman*? Maybe that's the only way she knew how to deal with the hurt? And to have everyone at school turn on her. It beggars belief.' That poor child.

'So you're on her side?'

My heart bongoes painfully against my chest. 'What's gotten into you? I've never seen this side that is needlessly cruel. I'm *so* disappointed, I really am.'

Even my *maman*, who's been quiet up to this point, shakes her head.

'She didn't cut your hair on purpose, did she?'

My daughter shakes her head. 'No. It really was an accident.'

'And the other two girls have been rude to you but Léa hasn't?'

She takes a shuddery breath. 'Uh – not exactly. I've been rude to them. *I'm* the problem.'

Lies upon lies. I'm shocked to my core.

Eloise bursts into messy tears. 'I felt so alone without Harriet and Daisy. I figured if I messed up royally here that you'd be forced to take me back to London…'

She lets out a wail that makes my heart seize up. There are no winners in this situation, least of all Henri and Léa.

'I've ruined everything and I feel awful. Léa is a really nice person and I treated her so badly. I can't even explain it. I just didn't feel like me here and I wanted to go home so bad.'

I think back to Eloise telling the principal I couldn't take phone calls at work. Another lie so she wouldn't be found out. The more I put it all together the more obvious it gets. Blind faith and an abundance of love for my daughter stopped me from seeing it.

'Perhaps it's time to get Henri and Léa over here?' Maman suggests.

I nod. 'I'll try.'

* * *

A couple of hours later, Henri and Léa arrive and Maman ushers them in, asking if they want coffee, apple juice, or wine. She's covering all bases.

'Do you want a glass of wine, Léa?' he says, and I melt a bit because we make the same joke with Eloise.

When he comes face to face me with me, the smile fades. 'Hey.' He nods.

'Hi,' Léa says. I can't even look at her without remorse knocking me sideways.

We sit around my parents' kitchen table. I clear my throat. 'Thank you both for coming here this evening. We appreciate it considering the way things were left. I had a long and *honest* chat with Eloise this afternoon and now I realise we're the ones who have a lot of apologising to do. From me personally, I'm so sorry, Léa...'

We spend the next hour discussing everything and resolve it all as much as it can be resolved when so much has happened. Eloise promises that it's all in the past and Léa is happy enough to give her a second chance, which I find noble of her. Henri remains aloof, but I get it. I would be too if the tables were turned. After they leave, I sit with Eloise for a while. Her eyes are red and puffy from crying, but she is truly remorseful. 'That was so hard.'

'It was,' I agree.

36

I wake with a start, still reeling from the evening before, trying to reconcile my daughter as the bully.

Once I'm ready for work, I wake Eloise.

'I made you breakfast.'

'*Merci.*'

She eats ravenously, and when she's done, I sit opposite her, ready for one last chat on the matter. 'What's your plan going into school today?'

'I'm going to tell the principal everything, like we discussed.'

'Are you sure? I can call her and explain if you'd prefer.' As much as Eloise needs to face the consequences, last night took its toll on her and I'm mindful of her mental health too. She made a mistake, and she's owned up to it.

'I'm sure. And I'm going to ask Léa if she wants to be friends again, but I'll understand if she doesn't want to.'

I suck in a breath. 'OK, if you think that's best. She said she was happy to give it a second chance, but the friendship part of things might take a little longer.' Henri didn't seem very forgiving last night, and rightly so. But Eloise does seem genuinely remorseful to me, and almost relieved that the truth has come to light.

'I know, I can be patient.'

'OK, I'm proud of you for trying to make it right.'

'I'm not going to sit with those other kids, the ones Mémère saw me with at the gates. I'm not blaming them, but I acted differently around them. Trying to fit in, trying to be someone I'm not.'

'It's great that you recognise that. Who will you sit with at lunch then?'

She smiles. 'Music nerds? Myself? I'm really sorry, Mum. I'm so embarrassed by what I did. And I've ruined your chance with the Jude Law guy.'

'You forgot the old part.'

'It's the new me, trying not to be so nasty all the time.'

'Well, don't go changing too much, I love you as you are. This is a hard lesson you've had to learn, but I feel like you and I can let it go now. I trust you'll make better choices in future.'

With a solemn nod she says, 'I promise I will.'

'Also, I had an idea. On the school holidays, Mémère has offered to take you for a long weekend to London to visit Harriet and Daisy. That should give you something to look forward to.'

Her face lights up. 'Really? What about your whole thing about not rewarding bad behaviour?'

I wave her away. 'I put those parenting books in the bargain bin at the bookshop. All I want is for you to be happy. And if seeing Harriet and Daisy every so often helps, then I'm all for it.'

'You're the best.'

I feign shock. 'Wow, can you write that down so I can wave it at you when you're reminding me I'm the worst?'

'I've been such a brat.'

I move around the table to kiss the top of her head. 'Yes, but you're my brat. Be strong today and don't expect miracles. Grandad is walking you to school.'

She stands and give me a hug. 'OK.'

When I get to the bookshop, Valérie is distracted. She barely looks up when I come in.

'Bonjour.'

'Coco.'

'*Oui?*'

'Nothing, nothing.'

She doesn't offer coffee as usual and it's obvious her mind is elsewhere. I stash my handbag in the cupboard and get to work. The new writers' group is meeting this afternoon. I want to check upstairs is clean and ready for them. They're running the group themselves and have paid to hire the space, so it's another small stream of income and hopefully one we can build on by possibly hiring the space to other community groups.

'Yell out if you need me, I'm just going to clean the book loft.'

Valérie wipes down the already pristine surface of the bar, almost as though she's in a trance, going up and down and back again. 'Just leave it, Coco. That area is better left shut off from the public.'

I frown. 'We've got the writers' group coming today though, remember?'

'Do they have to use that space?' She sighs. 'I'd rather they didn't.' This is the first I've heard of this.

'Oh, why's that? Customers love the book loft and it's a lot quieter up there for a writing group, don't you think?'

She exhales a frustrated breath. 'I really don't care how

quiet it is. What *I* want is for that space to be closed to customers. Now, I don't want to talk about this again.'

I double blink, taken aback by the abruptness in Valérie's voice. 'Why didn't you mention that to me before when I asked if they could hire the space? I've already told them all about it.'

'*Coco.*'

'I'm curious what prompted the about-face, that's all? The book loft is such a great space. I've come up with a lot of ideas of how we can use it to make more income. I don't want to overstep, but I do worry that the bookshop isn't making a profit. And I'm sure you've got plenty of overheads that you—'

'*Coco,*' she says my name so sharply it throws me for a loop. 'Why won't you let it go? Who cares if the bookshop isn't making a profit? Who cares about money? I don't care about any of it.' Her voice rises with every inflection. She tosses the cloth to the floor. 'None of *this* is working! The potions, the passages, the TikToks lauding her; none of it's any good. It hasn't worked.'

The TikToks lauding who? What hasn't worked? I'm not brave enough to ask as tears form in Valérie's eyes. I've never seen her behave in such a way, like she's snapped. I'm frozen to the spot, unsure of what to do, how to react.

'There's a hole in my heart and nothing can fix it!' She deflates, all at once, as if the fight leaves her as quickly as it came. When she next speaks, her voice is laced with bitterness. 'For a while, I believed this place truly was the remedy, but it's not.'

I scramble to piece this together, still unsure of what to say.

Valérie comes around the bar and sits heavily on a stool. 'You're so like her, Coco, do you know that?'

I take the stool next to her. 'Like who?'

'Madeline, my daughter.'

Bibliothèque Madeline. Upstairs is her daughter's space and that's why she doesn't want strangers encroaching. This is connected to wherever Valérie disappears to most days, I'm certain of it. When she returns from wherever she goes, she's always less sunny, less like herself. 'The first day you walked in here, my heart stopped. I thought you were her. You are *so* alike. When I realised you weren't her, it still felt auspicious, some-how, like a visit from her. A reminder that she's still all around.' I recall that first meeting, when Valérie put a hand to her heart as she stared at me, and pain flashed across her face. Now I understand why.

'What happened to Madeline?'

Valérie takes a moment before she says, 'She died of cancer at twenty-seven. Young, far too young. We'd only just moved to Paris when she was diagnosed.'

'I'm so sorry, Valérie.'

She exhales a wobbly breath. 'So am I. She had so much to live for. So much to still do. Her dream was to get published.'

Ooh! 'Madeline's the poet? I knew those poems were connected to the view upstairs.'

Valérie smiles. 'She's the famous poet, posthumously at any rate. A literary genius. But this wasn't quite a bookshop then. We hadn't got that far yet. And then the bad news came, and all she wanted to do was finish her book, and that's what she did. While she penned her poems upstairs, I got the bookshop set up, but I didn't open it. I didn't want to waste any precious time she had left. It was just something to do while she napped. She died before she could submit her book to publishers in the hopes of getting a deal.'

My heart. What cruel fate that she never got to experience getting a book deal and then the huge success it's gone on to have. 'You got the book published for her?'

Valérie nods. 'And it took off. Became a hit with Gen Z on TikTok, of all things. No one could have predicted that, least of all me. I didn't even know what TikTok was, but I had to learn fast. I wanted to soak up every word they wrote about my beautiful daughter, wanted their praise to wash over me, hoping it would almost bring her back to life. But it didn't.'

'And why do the book club keep it a secret? I'm guessing from the sketchy way they all acted that they know your daughter wrote it.'

Valérie considers it. 'They all figured it out early on but understand that I won't discuss it. I don't tell anyone it's my daughter's book of poems, probably for self-preservation. Its success is a testament to her, but the poems are deeply personal so it's probably best it's not connected to me.' The abusive husband? In the poem they ran when they felt it was safe to go.

'In case he finds you?' I say gently. 'Just like the poem about fleeing violence in the family home? I'm guessing the poems were all autobiographical?'

'*Oui.* He still might find me. But there's nothing he could do to hurt me now. The very worst thing has already happened.'

It's so sad to contemplate that they were finally free of that dark past and then cancer stole Madeline away.

'After Madeline died, I opened the bookshop. I needed something tangible to keep me here. Soon it became a refuge for others just like me. I recognised the magic right away and figured it would be up to me to cure the broken hearted among us, and surely my own heart would heal. I made the bookshop a welcoming place where they could sink their sorrows with a potion and passage. Find comfort in a good book, which is one way to outrun grief for a while. But it's all a sham. I see that now.'

'You've helped so many people, Valérie. It's not a sham. You didn't do it for any other reason than wanting to help heal those who hurt just as much as you. And it hasn't been in vain.'

A tear runs down her cheek. 'I'm not sure about that, Coco. I figured the broken parts of me would one day heal over even though the scars would remain, but if anything, it actually gets worse. The success of Madeline's book makes me want to howl. Why couldn't it have been *me* who died?'

I give her a hug. As a mother I'd feel exactly the same way. There's no adequate response because it's not fair. No parent should lose their child. 'You know, someone once told me: "Grief is love that has nowhere to go". And that rings true. You directed all your love towards your daughter and then when she passed, instead of letting that consume you, you poured that love for Madeline into The Paris Bookshop for the Broken Hearted. That's why this place is so special that even a sceptic like me starts to believe, and that is really saying a lot.'

She gives me a rueful smile. 'You really were my toughest challenge, Coco.'

I laugh. 'I'm a facts person, or at least I was. This place has changed me for the better. I've learned to let go, not put such pressure on myself, and I can't help but think you *and* Madeline had a hand in it. You with your support and Madeline with her poetry.' Now I choke up a bit, which I really hate doing in public. 'Without you, Valérie, so many of us would have given up, on dreams, on love, on what comes next. You're the reason the magic works here. Bad days like today will come, but that's the cost of love, right?'

She takes a tissue from a box behind the bar. 'It's the third anniversary of Madeline's passing and it felt like the first day all over again.'

'Oh, Valérie, no wonder all this has come to the fore. Anniversaries such as these are so hard. Give yourself some grace, just as you freely give all your customers suffering in the same way.'

'You're right, I should. I don't know why I sit with sadness and let it consume me.'

'It's OK to sit with the sadness from time to time. Is there a place you go to do that?'

'*Oui.* Every day I go to the same crowded place and close my eyes and only see her. I'll take you there now. It's a happy place so I'm hoping that happiness eventually rubs off on me.'

We lock up the bookshop and put the "Back Soon" sign on the door. We walk in the direction of the River Seine and come to a stop at the square in front of the Notre Dame cathedral. Even though it's early morning, it's already bustling with people. 'Here it is.' She points to the ground where there's a sunken plaque with a brass insert shaped like a star that says 'Point Zero'. It's littered with coins.

'I was not expecting that.' I presumed we'd go inside a beautiful church and find a special pew or sit on a bench in a flower-filled garden.

'It's a wishing spot for some, and a wishing well for others. Paris is famous for them.'

'Really?' In light of Valérie's upset, I try my best to hide my doubt about such a thing. 'How are they different?'

'Oh, Coco! If you want to find true love, you spin on the brass star three times and make a wish. You use the wishing well if you want to wish for anything else. You close your eyes and throw some coins on there while you make your wish.'

'Sorry, sorry, it's just... a wishing well? As far as I know, Point Zero is the exact centre of Paris that all distances are measured from.' But I hastily add, 'I'm willing to suspend my disbelief for you.'

Valérie laughs. 'You know, Madeline didn't believe it at first either. In fact, when I'd throw my coins on there and make a wish, she'd hide behind her hands and tell me she was mortified. But it became our thing. After she was diagnosed, I snuck here every single day to wish on it, hoping against hope it would save her.'

Here come the tears again. I'm picturing Valérie trying everything in her toolbox to save her daughter, including using a wishing spot. I'd have done the same even though I'm not a real believer. You never know.

'A week or so before the end, she asked to come here. She was in a wheelchair then. She closed her eyes for the longest time before she threw the coins down.'

'What did she wish for?'

Valérie shakes her head. 'You can't share your wishes or they won't come true.'

'I'm sure her last wish was that you'd find peace.'

'How do you know?'

'Because I'm a daughter too.'

Valérie's musters up a smile. '*Merci*, Coco. So...?'

'So?'

She motions with her head to the plaque.

'You're not serious?'

'I am so.'

I can't exactly say no since this is her special spot. 'Do you have any coins?'

She frowns. 'Coins? Get on there and spin three times and wish for true love.'

'Everyone will see.'

'Then do it fast.'

There's no point arguing with her, it's only going to delay my mortification. Spinning on a circle to wish for love, indeed!

Still, I do as ordered and I picture Henri's smiling face, just for kicks. Not because I believe there's anything in it.

'Now let's see if that changes anything between you and Henri.'

'I don't think so somehow.' I don't bother telling her about Eloise and Léa. It's not the right time to be mentioning daughters, especially badly behaved ones like mine.

Valérie closes her eyes and throws some coins down. Soon we're surrounded by tourists who ask what the significance of the circle is and what we're doing. Valérie regales them with all the folklore about Point Zero, including that if you stand on it with your significant other and kiss, it means your relationship will last forever. Tourists also use it to say au revoir to Paris, and it's believed if you stand on the plaque at the end of your trip and say a word of thanks, it means you'll return to Paris again one day. Their faces light up and there's much jostling for space on Point Zero. We leave them to it.

'I see why you go there, Valérie. It is a happy place, a place to make a wish and most of all have hope.'

'Exactly. *Have hope.* I love sharing Point Zero with people, but afterwards that sadness catches me once more, but that's OK. It's my love for my daughter, and it's bound to hurt.'

We slowly walk back to the bookshop. I loop my arm around her elbow as Valérie tells me more about Madeline, as if her earlier heartache has lightened a little. That's the thing with grief – you can't outrun it. The pain of a broken heart demands to be felt. And while the eccentric bookseller has been busy helping others heal, she's put her own hurt on the backburner, or else she's tried to outpace it, but it's not something you can outrun.

Has anyone sprinkled the potion and passage magic dust

over Valérie? Maybe what she's missing is a bit of her own medicine?

Back at the bookshop, I get on the book club group chat and call an impromptu meeting, giving them scant details except it's the third anniversary of Madeline's passing and I've got an idea. They quiz me on how I found out about Madeline and I tell them what unfolded. I love how they've all kept Valérie's past secret and tried to protect her. Everyone agrees to meet at the bookshop at the close of business.

I rope off the stairs that lead to Library Madeline. Valérie apologised for her outburst and told me to ignore her protests about the space, that it should be used and enjoyed. But I'm not too sure. Now that I know the full story, it feels sacrosanct, special. It's where Madeline sat and wrote her book as illness ravaged her body. It's where she slept and dreamed. The books are her own private collection.

As always, the day races away as I serve customers, organise an area downstairs for the writers' group and unpack boxes of stock. Valérie is behind the bar regaling customers with a potion and passage. I strain to hear the passage she's sharing with an elderly man with a small yappy dog: 'Sadness flies away on the wings of time – Jean de la Fontaine.'

It occurs to me that every wish made over a potion, every passage she's uttered, has been done in an effort to heal her grief too. A golden thread to mend her broken heart.

* * *

The book club members meet by Henri's chair, although Henri himself doesn't appear. Valérie glances over to us with a frown, probably wondering about all these impromptu meetings.

'Agnes!' I'm delighted to see her up on her feet again, complexion rosy.

'Don't make a big deal of it, Coco. I'm about ready to self-combust with hunger. The cardiologist has me on the most ridiculous diet. I'm sure he's not French. No Frenchman would suggest avoiding duck fat roasted potatoes.'

'I see your point, but you are looking great.'

'I know, I know.'

I shake my head. Ziggy and Lucy arrive. They're excited to see Agnes too. Nikolina is next, and sauntering behind her is Henri. I take a deep breath and will myself to remain professional. It's not like I'm going to argue with the man, since we were in the wrong and all, but it's just the ever-present awkwardness that goes with seeing him. We kissed! It's an intimacy and now I have to pretend all is fine and dandy. Isidore saves the day by tripping over the leg of a chair, taking the attention away from me.

Once everyone finishes catching up, I motion for them to come closer while I tell them my plan.

'Ooh.' Lucy's eyes go wide. 'That is so beautiful.'

'Do you think it will work?' Ziggy asks. 'We might not have the power she does.'

'We've got love in our hearts,' Agnes says. 'I think that's the most important element.'

Henri nods. 'Let's give it a shot. What's the worst that can happen?' We share a tentative smile.

Isidore agrees and says, 'Why didn't we think of this sooner?'

We chat about how to go about it and then make our way to the bar. I duck behind Valérie and I'm soon opening and closing cupboards finding what I need while the book club sit at the bar, big awkward smiles on their faces. Their acting skills are woeful.

'Is there any reason you're all sitting there like lame ducks staring at me?' Valérie asks.

'*Non*,' comes the reply. They're supposed to be distracting her so I can make the potion even though I'm not quite sure how she gets them to bubble like she does.

'What are you doing, Coco?'

'Can you please leave us for a moment, Valérie?' My tone brooks no argument.

'Come and sit with me for a minute,' Agnes says. 'I have a lot to tell you later so I hope you've got a nice chilled bottle of chardonnay with my name on it.'

'No wine. Doctor's orders,' Ziggy warns. It's sweet how protective Ziggy has become over Agnes.

'He can't take away everything.'

Valérie pats her hand. 'A small glass is medicinal.'

Ziggy shakes her head. While they're bickering about what Agnes can and can't have, I find what I need and manage to assemble it all.

I turn to the group and nod.

'Can we offer you a potion and a passage?' Lucy says to Valérie.

'Me?'

'You,' Lucy confirms. 'Coco came up with the idea that perhaps our fearless mender of hearts was in need of a little boost herself. While we might not have your magic fingers, what we do have is a whole lot of love for you and what you've achieved here. We're all better for having known you, Valérie.'

'Because of you, I'm going to Australia next week,' Ziggy says, and we all gasp. 'For a holiday! Don't worry, it's just for a few weeks.

The thing is, while I might come across as very confident what with all my famous author friends and all, in reality that's a bit of a front. They're not really my friends, those authors. And now I've found a guy I like and who knows what the future holds? It's much better than an online love, that's for sure. So *merci*, Valérie.'

'Actually, you have Coco to thank for that.' Valérie explains the story about when the Australian guy popped into the bookshop and asked me for a book "Tolstoy but make it fun".

'You knew?' Ziggy asks.

'I didn't know he meant you at the time.'

Ziggy slaps a hand over her mouth. 'She has the magic, just like Valérie!'

'No, I don't!'

We go down the line, expressing our thanks to Valérie for making us believe, for giving us hope. For picking up the pieces and helping put us back together.

When we've all said our piece, I say, 'Your bespoke cocktail, and your very own passage.'

She takes a sip of the bubbling drink. 'It tastes like sunshine! *Equis*.' And then she unwraps the scroll.

'Read it out loud,' Agnes says.

'A wound is a place where light enters your soul. Rumi.' When Valérie looks up, her eyes are glassy with tears. She lifts up her potion full of sunshiny flavours and bright light. 'Here's to letting the light back in.'

Valérie gives me a soft smile that conveys more than words ever could.

37

'Hi, DS Phillip, it's Coco.'

'Coco, how are you? Sick of French food yet?'

'Is that even possible?'

He cackles. 'I'm a meat and three veg man, so that would be an affirmative. Now listen, I know you've been hesitant to go down the civil suit road with Alexander.'

'That's it for small talk?' I can't help but tease. DS Phillip is a man of few words unless it's about policing matters or complaints about the state of the publishing industry.

'Don't make me ask about the weather.'

'Fine, I won't. Anyway, you were saying?'

'I felt so bad about what happened to you, we all did, but we were obligated by our legal team to follow their direction...'

'I understand. No hard feelings.'

'Well there are some hard feelings, directed towards the man of the hour, Alexander. It didn't sit well with us when all those articles came out about how he gives the less fortunate a leg up in the literary space, when we know he does no such thing.'

'Right.'

'I took it upon myself to call in a few favours, have a bit of a poke around in his past. Not illegal, I'll have you know.'

'I know you'd never break the law, Phillip.' God forbid.

'Good, good. Anyway, I managed to uncover a few things about our pal, Alexander, namely that this kind of theft isn't new to him. In fact, he's been caught twice before. Once he settled out of court and the second time the charges were dropped due to insufficient evidence, and then there's the third time with London Field Publishing. A mate of mine, an investigative reporter, got wind of it and wants to do an exposé on him. I told him to hold off, because if he does that it might affect your civil case, if all the information is shared to the public domain.'

'Hmm.' I consider it. Why does Alexander get to do this several times and get away with it? 'I've already been told by my lawyer that the costs to recoup my investment will outweigh the amount I'll get back, so I don't think there will be a civil case.'

'Figured as much.'

'Unless he settles with me out of court, like he did before.' Then I'd get at least some funds back. 'But the thing is, DC Phillip, if I did settle out of court then his misdeeds are hidden from the industry again, from his next victim and I don't like that one little bit.'

Do I want there to be an exposé on Alexander? It would be an efficient way to prove that I was not involved for those who still don't believe in me. And it would be just. I don't need my investment back as much I need him to be exposed for what he is. A thief.

Choice made, I say, 'If the investigative reporter wants to do a story, who am I to stop him?'

'It'll be big, Coco. He's top of his game.' He shares the name of the reporter and I'm suitably impressed.

'I'd quite like my reputation restored so I can get back to editing one of these days.'

'Say no more. And if you're planning on starting up your own thing, let me know. I'd love to work with you again. My new editor is great, but she doesn't seem to care about the state the publishing industry is in, no matter how many times I tell her.'

I laugh fondly over his penchant for just that very thing. 'Watch this space.'

* * *

That evening, Eloise and I walk along the Boulevard Montparnasse in search of ice cream. 'How did today go?'

'Well, it wasn't the most fun I ever had but that's to be expected. They were all fair, I suppose. The principal went over the bullying policy in great detail just so it sinks in this time.'

'And Léa?'

'She was really sweet. She said her dad has been happier since you came along, but now after all this he's sad again. Is that true?'

I'm surprised by that. 'He's been happier?'

'Yeah. She said he's finally been able to write again after struggling with it for so long. He's changed the type of articles he writes, and apparently now they're satirical, whatever that means.'

'Huh.'

'And she even said that at home, he'd changed. Became more of a fun dad again. He'd been a bit, like, down after the divorce and all.'

'You talked about a lot with Léa. Quite personal stuff.'

She lifts a shoulder. 'We are trying to figure out how to fix it. *I'm* trying, I guess, because I don't want to be the one responsible for you remaining a spinster.'

'Gee, thanks.'

'What?' she says innocently.

'It's fine, don't worry about my... spinsterhood.' I still feel a pang when I think of Henri and what might have been, and while it's been cordial, it hasn't gone back to the way it was. It might never go back to that. 'Right now, I'm more concerned about finding us the perfect abode.'

'We're ready to start looking?'

I nod. 'We are.'

She shrieks, high and loud. 'Can we stay close to Mémère and Grandad though? They'll be so sad when we move out.'

'Of course. We'll stay as close as we can, if funds allow.' I've done some research already and if we're prepared to overlook an older style apartment, we'll be able to stay in the same arrondissement.

38

'Coco, could we borrow you for a minute?' Jaques from the writing group asks. I dust my hands on my jeans after moving a stack of books that never seem to get any attention because they're stuffed into a dark corner of the bookshop. I'm rotating stock as much as I can to give each book a chance to find a new home. It's working well so far, unearthing all these gems that have remained hidden for so long.

'Sure, what's up?' I follow him upstairs to the writing group, which Valérie insisted we continue to use as her daughter would have been tickled to know people were enjoying her space, especially other aspiring writers.

The group sit around a long table, notebooks and laptops in front.

'We've been chatting about next stages. A few of us have finished manuscripts that we'd love a trained eye to go over for us, give some editorial feedback and the like. Valérie told us you recently owned a boutique publishing house where you were editorial director, so we wondered if you might consider our proposal...'

Valérie!

'What proposal is that?'

'We were hoping you'd be amenable to reading our work for a fee and helping us on the path to publication.'

'That's really lovely of you to consider me but...' Before I think of all the systems I *don't* have in place, I stop myself. Isn't this actually perfect? Editorial projects I can do when I'm not working in the bookshop? 'I would love to. Let's discuss.'

After we've chatted about the details and what they should expect, I go downstairs with a spring in my step. Freelancing, could that be a way to keep my hand in without the pressure of running a business? And so I can continue to work in the bookshop, whose future I have big plans for, including hosting an upcoming summer series of author events.

At the bottom of the stairs, I slip and fall into the back of a man. 'Ooof!'

It's Henri. *Of course.*

'Throwing yourself at me again, Coco?'

I shake my head. 'Can you blame me? How else am I supposed to get your attention? We've missed you around here.'

'Really?'

'Really.'

'I've been writing.'

'So I hear. It's going well then?'

'Really well. Thanks to you.'

'Well, it's easy to give advice when you don't have to follow it yourself.'

'You always shrug these compliments off, but I'm not the only one who's remarked on the way in which you've fixed certain situations.' *And made others worse*, but I bite down on that particular sentiment.

'I do appreciate the praise, trust me. And good news from

me too. I've just landed three manuscript appraisals from the writers upstairs.'

'Congratulations. So freelance it is?' While we're chatting amiably, it still doesn't feel right, like we're missing that spark we once shared, or that things are still a little delicate between us.

'Looks that way.'

'Will you stay at the bookshop?'

I grin. 'I'll stay as long as Valérie will have me.' And I mean it. The bookshop has some hold over me, magical or not. I don't overthink it, it just is. It's a book utopia and I enjoy every minute; well, almost. I don't especially like the dust, but there's not much I can do about that.

'You're going to need an office here then?'

I raise a brow. 'What, like you? We can sit side by side and share notes. That's if you're coming back?'

'You're not having my chair.'

'Wouldn't dream of it.'

'Then it's a possibility.'

'Lucky me.'

'Likewise.' I'm sure we're almost flirting but I don't read too much into it. If we're meant to be, the bookshop will work its charms or Valérie will drag us kicking and screaming down the aisle to our fantasy wedding; one or the other.

'See you at book club tomorrow then?'

'*Oui.*'

He leaves with a backwards wave. Maybe his absence hasn't been just because of me. Maybe a change of scene helped with his writer's block. I hope it's that at any rate.

I go to the bar to share my good news with Valérie but she's got that faraway look in her eyes that can only mean one thing. 'Don't even start.'

Agnes is propped up on a stool drinking a glass of water.

'It's fait accompli.'

'Uh-huh. How are you, Agnes?'

'I'm well, Coco. In fact, I'm better than I've been in quite some time. Would you like to know why?'

'I'd like nothing more.'

'See over there?' I turn to where she's pointing. By the ornate gold door are a few boxes and a suitcase.

'You left your husband?'

She grins. 'Should have done it years ago. Dullest man alive. I'm moving in with Valérie.'

'And just what mischief will you two get up to?'

'Plenty, I expect. If only this blasted doctor would agree.'

'Everything in moderation,' Valérie says.

'See? She's already a bad influence.'

They're going to be good for each other, roommates who need a friend in this new season of their lives.

'And my manuscript, Coco. No rush but did you manage to read it?'

'I did. I read it and I loved it. You have quite the gift for punchy dialogue. I'll send you my notes soon. And I'll give you some advice of publishers to try.'

She frowns. 'Can't you be my publisher?'

'Well, no, I...' What's stopping me from expanding into a petit publisher who only handles passion projects like Agnes's book? 'We can definitely look at that, if you're sure you don't want to try a bigger publisher first?'

'I'm sure. I trust you and I want you to handle it all. I'm not expecting worldwide fame, I'm just happy to have a hobby that'll keep me occupied. The rest is just icing on the top.'

39

'ORDER!'

Ziggy covers her ears. 'Coco, you're getting just as bad as Henri. I'm sure you've pierced my eardrum, and that's not going to be ideal on the long-haul flight to Australia tomorrow.'

'That's rather dramatic, don't you think?' Agnes shakes her head. 'Have you got your holiday reads sorted?'

'I've got a few but I need more. Send me your recs.'

Agnes rolls her eyes dramatically. 'Why must everything be done by a handheld device? We're sitting directly opposite you. Can we not just use our voices?'

'OK, OK, don't get worked up, Agnes. I don't want you having another heart attack on account of me.' Ziggy shakes her head. These two always amuse me. Love to hate each other, but really, they just enjoy the bantering.

'We're just waiting on Henri,' Lucy says, toying with her phone. 'He said he'd be here soon.'

I remind members about the drinks and nibbles while we wait. Out of the corner of my eye, I catch Valérie shooting quick glances my way. What's that about?

When she does it again, I spin to face her and raise my eyebrows. She yelps and ducks. I'm about to ask what she's playing at when Henri walks in with a bunch of flowers.

'Ooooh,' says Lucy. 'No guesses who they're for.'

'Me?' Agnes says hopefully.

Ziggy scrunches up her face. 'I mean, he can be a gentleman and all but I don't think they're for you somehow.'

'*Bonsoir*, Henri.' I give him a welcoming smile.

'*Bonsoir*, everyone. Sorry I'm late. Can I borrow Coco for a few minutes?'

Agnes slumps. 'They're for Coco, I should have known.'

'Sure, take your time,' Lucy says.

Henri takes me gently by the arm. Is this connected to Valérie ducking for cover? 'I had this idea and I hope it wasn't too presumptuous...'

'OK?' He stands in front of a door I've never seen before because there was a bookshelf in front of it. 'Where did the books go?' How did I not notice? Is that what Valérie's been doing while I've been setting up the book club?

'Ready?'

I nod.

He pushes open the door to reveal a light-filled room with a small desk and lamp. It's spic and span. 'What's this?'

'Your new office. Valérie and I thought you might like to work among the books but still have your own dedicated space.'

He hands me the flowers. 'To brighten up the room until you put your personal touch on it.'

I go to the desk and open the drawers. They're filled with stationery, everything I might need to get started in my new little freelance business. 'I stocked up for you. And I've arranged for an ergonomic chair, because you just look like an ergometric chair person to me.'

I laugh and turn to him, touched that he's done all of this for me. We stand close, our faces within kissing distance, and just as I go to lean in, the book club come barrelling in, demanding to know what the big secret is.

40

The next evening, I'm locking up the bookshop when I get a text from Eloise.

> Meet me at the Eiffel Tower?

What! What is she doing out on her own? When I call she doesn't pick up. Is she sneaking out now? Is my girl really sliding off the rails? I call Maman – no answer. Then Dad. Nothing.

Maybe they're out looking for her? I send them both a text asking what's going on. Luckily the Eiffel Tower isn't far from the bookshop so I hastily make my way there. I'm going to kill her for sneaking out. Or at least ground her until she's thirty.

The night is balmy as stars shimmer in the dark sky above. It's the most beautiful time of year in Paris where everything is blooming and the air is fragrant with promise. When I arrive, I step around clusters of people, unable to see my daughter anywhere. What if she gets targeted by pickpockets? Have I even made her aware of such a thing?

Bad mother parenting alert goes off in my brain while I search for her.

I do a loop and come face to face with Henri, who's wearing a tense expression too.

'Have you seen Léa?'

'Have you seen Eloise?'

'What?'

'What?'

I hold up a hand. 'Stop speaking at the same time as me.' If I wasn't so panicked it'd be laughable. 'Did Léa tell you to meet her here?'

'*Oui*? But she's not allowed out alone, especially at night. And she's not answering her phone.'

'Ah. They've set this up.'

He slaps his forehead. 'The little minxes.'

It doesn't take long for us to spot them, giggling into their hands, my parents standing behind them like sentries. We go to join them.

'Seriously?' I can't help asking.

'Sorry.' Dad drops his head. 'They wouldn't be swayed.'

'I had to make it right,' Eloise says.

'She did,' confirms Léa.

Eloise fidgets with the zip on her cardigan. 'I've been the *worst* kind of brat all because I missed my friends. I had this warped idea that if I made a mess of school in Paris then we'd have no choice but to return to London where I'd be reunited with Daisy and Harriet. What I didn't think about was the people I was hurting along the way. *All* of you. Léa has forgiven me but I know I still have a way to go to make things up to her and the other two girls, as well.'

Léa gives Eloise's hand a supportive squeeze. 'Losing someone you love is hard. That loss can make a person go a little crazy.' Léa and Henri exchange a sad look, as if they're sharing a memory of their past and what they lost, namely a wife and a mother. 'It's not easy being the one left behind.'

My heart aches for the girl as I realise her and Eloise have that same awful circumstance in common. A missing parent. Can the love of the remaining parent do the job of two? I have certainly tried to make up for that lack, and I'm sure Henri has.

'It's not easy,' Eloise says with a tentative smile. 'But I'm lucky that I have the best Mum in the world. She fights for me even when I don't deserve it. She's patient when I'm being moody and rude. And you told me you have the best Dad in the world.' Her voice cracks. 'I just hope *I* haven't ruined the rest of their lives,' she says, bowing her head.

'What do you mean?' I take her in my arms and give her a hug.

When she composes herself, she says, 'You and Henri. I hope I haven't ruined things between you. I'm not joking when I say I can see you at eighty chatting away with your Alexa device, all alone, wearing one of those long night gowns, muttering.'

What a vivid portrait she paints! I wouldn't be surprised if Henri bolts, knowing how in demand I am, so much so, that I'm destined to spend eternity with a *machine* as my companion.

'I'm worried about you being alone too,' Léa says to her dad. She faces me. 'Before you came along, Coco, he mostly stared off into space. He would nod and pretend to hear me, but he wasn't really listening. It was almost as if he was a shell and the real him disappeared along with my Maman. Things changed recently. He came home and talked about you, like, *a lot*. I had to give him some hard truths when he told me about the attempted pickpocketing under the Eiffel Tower. Victim blaming, *much*?' Henri has the grace to blush. 'Suddenly he's making us fancy dinners, wondering: *if Coco likes steak tartare.*'

'Ooh, it is gross,' Eloise says. 'It's *raw*.'

'It's an acquired taste,' Henri and I say in unison and share a smile. My parents look fondly at us, as if we're all the best of friends and not four people who have been through the wringer of late. But I suppose that's real life. The good and the bad. The ups and the downs. We each have golden threads that stitch up the damage. That allow us to step in to the light again.

'So,' Eloise asks us. 'Did I ruin your chance of a happy ever after?'

Henri shakes his head. 'No, you haven't ruined anything. In fact, I think it's a good lesson for all of us.'

'In what way?' Eloise asks.

'Not to hide the hurt.' He clasps my hand and looks deep into my eyes, and I sense a shift, in the earth, in my heart. 'For me, the future is bright with possibility.' He pauses, and I like that he doesn't speak for me. He doesn't presume to know how I feel.

'For me too.' I'm not sure if it's because the four of us have opened up about our vulnerabilities, but I get this flash, this premonition about the future. A little family of four. And I shoot a wish into the inky night that it will come true. Can we each be that missing part of the puzzle for one another? Only time will tell. Maybe I've read too many romances and watched too many Hallmark movies, but why *can't* that be us? Four souls made stronger with some golden seams and an abundance of hope.

I think back to when I first met Valérie and she imagined my future fantastical wedding including my pretty flower girls. She knew all along. And so in the spirit of letting go and enjoying the ride, I make the decision to be bold and brave and say what's in my heart.

'I'm not a believer in fate, the stars guiding us, the universe intervening, Cupid's arrow or any of that kind of thing. Well, I *wasn't*. Until this pesky man kept being thrown in my way. Perhaps, I needed the hand of a higher power so I paid attention to the signs. I know, I know, it sounds ridiculous. Whatever it is, I've made a promise to myself that I'm going to do what makes me happy. And you make me happy, Henri. Your driving abilities leave a lot to be desired, but hey, that's why we have the Metro. No one is perfect.'

'His driving is shocking,' Léa says. 'Wait until he takes you on his motorbike.'

My eyebrows shoot up. 'You don't have a motorbike, do you?'

'I have two.'

'OK, well.' I gulp. 'This has been fun…'

He laughs. 'I promise I'm a better rider than I am a driver.'

'How is such a thing possible?'

'Because he can't talk on the motorbike with the helmet on, so he actually does manage to keep his eyes on the road,' Lea says.

'As long as I never have to be a passenger.'

'Never,' he swears. 'I will never put you at risk, Coco. And, yes, maybe in some ways I'm still a dinosaur, like the way I behaved that day with the pickpockets, but that was purely some protective instinct rising to the fore. I'd been so distracted by you, the way you'd held your face up to the sun, as if the rays themselves were recharging you. You stood out, like this bright light, and I was mesmerised. How could you be full colour when the rest of the world was so grey? And then those dodgy men snuck up on you, and you remained oblivious. I was mad at them, not you. But you didn't seem to care about your safety, not one iota. And then you got mad at me. Belligerent, even.'

'You deserved it. You called me a *banane*.'

'I did. You're right. Part of me had already fallen madly in love with you and how could that be? I worried I was losing my mind.'

I don't dare tell him I felt the exact same way, was taken in by the *sultry curve of his lips,* for crying out loud.

'You'd already sailed into my arms at the train station. When we crossed paths at the bookshop, I felt like Valérie must have orchestrated it, somehow. So intent was she on fixing all the broken parts of me. But it was soon obvious she didn't have a hand it in, although she recognised the spark between us right away.'

'How *does* she sense these things?' I ask, almost to myself.

'Duh,' Eloise says. 'The way you two stare at each other makes it pretty obvious.'

'It does,' confirms Léa.

Valérie fully believes in the power of love and how it can move mountains. And she also knows how it can be snatched away. When I think of her daughter's poems about how they'd finally found their freedom only for her life to draw to an end, it sends a shot down my spine. We can't wait. Tomorrow is not promised. The only thing that matters is letting go and hoping love follows.

Henri grins. 'Was it that obvious to everyone?'

When my parents make a *duh* face and nod their heads the girls fall about laughing. Well, it looks like we're both terrible actors...

'On that note,' Maman says, glancing at a watch she doesn't wear. 'We should be off.'

Can it be over so soon? The night feels magical somehow,

like the air is pulsing with anticipation of what may happen next.

'We're happy to have Léa over for pizza if you'd like to enjoy the evening together so these scamps can leave you alone?' Dad says, trying but failing to hide a smile.

Henri slides his arm around me like it's the most natural thing in the world. 'In that case, I'd love to. Coco?'

'Sure.' We hug them goodbye and soon they're off, giggling and shrieking, with my parents following safely behind.

When it's just the two of us, I pull him close. 'I suppose we should be happy they're on board with this.' Just then, three hoodie-wearing guys slink past. 'Lucky you're here to save me again?'

He gives me a gracious smile. 'It's you who saved me.'

We pay the trio no mind as Henri takes me in his arms and leans down to kiss me. The Eiffel Tower glitters in the background while my heart expands and fills with a blossoming love for Henri. I'd never usually consider L word this early on, but something tells me this time it's different but it's a delicious secret I'll keep to myself for now.

I'm swept away by the feeling of coming home, of recognising my perfect match, even if that makes me sound like a heroine in a romance novel.

Our love story is just beginning, and we have so many chapters that are yet to be written...

* * *

MORE FROM REBECCA RAISIN

Another book from Rebecca Raisin, *Christmas at the Little Paris Hotel* is available to order now here:

www.mybook.to/ParisChristmasBackAd

ACKNOWLEDGEMENTS

A huge thank you to my readers! You really make these solitary writing days brighter with your support. I appreciate every one of you! I look forward to bringing you more books.

Big thanks go to my editor Isobel Akenhead who helped shape this book with so many great ideas. Coco, the heroine of this story is an editor, and so I hope I did the bond of writer and editor justice. Editors really are the unsung heroes of the writing world and I aimed to show the importance of that relationship in this book. It's a team effort, bringing a book into the world and editors have a big hand in making that magic happen. This goes for copy editors and proofreaders too, who also weave in their wisdom and become part of the fabric of each and every page. Thanks to Jennifer Davies for amazing copy edits. And Arbaiah Aird for your eagle eyed proofreading. You are a joy to work with.

Team Boldwood, what a ride! Thank you so much. We're only just starting and look how much fun we're having! Niamh Wallace, you are an absolute super star and also a genius. Thanks, as ever, to Nia Beynon and Amanda Ridout for your vision and enthusiasm. And to Wendy Neale who is already so fun to work with.

Thank you to all my editors past and present. I've loved working with you all and have learned so much along the way.

ABOUT THE AUTHOR

Rebecca Raisin writes heartwarming romance from her home in sunny Perth, Australia. Her heroines tend to be on the quirky side and her books are usually set in exotic locations so her readers can armchair travel any day of the week. The only downfall about writing about gorgeous heroes who have brains as well as brawn, is falling in love with them–just as well they're fictional. Rebecca aims to write characters you can see yourself being friends with, people with big hearts who care about relationships and believe in true, once-in-a-life time love.

Sign up to Rebecca Raisin's mailing list for news, competitions and updates on future books.

Follow Rebecca on social media here:

facebook.com/RebeccaRaisinAuthor

x.com/jaxandwillsmum

instagram.com/rebeccaraisinwrites2

bookbub.com/authors/rebecca-raisin

tiktok.com/@rebeccaraisinwrites

ALSO BY REBECCA RAISIN

A Love Letter to Paris

Christmas at the Little Paris Hotel

The Paris Bookshop for the Broken-Hearted

**WHERE ALL YOUR ROMANCE
DREAMS COME TRUE!**

**THE HOME OF BESTSELLING
ROMANCE AND WOMEN'S
FICTION**

 **WARNING:
MAY CONTAIN SPICE**

SIGN UP TO OUR
NEWSLETTER

https://bit.ly/Lovenotesnews

Boldwood

Printed in Great Britain
by Amazon

57631458R00175